# Even Cat Sitters Get the Blues

*A Dixie Hemingway Mystery*

# BLAIZE CLEMENT

Thomas Dunne Books
St. Martin's Minotaur   New York

This is a work of fiction. All of the characters, organizations, and events portrayed in this novel are either products of the author's imagination or are used fictitiously.

THOMAS DUNNE BOOKS.
An imprint of St. Martin's Press.

www.thomasdunnebooks.com
www.minotaurbooks.com

Library of Congress Cataloging-in-Publication Data

Clement, Blaize.
    Even cat sitters get the blues : a Dixie Hemingway mystery / Blaize Clement.—
1st U.S. ed.
        p. cm.
    ISBN 13: 978-0-312-34093-3
    ISBN 10: 0-312-34093-1
    1. Hemingway, Dixie (Fictitious character)—Fiction. 2. Women detectives—
Florida—Sarasota—Fiction. 3. Sarasota (Fla.)—Fiction. 4. Pet sitting—
Fiction. 5. Iguanas—Fiction. 6. Cats—Fiction. I. Title.
    PS3603.L463E94 2008
    813'.6—dc22

                                                                    2007038735

First Edition: January 2008

10  9  8  7  6  5  4  3  2  1

Even Cat Sitters
Get the Blues

ALSO BY BLAIZE CLEMENT

*Curiosity Killed the Cat Sitter*
*Duplicity Dogged the Dachshund*

# Acknowledgments

It may not take a village to write a book, but it sure takes a lot of help from a lot of people. As ever, I am indebted to the Thursday Morning Writing Group—Kate Holmes, Greg Jorgensen, Clark Lauren, and Roger Drouin—for their encouragement, suggestions, information, and friendship; to Annelise Robey and the rest of the Jane Rotrosen Agency for trusting me; and to Marcia Markland and her able editorial assistant, Diana Szu, for giving me unconditional support. A big thank-you as well to copyeditor Janet Baker, who winces when Dixie says "than me" instead of "than I" but allows it because I insist that's how Dixie talks. Any grammatical blips are from my pig-headedness, not Janet's oversights.

Thanks, too, to Spike, who served as model for Ziggy, and to Rob Crafts for many things, one of which was patiently teaching me about iguanas.

Even Cat Sitters
Get the Blues

# 1

Christmas was coming, and I had killed a man.

Either of those facts was enough to make me want to stay in bed and pull the covers over my head for a long, long time.

Not to mention the fact that I was having feelings for two men, when I'd never expected or wanted to love even one man again, ever.

Not to also mention the fact that I'd agreed to take care of an unknown freewheeling iguana today.

It was all too much for any one person, especially this person. I figured I had every right to put the brakes on my life and refuse to go on. To just stand up and yell, "Okay, time out! No more life for me for a while. I'll get back to you when I'm ready."

Instead, I crawled out of bed at 4 A.M., just like I do every friggin' morning, and gutted up to face whatever the day would bring. It's a genetic curse, coming as I do from a long line of people who just keep on keeping on, even when anybody in their right mind would step aside for a while.

I'm Dixie Hemingway, no relation to you-know-who. I'm a pet sitter on Siesta Key, which is a semitropical barrier island off Sarasota, Florida. Until almost four years ago, I was a deputy with the Sarasota County Sheriff's Department. My husband was a deputy too. His name was Todd. We had a beautiful little girl. Her name was Christy. We were happy in the way of all young families, aware that bad things happened to other people but blocking out how exquisitely tenuous life really is. That all changed in a heartbeat. Two heartbeats, actually—the last of Todd's and Christy's.

I've read somewhere that excavators in Siberia found an intact woolly mammoth that had been entombed in ice for millennia. A butterfly was on the mammoth's tongue. I think about that woolly mammoth a lot, because life's like that. One second you can be blissfully standing in golden sunshine with butterflies flitting around you, and the next second—*whap!*—the world goes dark and you're totally alone and frozen.

I went a little bit crazy when that happened to me. To tell the truth, I went more than a little crazy. My rage was so great that the Sheriff's Department wisely decided that sending me out in public with a gun on my belt was like dropping a piranha in a goldfish bowl. But grief held too long eventually becomes a memorial to yourself, and you have to let it go.

When I was able to function again, I became a pet sitter. I like pets and they like me, and I'm not often in situations where I might revert to the old fury that buzzed in my veins for so long. I can't say I'm completely free of either the grief or the craziness that goes with it, but I'm a lot better.

At least I was until I killed that man.

Not that he didn't need killing. He did, and the grand jury agreed that he did. Actually, they agreed that I had killed him in self-defense and that it was a damn good thing I had, given the awful things he had done and would have done again, but that didn't change the fact that I have to live with knowing I've killed somebody.

Killing changes a person. Ask any combat veteran responsible for enemy deaths. Ask any cop who's had to take out a criminal. You can justify it, you can know that it was your job, that it was necessary, and that you'd do it again in the same circumstance, but it still changes you, even if nobody else knows it.

That, plus the fact that Christmas would be here in exactly twelve days, was causing me to avoid almost all human contact.

In my line of work, avoiding human contact is actually pretty easy. If a pet client is new, I have one meeting with its humans when we sign a contract and make sure everybody understands exactly what I will and will not do. I'm pretty much a pushover when it comes to pets, so I'll do whatever they need, but I try not to let the humans know that right up front. They give me a key to their house and a security code number if they have an alarm system, show me their pet's toys and favorite hiding places, and tell me what they want done in the event they both die while they're away. Living in a retirement mecca where the majority of the inhabitants are over the age of sixty-five makes that an issue that comes up more frequently than you'd think. Sometimes it's the other way around; they tell me what they want done with the pet in the event it dies while they're away. That also happens more frequently than you'd think. Once we've all made sure we're in accord about what's best for the pet, they leave and I don't have any more contact with them until they return.

That's my modus operandi and it's practically set in stone. The fact that I'd deviated so much from it when I agreed to take care of an iguana that day was a mystery. His owner had called the night before and talked me into taking the job even though he wasn't one of my regular clients, and even though it is absolutely against my professional standards to take on a pet without first meeting both pet and owner. We'd had a bad connection and I'd had to strain to hear him. To this day, I'm not exactly sure what he said that was so persuasive—the husky Irish accent, maybe, not full-blown faith-and-begorra Irish but with enough of a lilt to make my mouth want to smile. Or maybe it was just that I have a soft spot in my heart for iguanas because my grandfather had one.

I said, "The iguana is in a cage?"

"No, no, he runs free. I don't fancy cages."

I nodded at the phone. My grandfather had felt the same way.

He said, "Somebody will be there to let you in. All you have to do is put out fresh vegetables. He dotes on yellow squash, and there's some romaine and red chard. I'm forever in your debt for doing this, miss. Leave me a bill and I'll get a check off to you the instant I get home."

"You want me to go just the one time?"

"Yes, that's all. Oh, and this is very important—his name is Ziggy. Zig-ee."

He gave me his address on Midnight Pass Road and rang off before I could get a phone number. When I looked at the notes I'd scrawled, they were pathetic. I'd written *Ken Curtis (?) Vegs Yellow sqsh Ziggy.*

Except for the address, that was it. I hadn't even verified the caller's name, and he had said it so fast I wasn't sure I'd caught it right. I pride myself on handling my business in a professional manner, but any half-assed amateur could have handled that call better. I consoled myself that it would be an easy twenty bucks. Iguanas don't have to be walked or groomed, so all I'd have to do was put out some veggies for him and I'd be out in no time.

The weather for the last few days had been what Southwest Floridians call cold and wintry, meaning night temperatures had dipped into the high fifties, and the days' highs hovered just below seventy. For tourists and seasonal snowbirds, the cold weather was a major disappointment. For thin-blooded year-round locals like me, it was an aberrant misery.

My apartment is above a four-stall carport, with a long covered porch running its length. The porch faces the Gulf of Mexico, where time and capricious tides have carved a narrow hiccup of beachfront property that shifts and transforms itself every few months, making it an undesirable spot for developers and investors. When I opened the French doors that morning and stepped out on the porch, it was so chilly I could see my breath in the pale light of a coconut sky. Rain clouds were building purple mountains over the Gulf, but they looked several hours away. At least that's what I told myself when I decided to take my bike instead of the Bronco. The truth is that at that pre-dawn hour, when the birds are still sleeping in the palms, oaks, pines, and sea grape, I feel invincible on my bike, gliding down empty streets and breathing in the salty air as if I were a bird myself.

Siesta Key is eight miles long, north to south, with one main thoroughfare named Midnight Pass Road. Sarasota Bay lies on our east side, and the Gulf of Mexico is on the west. Two drawbridges connect us to Sarasota, each with a bathroom-sized bridge house where a tender pushes buttons and flips switches to open the bridge when a boat needs to pass through. The entire operation only takes about ten minutes for one boat, but if several boats sail through, it takes a lot longer. One of our favorite bitch topics is how long we had to wait for a sailboat to pass, but the bridges also make for great excuses for being late to appointments. All we have to say is, "The bridge was up," and people roll their eyes and groan in understanding.

About seven thousand permanent people call the key home, but during the season, from October to May, our population swells to around twenty-four thousand. Except for times when our streets are clogged with sun-bemused snowbirds, tourists, or carousing students on spring break, we're a fairly laid-back bunch.

I live near the south end so I always begin the day working my way north, just taking care of dogs. Dogs can't wait for you the way other pets can. Once all the dogs have been walked and fed and groomed, I retrace my route and call on the pets who don't have to pee outside— cats and hamsters and rabbits and guinea pigs and birds. Not snakes. I don't take care of snakes. I'm not exactly snake-phobic, but it makes me go swimmy-headed to hold a squirming little mouse above a gaping snake's mouth, so I refer those jobs to other pet sitters.

No matter who else is on my daily list of calls, I always start with Billy Elliot. Billy's a former racing greyhound who lives with Tom Hale in the Sea Breeze condos. Tom's a CPA whose spine was crushed a few years ago when a wall of lumber at a home-improvement store fell on him. Then, to make his misery complete, his wife left him and took their children and most of their possessions. Eventually, Tom got his act together, moved into the Sea Breeze, and started doing whatever it is that CPAs do at his kitchen table. He and I trade services. I go by twice a day and run with Billy Elliot, and Tom handles anything having to do with me and money.

With all that had happened to him, Tom was about as closed off from the world as I was, but when I got to his condo that morning, there was a big Christmas wreath on his door. It wasn't just a generic wreath, either, but a customized affair with a sassy red velvet bow and a toy greyhound perched above a nest of gilded pinecones. I stood a moment gaping at the thing before I unlocked the door and let myself into the dark foyer where Billy Elliot was nervously prancing on the tile floor. We kissed hello, I clipped the leash on his collar, and we slipped out of the apartment as quietly as thieves. On the ride down in the elevator, I considered asking him what had possessed Tom to have such a fancy wreath made for his door, but I thought it might hurt Billy Elliot's feelings, seeing as his facsimile was the focal point of the wreath.

We ran tippy-toe across the downstairs lobby and went outside to the parking lot for our run. Billy Elliot knew the routine—run fairly slowly and pee on selected bushes until we come to the oval track encircled by parked cars, and then stretch out and run like hell, full out, galloping like crazy, just like when he was a young dog chasing a mechanical rabbit while crowds cheered and bet money on him. Except this time he had a wheezing blond human slowing him down because her thigh muscles weren't nearly as strong as his. When he had finally run out all his nervous energy and I was about to fall over from breathing so hard, we ran at a slower pace back to the Sea Breeze's front door.

A woman with a corgi on a short leash was just coming out, and we stood aside while they passed. The woman nodded, but the corgi was embarrassed on account of wearing a pair of miniature deer antlers and an ermine-trimmed red velvet jacket, so he kept his head averted. Billy Elliot and I exchanged a *can-you-believe-that?* look, but we didn't let on how dorky we thought it was.

Upstairs, I could smell coffee brewing in the kitchen, and the lights were on in Tom's living room. I hadn't noticed it before, but there was a lavishly decorated Christmas tree in the corner. Now that I knew it was there, I could smell it, too, a pleasant balsam odor. My gosh, not only a wreath but a real Christmas tree! Tom and I don't always talk when I pop in and out of his apartment, but you'd think something like plans to buy a Christmas tree would have come up at least once. I wondered how he'd managed to get the top ornaments on. To tell the truth, I felt a little put out that he hadn't asked me to help him. I mean, I didn't want a tree of my own, but if he wanted to have one I would have been happy to help him with it.

I yelled toward the kitchen, "Morning, Tom! Nice tree!"

He wheeled into the living room with a curious grin on his face and his mop of curly black hair looking slept on. Instead of his usual sloppy sweats, he wore a snazzy red velour bathrobe. He looked a little bit like the corgi.

I said, "Wow, you've really got the Christmas spirit, don't you?" I could hear the little defensive whine in my voice, but I couldn't do anything about it.

He grinned even wider and made some inarticulate sounds that sounded like he was trying to deny it and claim it at the same time. Clinking sounds came from the kitchen, the sounds of mugs being removed from a cupboard, and a silky woman's voice called, "Darlin', did you ask me something?"

Oh. Now I understood. Tom hadn't been hit by the Christmas spirit, he'd been hit by romance. And he hadn't told me. He hadn't said, "Hey, Dixie, I've got a woman in my life now, so when you come to run with Billy Elliot, you may meet her."

For some reason, that made me vaguely angry, which was stupid, because Tom's personal life wasn't any of my business, and I was actually glad that he had a girlfriend after being alone for so long. But I was still sulky at the change in him.

I said, "Oh, excuse me," and beat a fast retreat, knowing all the time that Tom would feel bad at the way I acted, but not able to do anything about that, either. I didn't even hang Billy Elliot's leash in the hall closet before I left, just left it sloppily looped over the arm of a chair.

The nasty truth was that I was jealous. Not like a woman jealous that another woman is with a man she wants, but jealous that Tom had found the strength to let his old love go and be happy with somebody new. I wasn't sure I'd ever be able to do that, and I was afraid I would self-destruct if I didn't—and soon.

# 2

An hour later, the sky was beginning to go lemon as I led a miniature beagle from her driveway to the sidewalk. Funny how I remember the moment so well, as if that were the real beginning of all the awfulness to come. It wasn't, of course, but it seemed so at the time.

A flurry of fish crows flew overhead, and the beagle and I both looked up to watch their flight. Either by accident or design, I was never sure which, a miniature English bulldog careened around the hedge by the driveway and almost collided with the beagle. The bulldog was white, with a brown hand-sized mark on his back, another covering his right eye, and a wrinkled, squashed face so ugly it was adorable. The two miniature dogs lunged toward each other like long-lost cousins, with lots of tail-wagging and butt-sniffing and leash-tangling.

At the other end of the bulldog's leash was a tall woman whose back and shoulders were so erect and squared that the open smile she gave me was a little surprising. By the time we'd got the dogs separated and they were at our feet panting and grinning—and drooling, in the bulldog's case—the woman and I were as friendly as the dogs, except without the tail-wagging and butt-sniffing.

I guessed her about five years older than me, which would make her around thirty-seven, with the long-boned, athletic, Katharine-Hepburn-type beauty that always makes me feel short and dumpy. She was wearing jeans and a hooded gray sweatshirt that hid her hair, but I had the impression the hair was dark, like her eyes. I noticed she wore the same kind of Keds I wore, the washable kind you can get at Sears for twenty bucks. The only unusual thing about her was that she had a nervous way of looking over her shoulder, and her dark eyes tended to dart from side to side as she talked, as if she were checking to see if somebody lurked behind the thick foliage lining the street.

In one of those husky voices that make every word sound full of portent, she said, "I guess the cooler weather has made Ziggy friskier. He's usually not so aggressive."

"Your dog's name is Ziggy?"

She laughed. "Ziggy Stardust, actually. I'm a big David Bowie fan."

"That's the second time I've heard about a pet named Ziggy."

Her smile flashed again. "Another dog?"

"No, an iguana."

"Really? How interesting. But you've just *heard* about him? You haven't seen him?"

"Not yet. I'm on my way there now."

"Okay, that's good. Well, see you later then."

She jerked on the bulldog's leash and ran off in the direction she'd come. Halfway down the block, she stooped and picked the bulldog up and broke into a hard run. At the end of the block, she turned the corner and disappeared, and in a minute or two I saw a dark sedan drive from the direction she'd gone.

The beagle and I continued our walk, but I felt uneasy. One of the cardinal rules of professional pet sitting is not to carry gossip from one client to another. I don't tell one cat owner that somebody else's cat vomited up decapitated lizard on a guest's shoes. I don't tell when somebody's valuable stud dog failed in his studly duties when presented with a voluptuous bitch in heat. I keep all those things to myself, both because it's confidential information and because I'm not the kind of person who runs around telling everything I know.

But I had a nagging feeling that I had just betrayed a confidence in telling the woman that I was going to see an iguana named Ziggy. I also had a nagging feeling that she had been ever so deliberately mining me for information, and that I'd given her what she wanted. Even worse, in retrospect I was beginning to think our encounter hadn't been an accident at all but that she'd been waiting for me to come out. I wished I'd kept my mouth shut about the coincidence of two pets named Ziggy. I felt as if I had given away an important secret.

That was such a nutty, paranoid idea, I took it as evidence that I had lost some ground in the move toward complete sanity.

Still, just because you're paranoid doesn't mean people aren't plotting against you.

After I left the beagle's house, I started retracing my way south, calling on cats. No matter what kind of pet it is, I always do a fast check to make sure they haven't had any embarrassing accidents or done anything naughty to get attention, then I spend about thirty minutes concentrating on them as the unique individuals they are. I feed them, exercise them, groom them, and do whatever else they need to feel special. Pets are like people; their need to feel important is as great as their need for food and water. Before I leave, I turn on their favorite TV station. When I tell them goodbye, they always look happier than they did when I arrived. That may not seem like a great accomplishment to a lot of people, but I like knowing I've made somebody happier, even if the somebody has four legs.

The exception was Muddy Cramer, who never seemed happy no matter what I did. Muddy's full name was Mud Fence, because when he was found huddled in the Cramers' backyard, Mark Cramer had declared him ugly as one. Muddy was a two- or three-year-old mixed breed shorthair whose tailless rump indicated an ancestor in the Manx family. He had a dull orange and black tortoiseshell coat, one of his ears had been partially chewed off, and his left eye squinted like a Caribbean pirate's.

Instead of showing gratitude for being rescued from the wild, Muddy seemed hell-bent to test his humans' loyalty. He sprayed the curtains, upchucked on the carpet, and clawed the furniture. The Cramers loved him anyway, which proves that love is not only blind, it also can't smell. I always carried my quart bottle of Anti-Icky-Poo spray to Muddy's house to neutralize the urine odors, but it was an uphill battle.

I left Muddy's house feeling sad for both Muddy and his humans—and thinking there is nothing in the world that smells worse than male cat pee. The sky had darkened, and the rain clouds that had seemed hours away were moving in fast. Nuts. I still had several pets to call on, and if there was anything I didn't need today, it was to get caught on my bike in a cold rain.

Home was just a couple of miles away, so I headed that way to get the Bronco, but I was too late. In seconds, driving rain was slamming me hard, and passing cars were ever so slightly hydroplaning on the oil-slick asphalt. Terrific. I was not only soaked, I could be hit by a flying car.

One of the sucky things about life is that your problems always begin with choices you make. Even worse, you usually know a bad choice when you make it, but you barrel on with it anyway. I had one of those moments when I came to a bricked driveway and saw a small guardhouse set well back from the street. We don't have many private guardhouses on Siesta Key, so I knew this one was there to preserve the seclusion of somebody who was either very wealthy or very famous or both. I didn't know the owner of that place. I didn't know the guard working in the guardhouse, and private guardhouses aren't known for being refuges for people caught in rainstorms. I knew all that. Nevertheless, I pedaled toward it. With luck, there would be a guard who would let me come inside and wait out the storm. If not, I thought I could at least huddle under its roof overhang until the rain stopped.

Bad choice number one. Or maybe it was number two or three. It's always hard to trace back to the true start of things.

As I drew closer, I could see the square window in the side of the guardhouse was open. Good. That meant a living person was inside, not a voice box manned from some other location.

The main house was beyond a tall areca palm hedge, and that was good too, because if a kind guard befriended me, his employers wouldn't be able to see.

With my mouth half open to charm the guard into helping me, I rode under the roof's overhang and looked through the open window. Then my mouth snapped shut and I jerked my bike to make a U-turn back to the street.

No way was I getting involved in what I saw. No way was I going to have anything to do with it. The last time I'd seen something like that, I had ended up killing somebody before he killed me. Uh-uh, no way. I wasn't doing it again.

I think I may have actually spoken out loud to the rain. I think I may have actually said, "I don't care! Somebody else can handle this! Not me!"

The guard was sprawled in his chair with an ugly red welt running up his cheek and a contact bullet hole in his left temple. It could have been a suicide, but I had a bad feeling that somebody had pressed the barrel of a gun against his head and pulled the trigger.

No matter how it had happened, the man was dead, dead, dead, and it didn't make any difference how soon his death was reported, he was still going to be dead.

At the end of the driveway, my conscience made me come to a guilty stop. Inside the hidden house, somebody might be looking down the barrel of a gun held by the person who'd shot the guard. Somebody's life might be saved if I called 911 and reported what I'd seen.

While I teetered between conscience and cowardice, a dark blue panel truck pulled into the driveway and sped toward the guardhouse. Within two nanoseconds, I was on Midnight Pass Road and pedaling like hell toward home, not minding the cold rain at all now, just glad that somebody else would see the murdered guard and call 911.

As if to let me know that my decision to stop at the guardhouse had been not only stupid but unnecessary, the rain stopped as abruptly as it had begun. By the time I got home, the sun was shining and all the clouds were moving toward the southeast. My brother was out on his deck, wiping water off the plank table. As I started up the stairs to my apartment he turned and yelled.

"Anybody ever tell you not to play in the rain?"

I gave him the finger and kept slogging up the stairs in my wet Keds.

My brother is Michael. He's two years older than me, which makes him thirty-four, and he's been feeding me and taking care of me since I was two and our mother decided that the demands of motherhood—like putting food on the table and staying with her children—weren't her favorite way to spend a life.

Michael is a blond, blue-eyed firefighter with the Sarasota Fire De-partment, so good-looking that women tend to arch their backs like cats in heat in his presence. Fat lot of good it does them. He's been with Paco for over twelve years, and they're as committed to each other as the pope is to celibacy.

Paco is also thirty-four, also a dreamboat that women vainly drool over. As dark and slim as Michael is broad and blond, he's with the Sarasota County Special Forces Unit, which means he does under-cover work, often in disguises that even I don't recognize. Michael and Paco live next door in the frame house where Michael and I grew up with our grandparents after our parents left us. They're my closest friends in the whole world. I don't like to admit it, but I'm not sure I would have survived without them after Todd and Christy were killed.

Using the remote to raise the hurricane shutters, I unlocked the French doors to my minuscule living room, left my wet Keds on the porch, and padded barefoot over the Mexican tile to the bathroom, shedding clothes as I went. My apartment is small—living room-kitchen with a one-person eating bar, bedroom barely big enough for a single bed and dresser, tiny bathroom next to a narrow laundry room with stacked appliances. But I have a large closet with a desk on one side and my T-shirts and shorts stacked on shelves on the other side. I like the fact that my living space is spare and utilitarian without any unnec-essary color or life. It suits me just fine.

Or at least it used to. Lately I'd been feeling a tad cramped.

I stood in a hot shower until my skin was rosy all over, but it didn't make me feel normal. Instead, I felt more and more disappointed in myself. I might not be a deputy anymore, but I was a human being, and it had been wrong to run from the scene of a murder. Maybe the driver of the panel truck had done the same thing. Maybe he had cut and run too, and the guard was still sprawled in his chair with that strange angry weal on his cheek and a bullet hole in his temple.

Avoiding my eyes in the bathroom mirror, I screwed my damp hair into a ponytail. Then I padded to the kitchen and put on water to make tea. While I waited for the kettle to boil, I put a Patsy Cline CD on the player. Sometimes I listen to Roy Orbison and sometimes to Ella, but mostly I listen to Patsy because she never lets me down. I can feel like buzzards are roosting in my brain, and Patsy's straight-at-you, tell-it-like-it-is, love-wasted transparency makes me feel like the world isn't such a bad place after all.

I carried my tea to my combination office-closet, where I pulled on clean underwear, a pair of faded jeans, a white T-shirt, and fresh Keds. Then I sat down at the desk and pretended to be businesslike. I checked the answering machine, but it was still too early in the morning for business calls. I squared up some pieces of paper. Then I went back to the bathroom and brushed my teeth again, even though I'd done it earlier at four o'clock. It didn't sweeten the nasty taste of guilt in my mouth. Even with Patsy Cline belting out lyrics designed to make life seem simple, right now mine seemed more complicated than I could handle.

In my head, I heard a voice quoting the Bible—or maybe it was Shakespeare—"Let the dead bury the dead," which doesn't make any sense at all when you think of it, but then nothing was making much sense right then, least of all me.

I still had a couple of cats and the iguana to take care of, so I grabbed my backpack, went out the French doors, and clattered down the stairs while the remote lowered the storm shutters behind me.

Michael stuck his head out his kitchen door and yelled, "Want some breakfast?"

Michael cooks the way other people breathe; it's a necessary rhythm to his life. If the world were poised for a direct hit from a meteor, Michael would probably ladle out soup. Since he's one of the world's best chefs, a lot of doomed people would line up to get it and feel a lot more cheerful about their prospects.

Ordinarily, I would have jumped at the chance to have one of Michael's breakfasts, but I didn't want him scrutinizing me this morning. He had been almost as traumatized as I was by the things that happened after I found the last dead man. If he learned I'd found another one, he was liable to insist that I get another line of work. One that didn't have so many corpses in it.

I said, "No, thanks. I just came home to get the Bronco. I've still got two cats and an iguana."

His face brightened. "No kidding? An iguana?"

"Yep. Haven't met him yet."

We grinned at each other with one of those coded memory-smiles that siblings have. Our grandfather had brought home a near-dead baby iguana when Michael was about twelve, and we had helped give it round-the-clock antibiotics sold for chickens—iguanas and chickens, having evolved from the same reptilian ancestor, have identical respiratory and digestive systems. By the time the baby iguana had gone from sick black to healthy green, Michael and I were both enchanted with it. For reasons that now escape me, we named it Bobby.

My grandmother never took to Bobby the way the rest of us did, and when he grew to be about four feet long, she banished him from the house. He lived the rest of his life in the trees, just coming down to nibble on the hibiscus and eat fruits and vegetables we left out for him. Except for a time when he sacrificed his tail to some unknown predator, his life was peaceful. His tail grew back darker and shorter than the original, but he seemed quite happy. He lived over ten years and died during an unexpected freeze that wiped out Florida's citrus crop. When he died, our grandfather wept. Neither Michael nor I had ever seen our grandfather shed a tear before, and his grief over an iguana's death had been as sobering as losing Bobby.

In the carport, a couple of great blue herons were sitting on the hood of my Bronco, where they'd taken shelter from the rain. Down on the shore, black gulls were putting on an aerialist show a few feet above the waves, while a few snowy egrets ignored them and made fresh tracks in the sand as they gathered up sand crabs washed in by the rain. I shooed the herons away and pulled the Bronco out of the carport onto the drive that winds to Midnight Pass Road. I told myself I wasn't going to think about the dead guard again, but I knew I was lying.

For the next hour, I concentrated on feeding and grooming the two cats on my schedule. I played chase-the-peacock-feather with each of them, and I cleaned their litter boxes. Before I left them, I turned on their TV sets—the wild-life channel, but with the sound muted—and made sure they had plenty of fresh water. They both gave me a couple of tail swishes to let me know they approved of my performance and then pretended to ignore me when I left. I love that about cats. They may be secretly gloating that they've made a human wait on them like they're royalty, but they never lose their cool and actually show what they're feeling. I wish I were more like a cat.

When I finished grooming the second cat, I checked the iguana's address again and headed north, looking for the number. For private houses, street numbers are rare along that stretch of Midnight Pass Road. The general attitude is that nobody has any business going to a person's house if they don't already know where they live anyway, so why post street numbers just for the curious?

When I drove past the mansion with the dead guard in the guardhouse, I allowed my head to turn and look down the drive. Two ambulances, three green-and-white sheriff's cars, and a Medical Examiner's van were parked along the edge of the drive. At least I could stop worrying that the murdered guard was still alone in there.

A block or so later, I saw a street number and realized I'd passed the iguana's house. I pulled into a condo parking lot and doubled back, driving slowly while I tried to find another house number. At the driveway to the guardhouse, the Bronco sort of turned itself in, and I sat staring at the crime scene cars while a horrible realization trickled into my brain.

My new iguana client lived in the house where the guard had been shot in the head.

# 3

I parked behind the sheriff's vehicles and crawled out of the Bronco like a possum slinking out of a tree. The last thing I wanted was to explain to the crime-scene people why I was there.

Sergeant Woodrow Owens saw me first. A pained expression crossed his face, and he put his hand over his eyes for a moment like he hoped I was an apparition that would go away. Sergeant Owens is a tall, loose-jointed, sad-eyed African American who, if he were a dog, would be a basset hound. He was my commanding officer when I was a deputy. When Todd and Christy were killed and everybody else expected me to get my act together and come back to work, it was Sergeant Owens who finally had the grit to tell me the honest truth—I was way too fucked up to carry a gun for the county. I've always respected him for coming right out and saying it and not pussyfooting around. There's something reassuring about having your own emotional instability recognized and authenticated. Once that's done, you can get on with the business of getting through life without the added stress of trying to fake normal.

He said, "Dixie, I'm almost afraid to ask why you're here."

I said, "I have a pet client in this house."

"You know Kurtz?"

"Who?"

"Ken Kurtz, the man who lives here."

So that was his name. Not Curtis, like I'd written when we talked.

"Never met him, but he called last night and asked me to come to-day and feed his iguana."

I glanced at the yellow crime-scene tape around the guardhouse and tried to look innocent. "What's going on?"

"Somebody shot the guard."

"Anybody else hurt?"

"Just the guard."

Well, that was a relief.

Sergeant Owens said, "When Kurtz called you, did he say where he was?"

"New York. He said he'd be home today."

"You get a number?"

I felt myself redden. Heck, I hadn't even got the man's name right.

"He hung up before I could, and the ID thing said NUMBER UN-AVAILABLE."

"Okay, come with me."

He went loping off down the driveway toward the areca palm hedge so fast I had to trot to keep up with him. Beyond the hedge, the drive-way curved and widened to a four-car garage. At first I thought the garage formed one wing of an L-shaped single-story house, but then I realized the house was built around a courtyard with a tall oak tree in its center. Sergeant Owens made a sharp right angle and walked down a long paved path between the privacy hedge and the side wall of the garage. We passed an expanse of clear glass and stopped at double doors painted glossy lipstick red. I had seen so much Christmas stuff that morning that I caught myself thinking a tasteful pinecone wreath would have looked good on the red door, but it was bare.

Looking over his shoulder to make sure I was still with him, Sergeant Owens jabbed one bony finger at the bell, and then we both took a step back and gawked through the glass like people in a depart-ment store staring at whatever dumb show is being flashed across a row of TV screens. The living room was decorated in low-slung, honey-hued, leather-steel-and-polished-stone furnishings like you see in *Architectural Digest,* the sort of room that makes me want to run amok flinging cat hair and peanut shells.

The back wall was dominated by a fireplace big enough to roast an ox, with a wide hearth and a bunch of brass and black iron tools for poking and shoveling fire stuff. Good-sized flames were leaping in the thing right now, which was downright bizarre. I mean, the weather was chilly but not *that* chilly. Even having a fireplace that size was an anomaly on Siesta Key, since we have maybe two weeks a year when a fireplace is inviting. The rest of the time it makes you feel sweaty just to look at one. People on the key who can't resist the nostalgic feel of a fireplace keep them small and unobtrusive, little hollows where they can grow bromeliads or ferns, but this baby was meant for serious roaring fires.

A woman came streaking past the fireplace toward the front door, and Sergeant Owens and I got our faces into neutral expressions.

The woman who opened the door took the term "drop-dead gorgeous" to a whole new level. She was the kind of woman who makes me remember that my split ends need trimming, my eyebrows need shaping, I need a manicure, and a facial wouldn't hurt. Not that she looked like she tried to be gorgeous, it was just how she was. Pale-gold Eurasian skin, almond-shaped topaz eyes, masses of long red curls carelessly caught up at the top of her head to cascade around a graceful neck. Sweeping eyelashes a foot long. Naturally rosy full lips, with a tiny dark beauty mark beside them, as if the angel who'd made her had been so carried away by the perfection he'd created that he'd taken a little brush and added a coded signature. Her hands were in thin latex gloves like surgeons use, and instead of a Miss America sash draped shoulder to hip she wore wrinkled blue-green surgical scrubs and white running shoes.

She smiled at Sergeant Owens, revealing even white teeth like the dentist uses as the ideal when he's telling you it's time to bleach yours. From the corner of my eye, I could see Sergeant Owens suck in his skinny stomach and straighten his sloping shoulders. I could only imagine what other male responses he was having.

Sergeant Owens said, "Ma'am, the pet sitter is here."

He said it so smoothly that anybody would have thought he gave a gnat's ass that I had arrived. He was up to something, I just didn't know what.

She looked at me with a harder expression in her eyes than she'd shown Sergeant Owens.

"I do not understand." She spoke with an accent—not Caribbean, not French, not South American, but something I couldn't place—and enunciated each syllable carefully, the way people do when English isn't their first language.

Sergeant Owens said, "The pet sitter that Mr. Kurtz hired. She's here to do her job. So if you'll just show her the . . ."

He turned to me with a look that said *Help me out here,* so I said, "Iguana."

She drew back a bit as if I had threatened her, and her big eyes got even wider. Considering that a murder had been committed not fifty feet away, I wasn't surprised that she was jumpy. What surprised me was that she seemed suddenly scared of me.

"But no, he did not. Is impossible. No. He did not call."

I decided her accent was fake and opened my mouth to tell her how I felt about being called a liar. Sergeant Owens wrapped his bony hand around my arm and squeezed. His face was as bland as buttermilk, but his grip said *Watch your mouth, Dixie*—words he'd said more than once when I was a deputy.

He said, "Ma'am, I'd like to talk to Miz Hemingway for a minute. We'll be back."

He steered me down the walk to the front of the garage. The look on his face approached excitement, or at least what passed for excitement for Sergeant Owens.

He said, "Okay, Dixie, this is good. Let's move on this. Something funny is going on in that house, but I don't have any valid reason to get a search warrant. Go in there and look the place over. I'll square it with Lieutenant Guidry when he gets here."

My heart did a little blip, either because Guidry would be the homicide detective on the case or because Sergeant Owens still had faith in my deputy skills, even though I hadn't worn a badge in almost four years.

"Is that woman Mrs. Kurtz?"

"No, she's Kurtz's nurse. Or at least she says she is. She claims Kurtz is sick in bed, too drugged up to talk to me. See if you can find him."

Without waiting for me to agree, he lurched back down the path with my arm still clamped in his big hand. The gorgeous woman was still in the open doorway, but now she looked as if she had remembered the influence she had on men and was ready to use it.

Sergeant Owens said, "Ma'am, I'm afraid I've forgotten your name."

"Is Gilda."

He waited a beat for a last name and then smiled toothily. "Well, Gilda, I have to ask you to let Miz Hemingway come in and do her job."

She shook her head so hard her trailing curls flew around her shoulders. "I say to you Mr. Kurtz no ask nobody to come. He no call nobody. Is impossible."

She pronounced his name *Meester Koots,* and I decided the accent was too consistent to be phony.

Sergeant Owens gave her a loose-lipped grin and played the kind of dumb that only a really smart cop can play.

"Well, Gilda, I guess this time he did something by himself, now, didn't he? He must be feeling stronger, is what I'd say, so good for him. Now Miz Hemingway is just going to go in and make sure the whatchamacallit is okay. She won't get in your way, will you, Miz Hemingway?"

He gave me a little shove while he talked, and Nurse Beauty was forced to step out of the way. Up close, she had a funny medicinal smell, sort of like the iodine my grandmother used to swear was the only thing that really killed germs dead. I walked fast into the living room, half expecting her to tackle me from behind. Instead, she slammed the door as hard as she could, I suppose to show her annoyance.

The room was even more impersonal than it had seemed through the glass. No Christmas stuff, no Hanukkah stuff. No flowers or plants, no books or magazines, no decorative objects, no framed snapshots. It looked as if a furniture company had delivered a truckload of expensive contemporary furniture one day and nobody had looked at it since. Except for the fire in the fireplace, the room had all the warmth of a morgue.

Over my shoulder, I said, "Where will I find Ziggy, ma'am?"

"Who?"

"Ziggy. That's the iguana's name, isn't it?"

"Oh. I don't . . . I don't know."

I stopped and turned, but she was looking off to the side with an apprehensive nervousness. Sergeant Owens was right. Something odd was going on, because she definitely didn't want me inside the house.

I said, "He hasn't been moved to a warm place?"

She gave a vague wave of her latex-gloved hand. "I do not know about animal."

At temperatures lower than 60 degrees, iguanas begin to shut down. If they get too cold for very long, they die. Our temperature had been in the fifties for two or three nights.

A dragging sound came from around the corner, like the sound of tough iguana skin sliding across hard tile.

The nurse stiffened and raised her head, her topaz eyes darting side to side as if searching for a place to hide. Now I understood why Kurtz had wanted somebody else to feed his iguana. Some people are terrified of all reptiles, even the ones with four legs, and Kurtz's nurse must be one of them.

I watched the floor, waiting for the first show of green lizard skin. What appeared was a man's foot in heavy socks and slippers. When he came into full view, I felt an internal shudder of revulsion. I think I may actually have gasped. A haggard man, he wore a red plaid bathrobe loosely tied so that a lot of chest and lower leg were exposed, along with continent-shaped scars that glowed like abalone shell. His skin was a mottled plum-blue color that reminded me of a cadaver's blood-puddled epidermis, and it was contorted by active minute contractions as if randomly jerked by internal wires. It gave his visage the quivering look of water's surface when it's being dimpled by fine rain droplets.

When I looked into his eyes, I saw such agony that I almost gasped again.

Involuntarily, I said, "I'm sorry."

His voice was raspy and wheezing. "Yes, so am I."

"I meant—"

"I know what you meant. It's a common reaction when people see me for the first time, a kind of knee-jerk horror that such ugliness has a mind and a beating heart."

"Actually, I meant I'm sorry you're in so much pain."

"Perhaps you can share your pity another time. For now, tell me who you are and what you're doing in my house."

Gilda said, "I say to her no, but policeman say I must let her in."

He raised pain-glazed eyes to her. "Policeman?"

"Ramón has been in accident. Is hurt."

I was getting fed up with her delicate twitchiness.

I said, "If Ramón was the guard, he wasn't hurt, he was murdered. I'm here because a man who said his name was Ken Kurtz called me last night and asked me to come today and feed his iguana. My name is Dixie Hemingway. I'm a professional pet sitter."

Both he and the nurse had gone very still, and for a second his bizarre skin seemed to pale.

In a guttural rasp, he said, "Don't take me for a fool! Who sent you?"

I'd have traded six weeks of my life right then for a badge or a gun or at least a name tag that gave me a deputy's authority. Since I didn't have any kind of authority at all, I put my hands on my hips and glared at him.

"What is it with you people? I know you've had a bad experience here, but that's no reason to be so damned rude. I was asked to do a job, and I'm here to do it. Now, do you want me to feed Ziggy or not?"

"Who?"

For a wild second, I thought this all might be a matter of mistaken identity or wrong iguana, since neither Kurtz nor his nurse seemed to know the iguana of the house by name.

I said, "The man who called said his iguana's name was Ziggy. He said that was very important."

Kurtz closed his eyes for a long moment, and I could see his chest rising and falling with deep breaths. The eddies under his skin twitched like living things trying to escape the light. When he opened his eyes, he seemed to have come to a conclusion that left him infinitely sad.

He said, "What else did he tell you?"

"He said Ziggy wasn't in a cage, and that he liked yellow squash."

He straightened his back, squared his shoulders, and lifted his neck. His hands came together at his waist to cinch his belt tighter. He was still grotesque, but now he was grotesque with pride.

He said, "I am Ken Kurtz, and I did not call you."

Sounding desperate, Gilda said, "I say to her you no call."

He ignored her. His eyes seemed to be piercing my skull, looking inside my brain, sifting all the information in it and coming up without the answer he wanted.

I said, "Do you have an iguana?"

"I do."

"Is his name Ziggy?"

He hesitated. "You could say that."

"Then somebody who knows you called me. Pretty funny that somebody would ask me to come here today, and then your guard gets shot in the head."

His chest rose again in a long sigh and I mentally kicked myself. I shouldn't have told him how the guard had been killed. I should have waited to see if he already knew that.

I said, "It's cold outside. If Ziggy is in the courtyard, he should be brought indoors."

He frowned and looked hard at Gilda. "The iguana is outside?"

Gilda's delicate color had gone flour white, and she looked genuinely terrified. Ken Kurtz apparently wasn't the kind of employer to cross. His mouth gashed and he made a sound of such rage that the nurse and I both backed up a couple of steps. It occurred to me that he might be even crazier than I was.

# 4

Gilda made motions with her hands like circling fish, then abruptly darted from the room.

Trying to sound more confident than I was, I said, "I noticed you have a big oak tree in your courtyard. Ziggy's probably up there. If you'll point me toward the kitchen, I'll see if I can coax him down with food."

Mutely, he pointed in the same direction Gilda had run, and I went down a hall to a kitchen that made me think of a hospital. White ceramic tile was everywhere—on the floor, on the wall between cabinets and countertops, and on the countertops themselves. Large squares of shiny ceramic linked by nurse-white grout and surrounded by nurse-white cupboards, nurse-white walls, and nurse-white appliances. Not a spot of color intruded. Even the dish towels folded next to the white porcelain sink were bright white. A magnolia would have looked dingy in all that stark whiteness.

Feeling like a large dirty germ, I clumped to the big white refrigerator and pulled the door open. These people didn't have color anywhere. No jars of purple jelly, no bottles of red ketchup, no green pickles. Nothing but stacks of packages neatly wrapped in white butcher paper, their corners and edges as squared as Christmas gift-wrapping. There was the same odd odor of iodine too. With my skin goose-bumping, either from the refrigerator's cold air or the weirdness of its contents, I pulled out one of the lower vegetable drawers. No squash. No romaine. No vegetables of any kind. It was full of white packages too, all with that funny iodine smell.

I suddenly remembered that in some parts of the world, iguanas are slaughtered and eaten. Feeling slightly nauseated, I closed the refrigerator door and went looking for the nurse.

In the hallway, I heard the sound of theatrical sobbing. I followed the sound to a room as laboratory white as the kitchen. White walls, white draperies, white carpet, white painted furniture. Still wearing her surgical gloves, Gilda was face down on a double bed covered with a stark-white *matelassé* spread.

Oh, this was terrific. An impostor had hired me to take care of an iguana that wasn't his. A guard hired to protect the iguana's actual owner had been killed, and the iguana was possibly in the refrigerator in little white packages. To make this my really lucky day, the owner's nurse was an incredibly beautiful flake. She might possibly be a murderous flake, guilty of killing both the guard and the iguana.

Since the house wrapped around a central courtyard, the layout was a bit disorienting. The four garages were on the south side, and the long living room with its huge fireplace took up the central part of the west wing. The dining room, kitchen, and Gilda's room were the north wing. I could see, at a right angle to Gilda's room, a long hallway running down the east side. Ken Kurtz's bedroom was either there or in a south wing between the garages and the courtyard. I wondered if he and Gilda had something other than a patient-nurse relationship. Not that I was judging. If they were lovers, Gilda wouldn't be the first beautiful woman to cozy up to a repulsive rich employer, nor would he be the first repulsive man to feel so grateful to have a beautiful woman in his bed that he'd give her anything she wanted.

I said, "Gilda, are those packages in the refrigerator iguana steaks?"

She raised a tearstained face and glared at me. "Who kill Ramón? How kill him? When? Why the policeman not tell me Ramón is dead?"

Even though she seemed too dramatic to be real, it occurred to me for the first time that she truly might not have known the guard was dead. Sergeant Owens might not have told her there had been a murder on the other side of the row of areca palms that separated the house from the guardhouse. Perhaps he had been waiting for Guidry to do it. Perhaps I shouldn't have done it either. Perhaps I had done something that would cause Guidry to want to wring my neck.

Well, it wouldn't be the first time.

I said, "I'm just a pet sitter, Gilda. I take care of animals. I don't know the answers to those questions."

"And I am nurse. I take care Mr. Kurtz. I don't know about animal."

"Okay, so taking care of the iguana isn't your job. Just tell me what's happened to him. Did somebody kill him?"

She buried her face in the bed and made some more sounds of racking sobs, but this time they seemed even more contrived. I had the feeling she was stalling for time while she thought up an answer.

The scraping sound of Ken Kurtz's approaching footsteps made Gilda raise her head. As if she wanted to get the words out before Kurtz got to her door, she blurted out, "Is not dead. Is in wine room."

I've stopped being surprised at the things rich people have in their houses. Poor people count themselves lucky to have running water and flush toilets. Middle-class people have living rooms and dining rooms, kitchens and bedrooms, bathrooms and closets. Rich people have things like ballrooms and movie rooms in their house. They have fitness centers that rival Gold's gyms, along with game rooms and bowling alleys. Ken Kurtz apparently had a wine cellar, which, given the fact that you hit water if you dig three feet under Siesta Key's sandy soil, meant he had a ground-level room dedicated to the storage of wines.

Being somewhere between poor and middle-class, the only thing I knew about wine cellars was that they were kept dark and at an even temperature. I wasn't sure what the temperature was, but I knew it wasn't warm enough for an iguana.

I moved away from Gilda's door to meet Kurtz. Each step seemed to cost him dearly in strength and endurance, but he had the look of a man with a mission. He also had the look of a man who always did what he intended to do.

I said, "Where's the wine room?"

His blue forehead furrowed suspiciously. "Why?"

"Gilda says Ziggy is in it."

Laboriously, he did a U-turn and headed back toward the kitchen. I gave one last look at Gilda, who appeared to be deep in thought, and followed him. Seen from the back, Kurtz presented a different persona—partly because his shoulders were surprisingly broad for such an emaciated man and partly because I could make out the outline of a small handgun nestled in a holster above his buttocks under his plaid bathrobe. It looked an awful lot like the kind of backup that every law enforcement officer carries somewhere on his person.

As I followed his agonized shuffle through the kitchen and dining room, I went over all the possible reasons that a man who had a private guard outside his house would also wear a gun inside. It could have been because he was crazy paranoid—a definite possibility—or it could have been because whoever killed the guard had intended to kill Ken Kurtz, and Kurtz knew it. Something strange was definitely going on in this house, and whatever it was had to do with the reason somebody had called me about the iguana.

We turned the corner into the living room, the west wing of the house, where the fire in the humongous fireplace was still blazing away. This part of the house seemed to be the only place without a glass wall looking out at the courtyard. Instead, glass walls flanked the double front doors and looked out at the palm privacy hedge. Kurtz hobbled past the fireplace and I trailed behind, walking so slowly to match his pace that it made me feel off-balance. The fireplace must have had a fan arrangement to blow heated air into the room, because I felt a welcome warmth on my legs as I heel-toed past it. Even Kurtz seemed to relax a bit when he felt it, if you can call easing one arm down to his side relaxed. The arm had been doubled in front of him before, crossed over his stomach as if he needed it to hold his skin down.

At the far end of the living room, the southern end, we came to a closed door. Kurtz took a key from his pocket and unlocked the door while I calculated that it led to a windowless room behind the row of garages. Kurtz pulled the door open, revealing a dark, cavernous space. He fumbled for a moment for a light switch, but when he found it the room wasn't much brighter than before. What light there was came from a red bulb like a photographer's darkroom illumination. In its eerie light, towering shelves leaped into view, all lined up like library stacks, each stack full of dark bottles that gave off odd purplish glints. The walls were lined with shelves of wine too. Overall, I estimated the room at about ten feet deep and twenty feet long—approximately a third the size of my apartment.

In my supermarket, wines are set upright with stickers on the fronts of the shelves to let me know which ones are on sale for less than ten dollars—my favorite vintage. Kurtz's wines were laid so their necks pointed down at an angle, and I was pretty sure the price of one bottle would be fifty times what I paid for mine.

I said, "What's the temperature in there?"

"Fifty-three degrees Fahrenheit."

Huh. Only a scientist or an intellectual show-off would have tacked on that "Fahrenheit," and Kurtz didn't strike me as a show-off.

"Can you turn on a brighter light?"

"Bright light isn't good for the wine."

Okay, maybe he was an intellectual show-off after all.

I said, "You don't need to go in. I'll find him."

Kurtz looked slightly relieved. He probably hadn't been looking forward to shuffling around between those stacks of wine bottles. I stepped into the room and stood a minute to get my bearings. The room wasn't frigid, but I wouldn't have wanted to spend much time in it. To an iguana, it would feel even colder. I turned to the right and moved along the outside wall, peering down each aisle between rows of shelves for the outline of a giant lizard. At the far end, I circled to the other side and walked straight along the long corridor to the stacks on the left side of the door. I found Ziggy with his head butted against the back wall and his long tail stretched out along the back corridor. He was immobile, with all his systems on hold. Poor guy didn't even know where he was. Iguanas locate themselves in space not by the view through their regular eyes but by light entering a parietal eye at the base of their skull. That "third eye" sloughs off like a contact lens when they shed their skins. In the dull red light of the wine room, Ziggy's navigational parietal eye was rendered useless.

I said, "Hey, boy. You okay?"

It was a dumb question. Ziggy didn't know I was there and didn't care. More than likely, Ziggy didn't know anything right then. He was totally tuned out, not just to what was going on outside himself but to what was going on inside too. If it hadn't been for his sides moving in and out with each breath, I would have thought he was dead. Even so, he was still capable of instinctive response, and I knew from painful experience that picking up an iguana so that he doesn't feel securely supported is a good way to make him panic and lash you with his powerful tail. Which won't kill you, but it hurts like hell. I knelt by his side and slid one arm under his neck to get a good grip on his front leg and the other arm under his back end to grip his back leg. When I lifted him off the floor, I pulled him snug so he was not only supported on my arms but close against my body. Then I sidestepped down the outside corridor until I came to the aisle leading to the door.

Kurtz was still in the doorway, one hand leaning against the door-jamb as if he might collapse any minute. The sleeve of his bathrobe had fallen away to expose a gauze dressing on the inside of his elbow, like the dressing that covers an indwelling catheter for receiving medication or blood transfusions. Gilda might be a flake, but she apparently was a competent nurse.

When he saw me, he straightened up in a way that made me think of a military man snapping to attention. No doubt about it, Kurtz was either an ex-cop or an ex-serviceman of some sort. But what kind of cop or serviceman retires with enough money for Kurtz's lifestyle?

When I sidled through the door, Kurtz looked down at Ziggy's cold-darkened body and a flicker of something like anguish moved across his face. My mind flashed to the way my grandfather had cried when our pet iguana died. I'd always thought it was because he'd been grieved to lose Bobby, but now I realized he'd wept because he was disappointed in himself for not protecting Bobby from the cold. We humans who take on the care of pets are really setting tests for ourselves of how responsible and caring we can be. If we fail our pets, we fail the test.

I said, "He's black because he's cold. When he warms up, his normal color will come back."

Kurtz made a rasping noise intended for a laugh. "Wish I could say the same for myself."

With Ziggy's side hard against my waist, I headed for the living room and the warmth of the fireplace. A basket filled with fireplace logs and kindling was at one side of the hearth, and a neat stack of large floor pillows sat at the other end. They invited people to sit on the floor and gaze into the fire and have a glass of wine, but I doubted that anybody in this house had ever sat on one. I kicked at the stack until I had enough pillows in front of the fire to make a soft bed for Ziggy, then gently lowered him and stretched his long tail out behind him. His eyelids were closed. He didn't move. If somebody who didn't know better had seen him, they would have thought he was a stone carving.

Kurtz had made it to the fire by this time. I heard him shuffle up and stop, but I didn't look at him. I was busy watching Ziggy.

Kurtz said, "I think those pillows are made from antique Persian rugs."

"Good, then they're probably not synthetic. I don't like synthetics around my pets."

"What did you say your name was?"

I looked at him then. "It's Dixie Hemingway."

"Any relation to—?"

"No, and I don't have any of his six-toed cats, either."

"I guess you get asked that a lot."

A form walked past the glass window, and I took a deep breath. I knew that form. Lieutenant Guidry had arrived and was about to ring the doorbell. Like a dog salivating to the ringing of a bell, various parts of my anatomy began to do all kinds of things, some of which are illegal in Republican states.

I had fairly recently come to realize that I had the hots for Guidry, and it scared me to death. I didn't want to want a man, and certainly not another deputy. Todd had been the love of my life, and when he died I had laid away all thoughts of romance or love or sex or any of those things that most thirty-two-year-old women have at the forefront of their minds. But my body was telling me it had an entirely different agenda. My mind could make whatever plans suited its ideals, but my body wasn't going along.

I said, "You might want to get rid of that gun before you talk to the homicide detective."

May God strike me dead, I don't know what possessed me to say that. Maybe it was a way to deny to myself that I was excited at seeing Guidry. Maybe it was because Kurtz had looked sad when he saw Ziggy's dark color. Maybe it was the fact that the man was so ugly he would scare little children, and probably crazy to boot. I've always been a pushover for the underdog, and Ken Kurtz had way too many strikes against him for his own good. Whatever it was, I suddenly wanted to protect him the same way I wanted to protect Ziggy.

# 5

The bell rang, and I moved to open the door.

As usual, instead of looking like the typical style-challenged cop, Guidry looked like he'd just stepped off the cover of *GQ*. He wore dark gray slacks most likely made from tender wool taken from some as yet undiscovered animal in the Andes, a black turtleneck, and a brown leather bomber jacket that had apparently been beaten into submission.

Guidry is fortyish, a head taller than me, with short-cropped dark hair showing a little silver at the temples. He has a beaky nose and calm gray eyes, and every cell in my body did a shivery little shimmy the minute I looked into those eyes. It was damned annoying, so I scowled at him.

"Good morning, Lieutenant."

"Some reason why you're answering the door at this house?"

I found that unnecessarily snippy, since I was sure Sergeant Owens had told him I was there and why. But before I could tell him so, Kurtz spoke from behind me.

"It's a courtesy Miss Hemingway is showing me, Lieutenant. It's difficult for me to move, and she was saving me some steps." He looked toward the kitchen wing and added, "Especially since my nurse seems to have stopped working."

If Guidry was shocked at what he saw, his eyes remained impassive as he took in Kurtz's blue color, the jerking whirlpools under his skin, his pain-racked face and emaciated frame in the red plaid bathrobe.

He said, "Mr. Kurtz, do you mind if I come in and talk to you for a few minutes?"

"Actually, I mind a great deal. I am in considerable pain and should be in bed. However, I am aware that a crime has been committed on my property, and I realize you have questions to ask, so come in, Lieutenant. Let's just get it over with as quickly as possible."

Guidry nodded and crossed to where Kurtz was still standing in front of the fireplace. Guidry's eyes swept the room, taking in the gigantic fireplace and its leaping flames, the closed door to the wine room, and then coming to rest on Ziggy. Ziggy remained stretched across the floor pillows on the hearth, dull and immobile as a rock.

Some people think iguanas are things of nightmares, but I think they're beautiful. Basically, they're big cold-blooded lizards with long banded tails, four legs, and clawed feet. They can run fast as a cat, and since their outer toes are made for gripping things, they can zip up a tree trunk in no time. Males have thin strips like Velcro on their inner thighs for sticking to a female when mating, which probably accounts for both sexes' lipless mouths lifting at the corners in perpetual smiles. Unless they want to smell something, they generally keep their mouths closed. Their olfactory centers are in the roof of their mouths, so if they're curious about how food or a threat smells, they stick out their tongues and touch it. Their tongues aren't forked like a snake's, but they have two sensory channels on their undersides that serve the same purpose—they feed back information about which way to go to be safer, warmer, or fed.

I especially like iguanas' dewlaps and back crests. The dewlaps hang from their necks, and if they're excited or scared they can puff them up so they look twice as big and threatening, which I think would come in really handy for humans. The dorsal crests are just cool—pointed dragonlike spikes running down their backbones. Who wouldn't like to have that?

Head to tail tip, Ziggy was about five feet long. On his best day, he would be a clear Granny Smith color, with creamy dorsal spikes and underbelly. But this definitely wasn't his best day. Instead of being green, he was dull and dark, almost black, and his eyes were hidden behind closed lids. He looked so unhandsome that I bristled in advance at the insulting things Guidry might say about him.

Guidry leaned to get a closer look. "Is he okay?"

I said, "Not really. He was left in a cold wine room and got chilled."

He turned to Kurtz. "Why was your iguana put in a cold room?"

Kurtz looked surprised. "I don't know, Lieutenant. I didn't put him there. My nurse may be able to tell you how he got there, since she knew about it."

"Who lives here, besides you?"

"My nurse has a room here. Nobody else."

"Your nurse is here now?"

"She's in her room. I expect she's upset about the guard being killed. I think they were good friends."

Guidry cut his eyes toward me, and I felt my face go hot. Yep, I had blown it by telling Kurtz there had been a murder. That should have come from Guidry, so he could see how Kurtz and the nurse reacted to the news. I had made it possible for them to concoct a story and rehearse it in their minds before time to tell it.

Guidry said, "Maybe the nurse put the iguana in the cold room?"

Kurtz said, "Lieutenant, I appreciate your concern about my iguana's well-being, but I fail to see what that has to do with a murder investigation."

Guidry gave him a level look. "I'd appreciate a look at the wine room."

Kurtz gave a suppressed snort of disgust, turned his back, and hobbled across the living room to the wine room door. The outline of a gun was no longer visible under his bathrobe, and I felt myself blush again. It had been stupid and wrong to warn him to get rid of the gun, and I still didn't know why I'd done it. I also didn't know where he'd stashed it.

Again, he took out a key and opened the door. Guidry ambled across the tile and stood in the doorway looking in.

Turning to me, he said, "Did you go in there?"

I nodded, already knowing where he was headed.

"Did you cover much of the room?"

"I walked around the perimeter, starting at the right side. I didn't go down any of the aisles except the one in front of the door."

"Uh-hunh. And you carried the iguana out?"

"Yes, and his tail was dragging."

Kurtz seemed to understand for the first time what was going on. "You're talking about footprints, right? Ms. Hemingway may have disturbed footprints?"

"And the iguana's tail," said Guidry. "Don't forget the dragging tail."

I said, "Oh, please!" and then saw Guidry's quick warning look that said, *Just once, Dixie, try to keep your mouth shut.*

He had some reason for wanting Kurtz to think I'd obliterated footprints in the wine room. It was possible I had, but ceramic tile isn't likely to yield good prints unless there was mud or blood on the shoes. Besides, it was more likely that whoever had put Ziggy in the room had simply deposited him inside the doorway. But since I'd blown it by blabbing about the dead guard, not to mention warning Kurtz to get rid of the gun, I figured I owed Guidry a bit of silence, so I went back to the hearth and stood next to Ziggy.

"Where did your guard come from?"

"I believe he was a Mexican national."

"I mean what agency supplied him."

"He was an independent."

"You hired him personally?"

"No, my nurse hired him."

"She vet him first?"

"I suppose. I haven't been able to attend to those kinds of details for a while."

Guidry said, "Did the guard spend time inside the house?"

Kurtz hesitated for just a fraction of a second too long. "Not to my knowledge, Lieutenant."

"But he may have come inside without your knowledge?"

"Sometimes I don't come out of my room for days at a time. On those occasions, I am not aware of anything in the rest of the house."

"You said your nurse was a good friend of the guard's?"

"I believe she was, yes."

"Any particular reason why you think that?"

Kurtz raised a hand to his face as if he hoped to calm the contracting areas under his skin. "It was just a general impression I had."

"Do you think they were friends before your nurse hired him?"

"No."

"The wine, is it drinking wine or investment wine?"

"Both."

Trust Guidry to think of wine as an investment. He was so secretive that I hadn't yet got the full story on him, but no man dresses like Guidry or handles himself like Guidry unless he's got a pedigree a mile long. About the only thing I knew about him was that he came from New Orleans and wasn't Italian. Also, he had called me a liar one time in French. That wasn't a lot to go on, and I didn't care anyway because it was none of my business, but he probably grew up in a mansion with well-stocked wine cellars and trusted old servants who lugged the stuff up the stairs and opened it. He probably wouldn't be caught dead drinking the supermarket stuff I bought.

He said, "Anything valuable enough for somebody to kill to get to it?"

"What a man will kill for, Lieutenant, is highly subjective, but I have a couple of cases of 1998 Pétrus that sells for about fourteen-fifty a bottle. I suppose a collector might murderously covet it. I also have a case of 1997 Romanée-Conti, somewhere over fifteen hundred a bottle, and quite a lot of Château Latour, some 1990, some 1993, some 1994. The Latour is cheaper, about seven or eight hundred a bottle."

Guidry didn't look shocked, but I was. I couldn't believe that a bottle of fifteen-hundred-dollar wine could taste a hundred and fifty times better than the ten-dollar-a-bottle stuff I drank.

Guidry said, "Anybody you know who might want your wine?"

"Until thirty minutes ago, Lieutenant, nobody even knew my wine existed."

"Somebody has to sell it to you. Somebody has to put it on the shelves."

"I order it flown in directly from the wineries. It's delivered in unmarked crates, and I put it on the shelves myself."

I thought, *And Gilda knew it was there, just like she knew Ziggy was in there with it.*

The man was not only blue and grotesquely ugly, he was a big liar.

Guidry said, "You know, under Florida law, it's a felony offense to ship wine in from out of state."

"Collector's wine falls under a different code, Lieutenant."

Guidry cocked an eyebrow at him, but he didn't challenge it. I didn't know diddly about Florida's laws about wine shipments, but I would have bet good money that Kurtz was bluffing.

Guidry said, "When's the last time the guard handled your iguana?"

Kurtz's face twisted, either from a spasm or from extreme annoyance. "Nobody *handles* my iguana, Lieutenant. And so far as I know, the guard never even saw my iguana."

"Never picked him up? Never had any contact with him?"

"As I said, Lieutenant, when I'm in pain, a lot can happen inside my house without my knowledge. My nurse may be able to give you more information about the guard's contact with the iguana."

I thought, *Oh, sure, let Gilda take all the blame.*

Honest to God, some men aren't worth the money it would take to buy a rope to hang them. With each answer Kurtz gave, I was regretting more and more my impulsive advice to ditch the gun he'd worn under his robe.

Guidry said, "How long has your nurse worked for you?"

Kurtz's eyes flicked up and to the right for a quick instant, a sure sign a person's preparing to lie.

"I hired her just before I moved here four months ago from New York."

"From an agency?"

"No, she also was independent."

"You mind asking the nurse to come in here?"

For a second, Kurtz's face betrayed how much effort it was taking to stand and talk. Asking him to make the long walk back to Gilda's room was like asking somebody who'd just had abdominal surgery without anesthesia to sew up his own incision.

I said, "I'll get her."

I nipped across the living room without waiting for either man's permission and headed through the dining room and kitchen toward Gilda's room. I hadn't much liked Gilda before, not because she was gorgeous but because she hadn't been concerned about Ziggy. Now I felt sorry for her. The thought even crossed my mind that I should warn her, one woman to another, that Kurtz was playing dumb about a lot of things. Not being a total idiot, I let the thought cross without flagging it down. I had already created enough trouble for myself by that inane protective gesture toward Kurtz. That decision was going to cost me, and I didn't want to add any more to it.

In Gilda's open doorway, I came to an abrupt spine-tingling stop. The room was still and silent as a coffin, and the bed's white cover was military smooth. An open doorway on the opposite side of the room showed a white-tiled bathroom, also empty and silent.

"Gilda?"

I don't know why I called. The room had a permanently empty feeling, the same deadness I remembered in my mother's room after she abandoned me and my brother.

I called a couple more times, just to confirm what I already knew. "Gilda? Are you here?"

I even trotted down the wide eastern corridor where a glass wall overlooked the courtyard. I pasted myself against the glass to look out at the oak tree and the landscaped lawn around it. Unless Gilda had scaled the tree and was hiding in its branches, she wasn't in the courtyard. The east wing had only one door and it was open—Kurtz's bedroom. I stepped inside and got a quick look at a big bed with black satin sheets. I called Gilda, but I knew she wasn't there. Gilda had left the house, and every instinct told me she hadn't left to run a quick errand. Gilda had run away, and she didn't intend to be found.

A hallway on the south side of the house held a door with a double dead bolt lock, the kind you have to use a key to open from either side. A key was inside the lock, one of two on a wire ring, probably left there all the time because it's a pain in the butt to always have to key open a door from the inside. I turned the key and opened the door to a narrow alcove at the far end of the row of garages. A sidewalk led to a utility area where garbage cans and recycle bins were located. Beyond the utility area, a wooden fence separated the Kurtz property from a bayside residential street. If Gilda's intention had been to run away, she was probably halfway to Tampa by now, or at least halfway to the Sarasota airport.

I shut the door and stuck the key ring in my pocket to give to Kurtz. With all the people who would be in the house when Guidry found out Gilda was gone, it wasn't a good idea to leave a key in a door, especially since I suspected the second key opened the precious wine room. I walked down the southern hallway, passed the wine room, and rounded the corner to the west wing where Kurtz and Guidry waited in front of the fireplace. Framed by the red glow of the fire, the two men could have been part of a medieval fresco of good and evil, with the iguana symbolizing a demon stretched on the hearth between them.

I said, "Lieutenant Guidry, could I speak to you for a moment?"

Both men gave me piercing looks that said secrecy wasn't an option.

Guidry said, "What is it, Dixie?"

"The nurse isn't in her room. She isn't anywhere in the house. She's gone."

Like a collapsed marionette, Kurtz suddenly clutched his thighs and gave a strangled groan. It didn't seem like the anguished cry of a man who'd lost a lover, more like a man who could not bear the implication of what he'd heard.

Guidry and I both rushed to support him.

Guidry said, "You know where his room is?"

I pointed toward the southern corridor. "It's this way."

In seconds, we had linked arms behind Kurtz's emaciated back and under his thighs to make a fireman's carry. Putting a suffering man to bed wasn't the usual kind of thing a homicide detective did. Not the kind of thing I usually did, either. But Guidry and I were both professionals, and professionals rise to the occasion in a professional manner—no matter what the occasion is.

We went down the southern corridor to the east wing and Kurtz's bedroom, where we turned sideways to maneuver him through the doorway. When we lowered him to a king-sized waterbed with rumpled black satin sheets, Kurtz seemed almost unconscious. With a heavy sigh, he stretched out on his back and held his arms close to his sides, as if he feared he might fly apart if he didn't keep his limbs close.

Guidry and I exchanged uneasy looks. With one mind, we both looked at the bedside table, where a clutter of prescription bottles stood next to a stack of magazines and a framed photograph. Guidry picked up a bottle and read the label.

I picked up the photograph. With a kind of eerie inevitability, I saw it was a snapshot of Ken Kurtz—as he had been before he turned blue and ugly—with his arm slung over the shoulders of the woman I'd met earlier—the one with the bulldog named Ziggy. They were both laughing into the camera with the unmistakable look of two people deliriously in love.

# 6

Seeing the photograph of the woman I'd met that morning made my head feel like somebody was setting off rockets inside it. Guidry didn't seem to notice. He shuffled through some more prescription bottles and then pushed them all into a clump.

"Mr. Kurtz, do you have your doctor's number?"

Kurtz opened his eyes and glared at Guidry. Between rasping breaths, he said, "No! Absolutely . . . no doctors! Understand?"

"But—"

"I said . . . no! You do not . . . have my . . . permission to . . . call anybody."

"Okay, no calls. Would any of these medications help you right now?"

"No . . . I just need . . . to rest . . . for a while."

Guidry stood a moment looking down at him and then nodded. I knew what he was probably thinking. Kurtz lived in agony every minute of his life, and he was probably the best judge of when he'd reached his limit. In any case, Kurtz's suffering wasn't the kind that could be fixed by a doctor. It would take angels to do that. Or at least aboriginal shamans.

Very gently, I put the photograph of the woman back on the bedside table next to the medicine bottles and magazines. I was positive now that she had contrived to talk to me so she could make sure I was going to his house.

Was the woman somebody with old scores to settle? A former wife or old lover who had vindictive reasons to pull strings by getting the Irishman to call me? If that were so, why had she wanted me there? And what was the deal with calling her dog Ziggy? None of it made any sense, but I didn't care. I had no intention of getting sucked into this weird situation. As soon as I was sure the iguana was okay, I was going to be out of there for good.

Guidry said, "Come on, Dixie."

He was standing at the door and his voice had a tinge of impatience in it, as if he might have been standing there a few seconds longer than his grand eloquence thought was necessary, and that he was holding me responsible for the delay.

I gave him a *What?* look. I was there as a pet sitter, not a deputy under the jurisdiction of a homicide detective, and he didn't have the authority to order me around like that.

On the other hand, I was in deep doo-doo already for not reporting the guard's murder and for warning Kurtz to ditch his gun. I wasn't the type of person to do either of those things. I was one of the good guys. Wasn't I? I was on the side of the law. Wasn't I?

As I moved to follow Guidry, it occurred to me that when I killed a man, I might have blurred my own line between good and evil. Maybe I wasn't so solidly in the good-guy camp anymore. Maybe I was straddling the line.

Guidry said, "Show me the nurse's room."

I moved ahead of him and walked the rest of the way down the eastern corridor to Gilda's room, glancing out the glass wall to the courtyard as I went. The plants still glistened with moisture from the rain, but except for the wet ground under the oak tree's shade, all the shadows had been eaten up by thin sunshine.

At Gilda's door, I stopped and took a deep breath.

Guidry said, "You okay, Dixie?"

Surprised, I looked up at him and pulled my shoulders back. "Sure. Why wouldn't I be?"

"I can think of several reasons why you might not be. You're allowed, you know."

"Allowed what?"

"Normal emotions."

For some fool reason, that made my eyes burn as if tiny little pinpricks were pushing against the undersides of my eyelids.

I pointed toward Gilda's door. "That's her room."

As he went around me, Guidry put an arm around me and squeezed my shoulder, almost as if he did it unconsciously. Guidry wasn't a shoulder-squeezing type of man, and I'm not the kind of woman who likes her shoulders squeezed. But his hand had been warm, and the touch had felt good. I watched his leather jacket move away and tried not to think about what it meant about me—that in the midst of all the bizarre things going on in this house, my main feeling was that I wished Guidry would touch me again.

Making my voice as cool as possible, I said, "If you don't need me, I'll go check on the iguana."

I scooted through the kitchen and dining room to the living room. Ziggy was still on the fireplace hearth, but he had raised his head and pushed his body up a little on his muscular forelegs. His Granny Smith color was returning, especially on the side close to the fire, and when he saw me he inflated his dewlap so he looked twice as wide. An iguana with a widely inflated dewlap looks alarming, like a miniature dragon about to breathe fire and brimstone. If I hadn't known iguanas, I would have found him scary. As it was, I stopped walking so he wouldn't get spooked and leave the warmth of the fire.

It takes about thirty minutes for a healthy iguana who has closed down on account of cold temperature to get back to normal. Ziggy was close to normal, but his household wasn't. Unless Gilda showed up with some plausible explanation for leaving, Kurtz and Ziggy were going to be here by themselves. Considering the shape Kurtz was in, it was a toss-up as to which of the two was less capable of taking care of the other. If Gilda's disappearance was as suspicious as I thought it was, there would be investigators in the house looking for evidence that would link her to the guard's murder.

I wasn't going to get involved, but I was a professional, and professionalism meant I had to find a place to put Ziggy so he would stay warm and still be out of the way.

I also had to feed him, which made me think of the odd packages stacked on the refrigerator shelves. I went back to Gilda's room, where Guidry was squatting on the floor in front of an opened cabinet in her bathroom.

Without looking at me, he said, "Tell me about the nurse. What's she like?"

"Beautiful redhead, late twenties, early thirties. She has an accent I couldn't place, sort of an island rhythm but more like French pronunciation. Her English isn't very good, and she smelled like iodine."

He closed the cabinet door and stood up. "Iodine?"

"That same smell is in the refrigerator, too. That's what I came back to tell you. The refrigerator doesn't have any food in it. It's filled with what looks like packages from a meat market, and there's a strong smell of iodine."

He was already moving past me toward the kitchen. I trailed behind him, wishing I could go get breakfast, wishing I hadn't agreed to take this job in the first place.

I said, "I have to go to the market and buy vegetables for Ziggy."

He stopped and frowned at me. "You call him Ziggy? You know him that well?"

"I don't know him at all, but that's his name."

"Kurtz's name is Ziggy?"

"No, the iguana's name is Ziggy."

"Oh."

He shrugged and moved on toward the refrigerator.

That's when I should have told him about the strange coincidence of the woman with the bulldog named Ziggy. And about the even stranger coincidence of the woman's photograph being on Kurtz's bedside table. But if I told him that, I'd have to tell him all the rest. I'd have to tell him that Kurtz had lied when he said nobody knew about the wine, because Gilda had known that Ziggy was in the wine room. Mostly, I'd have to tell him about the gun Kurtz had been wearing when I got there. And then I'd have to tell him I'd warned Kurtz to get rid of it before he talked to Guidry.

I wasn't ready to do that. I told myself that half the population of Florida carries concealed guns, so it wasn't unusual for Kurtz to have one. It wasn't even unusual for a gun toter to be paranoid enough to wear it inside his own house. Furthermore, I hadn't broken any laws when I advised Kurtz to get rid of his gun, I had simply suggested it might be a good idea not to meet a homicide detective while wearing it. It had been a friendly hint, nothing more. And so far as the woman in the photograph, maybe I was mistaken. Maybe it only looked a lot like the woman with the bulldog. And who's to say it's unusual for two pets in the same city to be named Ziggy? There are probably millions of pets named Ziggy, and several of them might live right there on Siesta Key. Mainly, I told myself I wasn't getting involved in this case, so the sensible thing was to keep my mouth shut.

Guidry opened the refrigerator door and turned to look at me with raised eyebrows.

The refrigerator was completely empty. All the packages in their neat white wrappings were gone.

I said, "That's odd. Gilda must have taken them with her when she left."

"You think it was meat?"

"I don't know what it was. It was packages like what you get from a meat market, you know, in that white butcher paper."

"And it smelled like iodine?"

"That's what it smelled like to me."

"Dixie, tell me again why you're here."

"A man who said he was Ken Kurtz called me last night and asked me to come today to feed his iguana. He said he was delayed in New

York, but that somebody would be here to let me in. He didn't leave a telephone number, and my Caller ID didn't register it, so I don't know where he was calling from."

"That's all he said?"

"He said the iguana's name was Ziggy and that he likes yellow squash."

Guidry closed his eyes and mumbled something that sounded like *Why me?*

I said, "I have to find a place to put the iguana while your people are here. I'm going to go ask Mr. Kurtz."

Guidry grunted, and I headed around the corner to the eastern corridor and Kurtz's room. Kurtz was sitting up with his eyes closed, leaning back against a headboard lined with shelves of tomes I could tell weren't light reading. The bottles of medicine were still on the bedside table. The photograph of the woman was gone, probably moved to the drawer in the table.

I said, "Mr. Kurtz? Is there someplace warm and safe where I can put Ziggy?"

He opened his eyes and gave me a level stare. "No place in the world is safe, Ms. Hemingway."

"Probably not, but some places are less problematic than others, especially for an iguana."

He tilted his head toward a closed door. "You can put him in the exercise room. It's warm in there. It's through the bathroom."

I left the side of his black satin bed and opened the door to the bathroom. More white ceramic tile, more white bathroom fixtures, more white walls. Whoever planned this house must have had a fixation with hospitals. Another door stood open from the bathroom, and I went through into a fully equipped home gym, with a glass-enclosed dry sauna in one corner and a compact swim-in-place pool in the other. I checked the size of the sauna and decided it would do. Ziggy would be cramped in it but warm.

Back at Kurtz's bedside, I opened my mouth to tell him I was on my way to get Ziggy and put him in the sauna. But the words that came out weren't what I had intended to say.

I said, "Who is that woman, Mr. Kurtz?"

He opened his eyes and looked up at me. "Gilda? She's my nurse."

"I mean the woman in the photograph."

"I believe you're here to take care of my iguana, Ms. Hemingway, not to pry into my personal life."

Every intelligent cell in my body was jumping up and down and yelling, *Let it go! Don't say anything else!*

I said, "She stopped me this morning. I think she wanted to make sure I was coming here."

The shock on his face was almost too painful to see. "You must be mistaken. It couldn't have been her."

"She had a miniature bulldog with her, and she said the dog's name was Ziggy."

For an instant, a look of wild joy flared in his eyes and just as quickly died.

"Sheer coincidence. You met somebody who resembled my old friend in the photo, and she had a pet also named Ziggy. That's all."

"Your old friend, does she have a name? In case she stops me again?"

He shot me a look that held poisoned arrows. "I'm warning you, Ms. Hemingway, drop it *now*."

I left him and headed toward the living room, taking the southern corridor so I wouldn't have to talk to Guidry again in the kitchen. My head was whirling, and I felt almost faint. Only pure idiocy could have moved me to ask Kurtz about the woman. Or insanity. Or both. It was entirely possible that I had gone completely round the bend. It was not only entirely possible, it seemed to be a proven fact. I had to get Ziggy safely stored in the sauna and get the hell out of this house before I did something even loonier than the things I'd already done.

# 7

Ziggy was still sluggish enough to spare me any tail-whipping resistance when I pulled him close again and carried him to Ken Kurtz's gym. Kurtz didn't even open his eyes when I sidled through his bedroom. I laid Ziggy on the floor of the spa, made sure the heat was set just warm enough for comfort but not warm enough to burn, and left him there. He looked a damn sight better than Kurtz. Lying back against his black satin pillows, Kurtz looked more comatose than asleep when I left his room.

I took the southern corridor back to the living room and slipped out the front door without telling anybody goodbye. I wanted to leave Ken Kurtz's house and never come back, but there was a good possibility Ziggy hadn't eaten in at least three days, and I hadn't seen anything that remotely resembled vegetables and fruit for him. Even though I'd been tricked into taking the job, I felt responsible for Ziggy. That meant getting him food.

Glumly, I clumped down the driveway past the crime scene investigators. I knew without having been there what they'd been doing. They had taken all their measurements and all their photographs. They had gone over every inch of the guardhouse and its surround for fibers, stray hairs, or latent prints, any minutiae that might point them toward the killer. They had slipped the corpse into a body bag and zipped it shut, and the body had been taken to the Medical Examiner's pathology lab for autopsy. Now technicians were widening their search, walking in slow circles around the grounds, looking for a weapon, shell casings, bullets, footprints—anything they could use to solve the crime.

Like them, I kept my eyes on the ground in front of me. I was minding my own business. This murder investigation had nothing to do with me, and as soon as I got food for Ziggy I was out of there.

On the way to the Crescent Beach Market, I met several cars with big red velvet Christmas bows attached to their hoods. On every street, Christmas stuff had suddenly appeared all over the place. Wreaths on doors, red velvet ribbons tied to outside security lights, baskets of poinsettias at every doorway. It was as if people had looked at the calendar and panicked when they saw we were only twelve days away from Christmas. Either all the Jews and Buddhists and agnostics and atheists on the key had converted, or there was a cosmic conspiracy to make me look Christmas square in the face.

Even in the best of circumstances, Christmas on Siesta Key has a surreal quality. We know from TV shows what a real Christmas is like. That's when families gather in the big house where they grew up, where their dying or divorced-but-friendly parents have festooned everything in sight with swags of fir, and where everybody ends up outside in the snow whooping like kids and rediscovering the true meaning of Christmas. We can never have that. On Siesta Key, our fir swags are fake, our snowmen are Styrofoam, and the closest we can come to a snowball fight is to kick sand at one another.

To children, of course, Christmas is Christmas no matter where it happens, and that was really what was causing my heart to ache. It would be the fourth Christmas since Christy had been killed. She had been three when she died, old enough to be thrilled with writing letters to Santa and sharing Christmas secrets and going shopping for presents for the people she loved. Every Christmas since she died has been a day of pain for me. For that matter, so has Valentine's Day and Mother's Day and Father's Day and Thanksgiving and Easter. All those holidays bring memories of Todd and Christy, and there have been times when I thought my heart would burst from them.

The best holiday is New Year's because it isn't imbued with images of children and loving families like all the others. Anybody can participate in New Year's. Old people who haven't seen their ungrateful progeny in years can still raise a glass to toast a new beginning. Single rejects who haven't had a date in decades can still see another year of possibilities opening like a portal to a deodorant ad of fields of flowers while they run in slow motion into the arms of a new beloved.

On all the other holidays, I stay to myself and dull the memories of Todd and Christy by thinking of new ways to groom belligerent cats or fresh approaches to flea dips. But on New Year's Day I live it up. I drink champagne and eat black-eyed peas and watch big men on TV chase a football and knock each other down. And at the end of the day, I look in the mirror and say, "Good girl, Dixie, you made it through another year. Now do it again."

But first I had to get through Christmas.

Outside the market, a Salvation Army Santa was ringing a bell with cheerful deliberation and calling out "God bless you" to people tossing coins in his pot. I didn't exactly say "Bah, humbug," when I passed, but that was how I felt.

Inside, "Jingle Bells" was playing. I tried to ignore the music while I filled a basket with kale, turnip greens, bok choy, escarole, collard greens, romaine, parsley, and yellow squash. As I hotfooted it to the TEN ITEMS OR LESS line, the music changed to "Here Comes Santa Claus." If I had to listen to that all day long, I'd be a blithering idiot.

Ahead of me, a white-haired woman was telling the checker that she and her husband had started the trip from Oregon to Sarasota this season via a cross-Canadian train ride.

She said, "It was my first train trip," and in an instant I was six years old and holding my mother's hand while we edged our way down a train car. Michael was behind me with his eight-year-old face set in stern, disapproving lines. It had been the Christmas season then, too. Our mother had wakened us early, with an exuberant giddiness that meant she'd already been drinking, and told us we were going on a trip. An adventure, she called it, but we both knew she was really taking us away from our father. The adventure came after she sobered up and found herself stranded in a little town in Georgia with two hungry kids and not even enough change in her purse to call home. It had been Michael who took control. He had marched up to a Salvation Army Santa at the train station and said, "My little sister and I need help. Our mother is sick and we have to take her home."

I think that was the moment our mother became afraid of Michael's strength and capability. It was also the moment when I knew I could always depend on him.

I hadn't thought about that train trip in ages, or about my mother. Just the possibility that I might be shirking responsibility like she'd always done was enough to jerk me to attention. As the checkout line moved forward, I stacked Ziggy's veggies on the conveyor and resolved to do what I had to do and not whine.

On the way out, I folded a five-dollar bill and put it in the Salvation Army Santa's pot. Not that I'd suddenly come down with the Christmas spirit, it was just the memory of that first Salvation Army Santa and how kind he had been. Maybe my five dollars would help some other stranded kids get home.

It was nearing noon and I'd been up since four o'clock without caffeine or food. Not having Ziggy's ability to store fat under my dewlap when food was scarce, I made a detour to the village and went into Anna's Deli, where the woman at the counter had hair almost as red and carelessly abundant as Gilda's.

I said, "I need a surfer sandwich bad."

Even as I spoke, part of my mind considered the odds of running across two women with messy red hair in one morning. I even considered the possibility that the entire morning was a dream, and that red-haired women were in it to symbolize something I needed to remember.

The woman must have sensed that I was spacing out because she barked out my order to the sandwich maker like a drill sergeant.

I said, "I need coffee, too."

"Sure you do," she said, in the tone one uses with a two-year-old about to have a tantrum or with a mental patient off her medication.

I wondered if my eyes were as big and white and staring as they felt.

While the sandwich person laid thin slices of ham, turkey, Swiss, and cucumber on thick marble bread, I thought of Ken Kurtz lying on his black satin sheets. He hadn't had breakfast either. For all I knew, he hadn't eaten in weeks.

The sandwich maker piled onion, lettuce, and tomato on my surfer, and topped the whole thing with Anna's special sauce. As she sliced it in half, I held out my empty coffee cup.

"Give me a refill, please, and another surfer. Also another coffee, large. And some pickles and chips, two of each. Oh, and give me four cups of chicken soup, too. And a couple of brownies."

Straight-faced, the woman said, "No salad?"

"Oh, yeah. One tuna and one garden. Ranch dressing."

With bags of veggies for Ziggy in the backseat and deli bags from Anna's in the front, I tore off for Kurtz's house, where a Contamination Sheet had been posted on the front door while I was gone. Technically speaking, a Contamination Sheet is only posted at a crime scene, and in this case the crime scene was solely the guardhouse. The presence of the sheet meant the nurse's disappearance had extended the range of investigation.

Through the window, I could see Guidry in the living room talking to some crime-scene techs. Looking at him gave me a fizzy feeling like my blood had turned to 7-Up. I signed in, noted the time, and opened the front door without ringing the bell. When I came in, Guidry looked up and I frowned at him.

I said, "I'm going back to feed the iguana."

He nodded, already bored with anything having to do with my pet-sitting duties, and I nipped down the southern corridor to the east wing and Ken Kurtz's room.

Propped on those black satin pillows, his blue skin gave him the look of a two-day decomposed corpse. Only the furrows of pain on his face and the neural chaos under his skin showed that he was alive. He was the most alone-looking human being I'd ever seen in my life.

I said, "I've brought food for Ziggy," and hurried through the bathroom to the gym.

Wide awake and bright green now, Ziggy looked like a not-so-miniature dragon. Even the spikes down his spine seemed to stand taller now that he was warm. When he saw me, he puffed out his dewlap to its fullest extent and bobbed his head at me. Iguanas bob their heads just when they see something unfamiliar, but if I hadn't known that he would have looked menacing.

I said, "Wow, I'll bet you scare the hell out of a lot of people."

I quickly knelt and put squash and romaine leaves in front of him, then nipped out so he could eat without the strain of trying to look dangerous.

Ken Kurtz was actually the scary, intimidating one, even though he still lay like a man half dead on his black satin bed.

Without any preamble, I set the bags of food on his bed and plopped myself down beside them.

"I brought you some food."

He opened his eyes and watched me haul out containers.

"I don't eat normal food. The nurse—"

"The nurse has flown the coop, and nobody else gives a hoot whether you eat or not. Since you won't let Lieutenant Guidry call anybody, I'm your last hope."

He groaned. I didn't blame him. I'd hate to think I was my own last hope.

I took the lid off the container of soup and moved it around in the air to waft the scent to him. "It's not like you don't have choices. There's a sandwich, with which you get chips and a pickle. There's tuna salad. There's a garden salad. And if all that's too solid for you, there's chicken soup."

I made a lap tray out of a magazine, and put half a sandwich and a cup of soup on it. It seemed to me that his eyes got a little brighter, but maybe I was projecting.

I said, "There's coffee too, and brownies."

"I don't drink coffee. The caffein mixes with the toxins in my body."

"And does what?"

He took a moment to consider. "I don't know what the fuck it does, it's just what the nurse always says."

"Uh-hunh. So do you want it with cream and sugar?"

He managed a weak smile. "Black's fine."

He took a tentative bite of his sandwich, then leaned his head back against the pillows as if the effort had cost him.

I said, "Who do you think telephoned me and told me to come here?"

He leaned forward to sip chicken broth directly from the cup. "I don't know who called you, Ms. Hemingway."

"Dixie. Call me Dixie."

He took another sip of soup and gazed at me. I had the strange feeling that he was waiting for me to ask a different question, and that if I asked the right one, he would answer it. It was senseless to probe for any answer at all, since every bit of information drew me deeper into a situation I didn't intend to be in.

It seems to me there are two kinds of people in the world, those with little endurance for the inevitable pain in life and those who dig in their toes and survive, no matter what. In my darkest moments, even when I think there's nothing to live for and no reason to go on, I remain a survivor. I could see the same hard determination in Kurtz's agony-darkened eyes. I couldn't even imagine the hell he'd gone through to cause him to end up as this pitiable figure who would frighten the toughest street thug, but whatever it was hadn't made him stop struggling to live.

I said, "I heard you tell Lieutenant Guidry that Gilda came from New York, but she didn't seem American to me."

His mouth quirked in wry amusement. "She claims her original home was one of the spice islands—the Bandas—and that may be true. With her coloring she might have Dutch or Spanish ancestors who went there to buy cloves and nutmeg. Nevertheless, she's an American citizen, and she'd been living in New York when she came to work for me."

He sounded derisive, as if claiming to be from a spice island was a far-fetched idea, but I could easily imagine Gilda among nutmeg trees or bushes or vines or whatever nutmeg grows on. She would look a lot more natural in a sarong than in surgical scrubs, and I found it a bit suspicious that Kurtz downplayed her exotic beauty as if he hadn't noticed it. I knew the man was sick, but only a dead man would be that oblivious.

I said, "The woman I met this morning had something to do with all this, didn't she?"

Lord help me, I couldn't seem to stop with the questions.

The smile left his eyes.

"Ms. Hemingway, you are far too nosy for your own good."

Squeakily, I said, "You can call me Dixie. I'm not formal. And I know she's the woman in the photo."

"The woman in the photo died two years ago."

"Then I met her twin this morning."

"They say we all have an identical twin somewhere in the world. If that's so, I pity the poor bastard who's my double."

A little stab at humor, I suppose, to get me off the subject of the woman.

"You lied to Lieutenant Guidry about the guard coming in the house. You also lied when you said nobody but you knew about the wine room."

"And have you told Lieutenant Guidry that I lied?"

I felt my face flame, and I took a drink of coffee. "Not yet."

"You won't tell him."

"Of course I will."

"You won't tell him I lied, and you won't tell him that you warned me to get rid of my gun. And do you know why?"

Trapped, I stared at him while my heart hammered against my ribs. This man had a strange effect on me that I couldn't explain.

Kurtz said, "You won't tell because you're like me, not like him."

I swallowed the last bite of sandwich and crumpled the paper it had been wrapped in.

"What's that supposed to mean?"

"It means you act on instinct, not on intellect, and your instinct tells you to keep quiet about my lies."

"My instinct also tells me you may be lying about a lot of things. Somebody chose me to come here, so I have a right to ask questions."

"The less you know, Dixie, the safer you'll be."

I didn't like the way this conversation was going, mainly because it made way too much sense. I stood up and gathered up the uneaten half of his sandwich and the unopened containers. "I'll put this stuff in the refrigerator so you can have it later."

"I appreciate your thinking of me, Dixie."

"Look, you have to have somebody here. Ziggy has to be fed, you have to be fed, you have to let somebody come in and help you."

"I was hoping that would be you."

"I'm a pet sitter, not a nurse."

"I'm more animal than human, so you're highly appropriate. All the iguana and I need is a bit of food once a day. You could do that for us, couldn't you? Just for a few days? Until Gilda returns?"

"What makes you think Gilda will come back?"

"Oh, she'll be back. And soon. I'm sure of that."

Now here's the thing about being a little bit off-center—you're never sure if you're a bona fide loon or if you have insight that other people don't have. You have to navigate through life using a kind of psychic gyroscope to keep from falling too far one way or another, and you feel a peculiar kinship with other people who are also a little bit off-center. Ken Kurtz was right. In some fundamental way, he and I were alike.

I said, "I'll give you a few days, but if Gilda's not back by the end of the week, you'll have to make other arrangements."

He made a sound halfway between a bitter laugh and a growl. "I wish it were that simple, Dixie."

I didn't ask what he meant by that. The house and the man were making me claustrophobic. I practically ran to the kitchen to stash Ziggy's veggies and Ken Kurtz's leftover food in the empty refrigerator. I had already crammed it on the shelves when it occurred to me that Guidry might have wanted the refrigerator to remain as Gilda had left it.

I could hear him in Gilda's room talking to some crime-scene people. No doubt about it, he was treating Gilda's disappearance as an important part of the murder investigation. I closed the refrigerator door and hurried to the living room and out the front door, pausing just long enough to log the time on the Contamination Sheet. Within seconds, I was in the Bronco and on my way home.

I didn't know whether I was shivering from the cool air or from the sure and certain knowledge that I was too involved in something bizarre and dangerous.

# 8

Michael and I learned that our mother had left us for good when we came home from school one day and found our grandparents sitting side by side on the living room sofa. Something about their stiff postures alerted both of us that something had happened in the mysterious world of grown-ups. My grandmother was the one who told us. She just came right out with it, as if she had to say it fast and get it over with.

"Your mother has run off with a man she's been seeing. He doesn't want any children, and she wants him."

My grandfather frowned and said, "I don't think that's necessary, Christina."

"Yes, it is," she said. "They need to know the truth of it." She turned to us and said, "We've already packed your things. You're going to live with us now, and I'm glad."

The thing was that when my mother had been there, she was really there, so her absence was all the more glaring. With hindsight, I decided she had probably always wanted to leave but she had waited until after our father died, putting out a fire to save somebody else's children. My mother never forgave him for dying. Perhaps she had never forgiven him for being a fireman.

At any rate, our grandparents took Michael and me in and finished doing what their daughter wasn't willing or capable of doing herself. Like the rhythm of the sea, they never changed, and in their frame house overlooking the Gulf I felt I'd come to a place of stability and safety. When they moved on to wherever we go when we die, they left the beachside property to Michael and me. Michael and Paco moved into the house, and after Todd and Christy were killed I moved into the apartment over the carport, where the sound of the surf anchored me.

Driving home from the Kurtz house, I decided not to tell Michael and Paco about the morning's bizarre events. They worried too much about me as it was, and Michael was still touchy about the man I'd killed. I guess no matter how old Michael and I get, he'll always feel it's his job to protect me. When he can't, he feels guilty, and when he feels guilty he gets grumpy.

Turning off Midnight Pass Road, I eased down our twisting lane. As usual, flocks of wild parakeets blossomed from the mossy oaks, pines, and sea grape as I passed, circled overhead in a kind of mock frenzy, then zoomed back to their perches as if they'd had a wild moment of excitement they'd never had before. Parakeets are such drama queens.

When I nosed the Bronco under the carport, I mentally groaned when I saw Michael in front of the shelves of a storage closet. He was meticulously rearranging tools and all the little jars of nails and touchup paint that men collect. There's something about laying things out so they all face the same way or lining them up in alphabetical order that makes super-organized people feel better. Not being a particularly organized person, I've never arranged stuff like that in my life, but I still find things when I need them. Usually.

I slid out of the Bronco and said, "What're you doing?"

He held up a jar of fish hooks. "Just sorting things."

"Uh-hunh. Michael, how long's it been since you used one of Granddad's old hooks?"

"You never know when you might need something like that. You hungry?"

"I had a sandwich a little while ago."

"You look funny. You looked funny when you were here before, too. What's wrong?"

"It's cold. I hate cold. I'm going to go take a hot shower."

I left him staring after me and hurried upstairs, raising the metal security shutters with my remote as I went.

Michael yelled, "I have chili on the stove when you get hungry."

I waved and smiled and opened the French doors. I kept the smile on my face all the way down the hall to the bathroom, as if Michael could see through walls. In the bathroom, I let the water turn steamy while I stepped out of my clothes, and then stood for a long time under water I was pretty sure was hot enough to kill germs. I even used germicidal soap. I didn't know what was wrong with Ken Kurtz, but I knew enough biology to know his weird whirlpooling skin pointed to something systemic and neural. Whatever it was, I didn't want it.

When I felt sufficiently decontaminated, I came out all red and hot, wrapped myself in a thick terry robe, and fell into bed and immediate dark sleep. I woke feeling a surprising clarity, as if the shock of the morning had put everything else into better perspective.

I mentally reviewed everything that had happened from the moment the phone call came from the man who claimed to be Ken Kurtz. I tried to recapture the timbre of the man's voice, the rhythm of his words, the Irish accent with its lulling calmness that had made me trust what he said. At the time, I'd thought we had a bad connection, but now I wondered if the fuzzy sound had been because the man had been speaking through layers of fabric that made the voice less distinct.

For the first time, I wondered how he had got my number. Other than a small display ad in the monthly *West Coast Woman*, I don't do any advertising. Half the time, I even forget to carry business cards. My business comes mostly from referrals, people I know well. And yet somebody had rejected all the pet sitters listed in the Yellow Pages and called me. Why?

With the question came the immediate answer. My name had been in the news just a few months ago when I'd killed that man, along with the information that I was a professional pet sitter. Somebody could have made note of the name and looked me up in the phone book. Maybe they'd thought I was a tough cookie, a former deputy who was a crack shot, a hard woman who didn't flinch at killing and who therefore wouldn't be sickened by Ken Kurtz.

If that were true, the person who called may have hoped I would do exactly what I'd done—feed the man as well as the iguana. Which would imply that he knew Gilda wouldn't be around. Which all came back to the guard being killed and to Gilda freaking out when she learned he was dead, and to her running away with the iodine-smelling packages in the refrigerator, whatever the hell they were.

I got up, collected the clothes I'd thrown on the bathroom floor, and rifled the pockets of my jeans before I tossed them in the clothes hamper. The key ring from Ken Kurtz's back door made a hard little *thunk* when I shook it into my hand. Damn, I'd forgotten to give it to him. Unless he had a spare, that meant nobody could get out the exit door from the inside. I went in the living room where I'd tossed my shoulder bag and dropped the keys in the bag. I would return them the next time I was at Kurtz's house.

Then I went to my office-closet, where the answering machine was blinking its little red eye. The readout said I'd had four calls. As I hit PLAY to listen to the messages, I shed my terry robe and reached for a pair of clean jeans. A fuzzy Irish voice from the answering machine made me freeze with the jeans dangling from my hand.

"Good afternoon, Dixie. I'm dreadful sorry that I lied to you, but it was the only way. And now I must ask you to do something else, something very important. Please write this down and repeat it to Ken Kurtz exactly as I give it to you: *Ziggy is no longer an option. You must act now.*"

I stood statue-still and stared at the machine, gripped by a strange malaise that made me unable to turn off the voice, either on the tape or in my head. It was the same man who had originally called claiming to be Kurtz.

I hit the REPEAT button. The voice said the same thing the second time, and the third and fourth. I replayed it at least a dozen times. I even wrote down every word. Then I played the other three messages while I pulled on jeans, a black T, and clean white Keds. I was stuffing the message in my pocket when I saw my forgotten underwear in the chair at the desk. Damn. Going braless is fine, I do that a lot. But wearing jeans without underwear is like sitting naked on the beach. Both take a certain masochism that I haven't yet developed, so I took an extra two minutes to get some satin between my crotch and the denim inseam.

I would deliver the message, and then I was going to insist that Kurtz find another pet sitter to feed Ziggy. I was through with both man and beast.

As I grabbed my shoulder bag from the living room sofa, I stopped short. It was two o'clock, and I didn't have to start my afternoon rounds for another hour. Why was I rushing? Why was I feeling an urgent need to get to Ken Kurtz and deliver the message? Why was I letting myself be used again by an unknown Irishman? Boy, talk about masochism! An inseam in the crotch is nothing compared to letting yourself be manipulated twice in twenty-four hours by a faceless voice.

I pulled out the message I'd written and read it again. Then I did what I should have done all along—I dialed Guidry's cell phone. I had called that number so many times in my last involvement with murder that I knew it by heart. He didn't answer, so I left a curt message.

"I have something to tell you about the guard's murder. Please call me ASAP."

I stuffed the note back in my pocket and went out the French doors and down the stairs to the carport. The sky was a clear expanse of blue now, all the clouds pushed away by a steady western breeze from the Gulf. A pelican stood on the shore congratulating himself on the catch in his pouch. A squadron of seagulls were flying straight into the wind like kamikaze pilots, then banking sharply and flying back to shore, arguing about who had flown the fastest before they headed out into the wind again.

I pulled the Bronco out and drove slowly down the lane so as not to alarm the parakeets, then turned north at Midnight Pass Road. I needed to talk to somebody smarter than me. That included most everybody in the world, but my actual possibilities were limited. I couldn't talk to Michael because he would freak out. I couldn't talk to Paco because that would put him in a position of keeping a secret from Michael, and he wouldn't do it. I couldn't talk to Tom Hale because he was too involved with his new girlfriend to have any energy left over for me or my problems. Cora Mathers was the only person I knew who was wise enough to give me good advice but not so emotionally close that talking to me would cause her problems.

Cora was the grandmother of a cat owner who'd got herself murdered on my watch, and Cora had sort of become a stand-in grandmother for me. She lived in the Bayfront Village, an exclusive gulfside retirement condo. Her granddaughter had plunked down an obscene amount of ill-gotten money so Cora could live in a large condo on the sixth floor where she had a view of the Gulf and the evening sunsets, but I suspected that Cora would have been just as happy in her old double-wide.

At the Bayfront Village, sliding glass doors breathed open for me, and the concierge waved to me from her desk. Chirpy as a spring robin, she trilled, "I saw you outside. I've already called Miz Mathers, and she said for you to go on up."

I mouthed, "Thanks," and threaded my way through gray-haired men and women milling around in the lobby. Some of them were smartly stepping along with tennis rackets or shopping bags in their hands, and some were stopping to take in all the Christmas and Hanukkah decorations.

A gentleman wearing bedroom slippers and cradling a teacup-sized white poodle in his arms got on the elevator with me. All the way to his floor, he talked to the poodle.

"You remember Elmer had one of those things, don't you? He seemed to like it well enough, but I never thought it was completely safe. If there had been a power failure, Elmer could have been trapped there in that house, stuck halfway up the stairs. I'm glad we don't have one of those, aren't you?"

The poodle listened intently, his round black eyes fixed on the man's face and shining with adoration. At the fifth floor, the doors opened and the man shuffled through, still talking.

"Elmer was always stubborn. He was a stubborn boy and a stubborn man. Not curious about anything, either. Not like you and me."

The doors closed, and I was left alone to be glad I had never known Elmer.

When I got off at the sixth floor, I saw Cora down the hall waiting for me in front of her door. Just the sight of her made me feel better, maybe because Cora reminds me a little bit of my own grandmother. From the top of her downy white hair to the soles of her little feet, Cora isn't quite five feet tall, and she weighs less than a hundred pounds. She moves in little jerky motions because her joints aren't what they used to be, but she's plenty active inside her head.

She hollered, "You must have smelled my chocolate bread! I just took it out of the oven."

That made me feel better too, because Cora's chocolate bread is Webster's second definition of *decadent*. She makes it with an old bread machine her granddaughter gave her, and she won't say what her secret is, but the result is dark and moist, with spots of yummy melted chocolate. Since I love chocolate second only to crisp fried bacon, the devil could leave a trail of it and I'd probably eat my way straight to hell.

I gave Cora a big hug, careful not to squeeze too hard and break her, and followed her half steps into her apartment. A jaunty red-berry wreath was on her front door, a sprig of mistletoe hung from the ceiling in the foyer, and a small fake Christmas tree with demented blinking lights stood in the corner of her living room. The tantalizing odor of gooey chocolate was heavy in the air, and I could hear Cora's teakettle whistling.

I said, "I'll get the tea things," and hurried to her narrow kitchen.

Cora transferred a stack of mail and some magazines from a small skirted round table set between her kitchen and living area while I put tea bags in her teapot and filled it with boiling water. She pulled out one of the ice cream chairs at the table and sat down with her elbows on the table and her chin resting in her hands. I could feel her keen old eyes watching me from under their hooded lids.

She said, "Don't slice the bread, just tear off hunks of it. It does better that way. And don't forget the butter."

"I know, I'm getting it."

I stacked bread plates and cups and saucers on a tray, added butter, a plate of fist-sized chunks of chocolate bread, and the teapot. When I carried it to the table, I moved my chair so I didn't face the blinking tree. Cora deftly set out the plates and poured the tea while I tore into a hunk of bread.

I closed my eyes and moaned. "God, that's good."

"It is, isn't it? I don't do too many things good, but I'm good at chocolate bread. What're you best at, Dixie?"

I stopped in mid-chew and considered. "I'm best with pets. Dogs. Cats. Right now I'm taking care of an iguana."

"A whata?"

"Iguana. They're big lizardlike animals. This one is a bright shade of green, about five feet long. Most of that length is tail, though."

"Do they bite?"

"They can, but they don't unless they feel attacked. They have little fish teeth, so their bite isn't dangerous, but they can break the skin."

"Huh. Imagine that."

I set my teacup down and took a deep breath. It was time to tell her why I was there.

# 9

I said, "Cora, I'm not doing so good."

She shrugged. "I imagine killing somebody would take the starch out of a person."

"It's not just that. It's something else, like I'm not myself anymore."

She sipped her tea and searched my face. "Who are you, if you're not yourself?"

I slid the butter knife down the stick of soft butter and sliced off a large piece of it. I laid it on a fresh chunk of hot chocolate bread and watched it ooze into the bread's pores. When it had totally disappeared, I took a big bite and chewed.

Cora waited until I swallowed and took a gulp of tea. Then she said, "Dixie?"

"I'm thinking. I guess I'm still myself, but I'm doing things I don't usually do."

"Well, sugar, nobody but a pure nincompoop spends their whole life doing the same things over and over. There comes a time when you start doing new things."

"I lied to a homicide detective, Cora."

She frowned. "You mixed up in something?"

"No, it's not like that. It's the iguana. Not the iguana itself, but the man who owns the iguana. See, somebody called me and said it was him, but it wasn't, and when I got there the guard had been shot in the head. I didn't want to get mixed up in anything again, so I left. I didn't report it. I just went home and took a shower and then when I went to find the iguana's house, it turned out that's where he lived. There where the guard got killed."

Cora blinked rapidly a few times. "I guess you should have reported it, but it's not exactly lying that you didn't. You just didn't tell what you knew."

I drained my teacup and set it down. "There's more. Before Lieutenant Guidry got there, I warned the iguana's owner to get rid of a gun he was carrying. Then I heard him tell a couple of lies to Guidry and I didn't tell Guidry they were lies. I didn't tell Guidry about the woman, either."

"What woman?"

"A strange woman stopped me this morning. She had a bulldog with the same name as the iguana, and I think she was watching me. The man had her picture on his bedside table. And he's blue, by the way. I think he's really sick."

Cora blinked some more. "Dixie, do you take vitamins? You know, you've been under a lot of stress lately, what with killing that man and all, and you need to take care of yourself. Get more rest, take vitamins. You shouldn't drink coffee either. I don't drink coffee at all anymore, just tea. It's better for you. They say green tea is healthiest, but I just drink it brown, and I'm pretty healthy."

"I sound crazy, don't I?"

"A little, but women go plumb loony when they're in love."

"I'm not in love, Cora."

"Well, of course you are, sugar. You're in love with that detective fella. Trouble is, you've forgotten how to do it."

"Believe me, I remember how to do it."

"Oh, I don't mean the sex kind of doing it. You don't ever forget that."

She paused for a while and smiled at whatever image had flitted through her head. I took a big bite of chocolate bread and waited for her to return to this century.

"I'm talking about how you're doing *love*," she said. "You've gotta be strict with love, or it'll just move in and take over your whole life. You have to give it a special room and make sure it stays there until you're ready for it to come out. That's what you've forgotten. Your problem is you're hauling love's butt around with you every place you go."

I swallowed wrong, and Cora eyed me while I had a coughing fit.

She said, "Men don't do that. You don't see men dragging love around with them every minute, worrying does it need a drink of water, is it hungry, does it need a sweater. Men just let love fend for itself while they go off and work or play or fight or fool around. They don't let love rule their lives like women do. You put love in its place, and you'll stop lying to people."

My cell phone rang and I leaped to snatch it from my purse. It was Guidry.

He said, "Dixie, we need to talk."

"I know, that's why I called you."

Cora rolled her eyes at how snippy I sounded.

Guidry said, "I'll be at your place in ten minutes."

He hung up without giving me time to tell him I wasn't at home. Well, okay, let him cool his heels while he waited for me.

I rushed the tea tray to the kitchen so Cora wouldn't have to lug it in there, then scooted to hug her thin shoulders and kiss the top of her feathery head. "I have to go, Cora. Thanks for the bread."

She said, "Don't worry about that man being sad, Dixie. After all, his guard got shot. That would make anybody blue."

"You're right. I won't think about it anymore."

I left her sitting at the table pensively staring into her teacup. I knew she hadn't understood a thing I'd said, but I actually felt a lot better.

During the summer months, I could easily drive from Cora's condo to my apartment in ten minutes. But during the season, when Sarasota's population triples, the streets became as congested as any large city, and half the drivers are of the opinion they are privileged people who should not be expected to obey traffic laws made for ordinary humans. You therefore have to be hyper-alert for expensive cars zooming out of driveways or running red lights, and if you get behind a blue-hair going fifteen miles an hour on Tamiami Trail, you have to resist the urge to gently tap her rear bumper to give her the idea to move along.

It took me a good thirty minutes to make the drive, and when I got home Guidry was nowhere in sight. Michael's car was in the carport, but his kitchen door was closed and all the shades were drawn. As I unlocked the French doors, Guidry's dark Blazer eased past the carport and parked in the open space next to Michael's cypress deck. I paused, hoping Guidry didn't guess that I'd raced home to meet him. He spotted me as he got out of his car, and then I started worrying that he might think I had been home all along and was so eager to see him that I'd come outside to wait for him.

He didn't seem put off by the fact that I didn't smile or wave or speak to him, just looked solemnly at me while he strolled across the ground to the stairs. The nip in the air had put extra color in his cheeks, and I couldn't help noticing that his usual golden tan was now more of a peachy color. I love that color. I could eat that color. It's warm and lush and makes me think of hot summer nights and homemade ice cream. But Guidry's gray eyes weren't warm at all. In fact, they were about as icy as the frigid slurry that firms homemade ice cream.

When he got to the top of the stairs, he said, "We have to talk."

He took my arm and sort of tugged me, not manhandling me, but not like I had a choice either. My heart did a crazy tango and my nipples turned to hot rubies, but at the same time I was afraid I might break out in hives or throw up. Cora was right. Men don't do that kind of crap.

Guidry pushed the French doors open, giving me a look as he stepped inside my apartment that made my jaws lock. I knew as surely as I knew the surf would roll on the beach every day that Guidry had feelings toward me too.

He said, "You have any coffee?"

Oh, that was good. Making coffee would give me a chance to do something with my hands. Guidry and I could sit and drink coffee and ease into a conversation about what had happened this morning.

I scurried to the kitchen and sloshed water in the coffeemaker, put in the little paper cone thing, filled it with coffee, and pushed the button. While it gurgled and spat, I got out mugs, but no cream or sugar because I remembered that Guidry drank it black, same as I do. When I turned around with my finger threaded through the mug handles, I met his calm eyes.

He said, "Dixie, the man who reported the guard's murder was there to deliver the *Herald-Tribune*. He says that when he turned into the driveway, he met a woman on a bicycle coming out. He describes her as about thirty years old, pretty, blond ponytail. Says her bike was black, with a roomy basket for carrying stuff."

Carefully, I settled the mugs on the bar and moved them so their handles pointed in the same direction. I pulled out the drawer under the bar and got out a stack of paper napkins. My mind flitted to the idea of cookies. We should have cookies with our coffee, it would be nicer.

"Dixie? Is there anything you want to tell me?"

I stepped back to the coffeemaker and watched the dark liquid rising in the glass bottom, climbing toward the four-cup line. When it reached the line, the machine burped and hiccuped a couple of times and a few more drops fell into the black lake. I waited a few seconds to give it time to squeeze out its all, and then lifted the pot and carried it to the bar. As careful as a prayer, I poured two mugs of coffee and took the pot back to its home base.

Then I turned around and folded my arms across my chest and met Guidry's gaze.

"Guidry, the guard was dead when I saw him. It wouldn't have changed anything if I'd called. Two or three minutes' difference, that's all."

"I'm not concerned about the timing, Dixie."

"Okay, I should have called. I know that. But I didn't want to get involved in another murder. You understand that, don't you? When the truck drove in, I knew the driver would report it, so I left."

"The guard's name was Ramón Gutierrez. Twenty-nine years old, no criminal record. Married, two kids. Killed by a single bullet to the left temple, probably a thirty-eight caliber."

I wrapped my arms around myself and shivered. "Why are you telling me this?"

"A witness saw you leaving the murder scene."

This time when my heart tripped it wasn't because I was close to Guidry. It was because I suddenly got the full import of why he was there.

"For God's sake, Guidry, *I* didn't kill him!"

His hand on his coffee mug was steady as he looked at me. "The call from the *Herald-Tribune* guy came in at six-fifteen. The Medical Examiner estimates the guard was shot no more than three or four hours before."

"You can't be serious about this! You know I didn't kill that man."

For the first time, I saw a glint of anger in Guidry's eyes. "What the hell were you thinking? Didn't you expect the deliveryman to tell us you were there? Why didn't you tell me? Why let me find it out this way?"

An undercurrent of some emotion I couldn't identify rang through his disappointment, some old hurt or resentment that didn't have anything to do with me or the current situation. We all carry such a bundle of old experiences, it's a wonder we're ever fully in the present.

By the way he compressed his lips and gave a slight shake of his head, it seemed he'd caught himself having feelings he regretted.

He said, "We have a new DA, Dixie—a woman with a lot of ambition and a lot of political connections. Here's how she's going to see it. You're a former deputy with sharpshooting awards. Your work takes you in and out of empty houses, so you probably carry a weapon. You were hired to take care of Ken Kurtz's iguana. You went to his house, but the guard wouldn't let you in. Maybe you had words with him, maybe he insulted you. You're emotionally stressed because of what happened back when you killed that guy, so you flipped out and shot him in the head. You came home, ditched the gun, and returned to the Kurtz house pretending it was the first time you'd been there."

"I don't carry a gun, and I didn't shoot the guard. I didn't even know that was the Kurtz house when I went to the guardhouse. I was trying to find a place to wait out the rain."

I thought about Ken Kurtz saying I would never tell Guidry that Kurtz had lied to him, or that I had warned Kurtz to get rid of his gun before he talked to Guidry. Instinct, Kurtz had called it. Acting on instinct rather than intellect. Now my instinct told me I had disappointed a man I greatly admired and respected. Maybe I had completely blown any chance of getting closer to him.

The weird thing was that I was as disappointed in Guidry as he was in me. He should have known me well enough to know I was innocent. Not just innocent of killing the guard but innocent, period. Sure, I might keep quiet about a few tidbits of information I'd overheard, and I might not tell him that Kurtz carried a gun under his bathrobe, but I was one of the world's good people, and I expected him to know it. If he didn't, maybe he wasn't the man I'd thought he was.

I said, "Do you want to take my thirty-eight for ballistics?"

He sighed. "Dixie, I don't think you killed the guard. I just wish you'd told me, that's all."

"But you want my gun."

"I'm sorry."

So furious I could hardly breathe, I left him sitting at the bar and went into my bedroom where the side of my single bed was pushed against the wall. Yanking the end of the bed away to get at its far side, I pulled out a drawer built into its base. The Sarasota Sheriff's Department issues 9-millimeter SigSauers to all personnel, but every deputy also has personal backup guns for which they are qualified. When a deputy retires or dies, his department-issued gun has to be turned in, so I no longer had either Todd's or my own, but I had all our backups. Todd's were a nine-millimeter Glock, his Colt .357, and his primary personal, a Smith & Wesson .40. My own were a Smith & Wesson .32 and a .38 that was my favorite. I kept them all in a specially built case in the drawer under my bed.

I lifted the .38 from its Styrofoam nesting place and laid it on the bed. I closed the case and slid the drawer back in. I pushed the bed back against the wall and stomped into the kitchen and put the gun on the bar in front of Guidry.

I said, "You'll note that it's clean and oiled. It hasn't been fired."

"I don't want to press the point, Dixie, but the gun could have been cleaned and oiled since this morning."

I slapped the counter and glared at him. "Guidry, this is nuts!"

"What was nuts was leaving the scene of a crime and pretending you didn't know anything about it."

I couldn't argue about that. I said, "My grandmother always said that wisdom came from knowing that every decision we make carries a consequence. I made a bad decision."

"That may be the understatement of the century."

"Guidry, tell me the truth. Do you really think I could have killed that guard?"

"The truth? The truth is that I have a better chance of winning the lottery than I have of finding the shooter."

The room seemed to grow dimmer for a second as it dawned on me that in the absence of an arrest of the real killer, I would look like a tasty suspect to a DA hungry to assure the public that all killers were speedily caught and executed.

When I was growing up, Sarasota was essentially lily white and essentially North American. Even Canadian snowbirds were considered foreigners. But as airfares from Europe got cheaper and European vacation spots more expensive, Florida became salted with temporary visitors from all over the world. Now criminal investigators have to think international. A serial rapist may follow an MO known to police in the Netherlands but not here. A burglar may leave a calling card familiar to French gendarmes but not to Sarasota law-enforcement officers. A tourist can commit a crime in Sarasota and be back home in Europe before the Forensics Department has had time to evaluate all their findings. Now when murders are committed, every homicide investigator has a secret fear that the perpetrator is halfway around the world laughing at him. The guard's killer could be safely across the Atlantic while the DA focused on me.

I said, "Kurtz was carrying a gun when I got there this morning. He had it in a fanny holster under his bathrobe. Looked like a backup gun a law-enforcement officer might carry."

"For Kurtz to kill that guard, somebody would have had to carry him out to the guardhouse."

"He lied when he said nobody knew about the wine room. The nurse knew about it, because she's the one who told me Ziggy was in there."

Guidry waved his fingers back and forth to show how insignificant my blabbing was.

"Dixie, can you account for your time this morning? Did anybody see you during the hours before the guard was found dead?"

I swallowed against a lump in my throat. "There was a woman, Guidry. She was out walking a miniature bulldog and she stopped me this morning. There was something odd about her. She said her dog's name was Ziggy, and she seemed relieved when I said I was going to see an iguana named Ziggy. She ran off and got in a car and drove away fast. The whole thing seemed phony somehow."

"Dixie, that's not—"

"Her picture was on the table beside Ken Kurtz's bed. He denied it, but I'm positive it's the same woman."

"What do you mean, he denied it?"

I licked lips that had suddenly gone bone dry. "I asked him about her. I know I shouldn't have, but I did."

# 10

Guidry's pupils contracted into little pinpoints, like a man about to jump up and ward off the devil. Half the people in Southwest Florida believe in a literal Satan, so for all I knew he might have caught the devil-believing bug, like catching chicken pox.

He said, "What're you doing, running your own investigation?"

"It may be an investigation to you, but it's my *life*! I'm the one who got tricked into going to that house. I'm the one the woman accosted. I'm the one somebody's using, and I have a right to know who's doing it and why."

"I'll agree that somebody tricked you into the house, but all that other stuff is your imagination—the woman didn't accost you, it doesn't mean a thing that her dog has the same name as the iguana, and the odds of her being the same woman in Kurtz's photograph are about a quadrillion-to-one."

"The photo was on his table when we carried him into the bedroom, and then later it was gone. He hid it. Why would he do that unless he didn't want anybody to see it?"

"I can think of a million reasons why a man might not want people to see whose photo he keeps beside his bed. The point is that you're there as a pet sitter, not as an investigator. If you see something you think is relevant, tell me about it, don't go blundering around asking questions. Furthermore, don't withhold information, *any* information, and don't put groceries in a refrigerator that may be an important part of a homicide investigation."

Uh-oh. I'd forgotten about putting Ziggy's veggies in the refrigerator.

Guidry's voice had got louder with each word, and by the time he ended his face had gone from an appetizing peachy color to a rather unhealthy rose.

In a little-bitty voice, I said, "Okay." Under the circumstances, that seemed like the best thing to do.

Visibly, he got control of himself. "I don't know what it is about you, but you always seem to pop up whenever something really weird is going on."

"So you agree the whole Kurtz thing is weird."

He slid my gun in his jacket pocket and headed toward my French doors. "I don't see how it could get any weirder."

He didn't even say goodbye, just left me wishing he hadn't said that it couldn't get any weirder. Call me superstitious, but I think it's a big mistake to challenge the universe to pull out all its weird possibilities. That's like declaring what you will not do, will not accept, or will not believe, ever, so long as you live, amen. Like parents who say about their baby boy, "No son of mine will ever have a motorcycle," are bound to look up one day and see him wearing a bug-eating grin and a biker chick glued to his road-calloused buns. You have to be careful about what you set into motion with what you say.

I went into my office-closet to check on messages. All but one were from people wanting to know my rates. I took their numbers to call back. The other was from Ethan Crane. Ethan's an attorney, but he's more interested in getting justice than in getting rich, so I don't hold that against him. I'd first met him when he handled the estate of a cat I was responsible for. Later, he took over the management of a foundation set up by a man whose murder indirectly led to my killing somebody. I don't hold that against him either.

Ethan is also one of the handsomest men I've ever seen in my life, and the second man I'd recently realized I was attracted to. In a sexual sort of way, I mean. In a holy-smokes-he's-hot kind of way.

Which was all very confusing because all my pores had only recently commenced salivating whenever I was around Guidry, so what the heck was I doing feeling sexual toward Ethan Crane? It was like my body had been without sex or romance for so long it had lost its ability to make choices.

Ethan's message was short and to the point. "Hi, Dixie, Ethan Crane here. Say, I was driving down Midnight Pass Road this morning and saw your Bronco in a driveway where there were a bunch of sheriff's cars and a crime scene tape. I hope everything is okay with you. I think about you a lot. Could we have dinner one evening? Give me a call, okay?"

There's a lot to be said for having dinner with a man who isn't mad at you, so I punched in his private number. He picked up the phone on the first ring.

"Hi, Dixie, how are you?"

Damn, I always forget about caller ID. Knowing he'd known it was me before he answered made me stutter a little bit.

"I'm fine. Good to hear from you."

"I know this is a busy time of the year, with the holidays and all, but if you're free this evening, I'd like to take you to dinner."

He had no idea how free all my evenings were. He also had no idea how I hated the whole idea of dating. I opened my mouth to tell him I was tied up until Easter.

My lips said, "Sure. Where shall I meet you?"

A beat passed while he registered that I would take my own wheels. "How about the Crab House at seven?"

"Better make it closer to eight-thirty. I have a full schedule today."

He chuckled lightly. "Okay, I'll meet you tonight at eight-thirty. Looking forward to it."

I nodded at the phone and then found my voice. "Good. 'Bye."

As I hung up, it occurred to me that I'd just said what sounded like a curt *Goodbye*. What I'd actually said hadn't been much less curt, but I had to fight myself to keep from calling him back and saying, "I didn't say *Goodbye,* I said *Good.* *'Bye.*" Another reason to hate dating and all the rules and crap that go with it.

I got up and pawed through my few clothes. If I was going to start going out with men, and it looked possible, I was going to have to buy a whole new wardrobe. Dresses. Skirts. Shoes and purses. The thought made me almost gag, but I had to start thinking like a grown-up, acting like a grown-up, dressing like a grown-up. I couldn't go through life forever in shorts and jeans and T-shirts and Keds.

It was time to leave for my afternoon pet visits—all of them except Ken Kurtz. I wasn't going to deliver a message to him, and I wasn't going back to his house for any reason except to feed Ziggy. Furthermore, I wasn't going until tomorrow. If either Ziggy or Kurtz got hungry before I came, they could damn well call out for pizza. But first I had to let Michael know what was going on.

I found him in his kitchen spreading freshly toasted chili-cayenne pecan halves on paper towels. When Michael and Paco moved into our grandparents' house, they left it pretty much the way it had always been, except for the kitchen. Now the kitchen is outfitted with Sub-Zero appliances, an enormous grill, and every gizmo ever made for professional cooks. A wide butcher-block island has a salad sink at one end and stools on each side at the other end for eating. Since Michael does the cooking at the firehouse as well as for me and Paco, his freezer is always stuffed and he spends a lot of his off time cooking things for fellow firefighters.

Firefighters must like things hot, because chili-cayenne pecans are Michael's annual Christmas treat for the firehouse. I popped one in my mouth and then did an Indian war dance while I fanned my lips and whimpered.

He waved a wooden spoon at me. "Coffee's fresh. Pour me a cup too, would you?"

Still fanning my lips, I got down mugs and splashed hot coffee into them. When I handed one to Michael, he stopped me with his spoon on my chest.

"Okay, something's wrong, and I want to know what it is."

I took my coffee to the big butcher-block island and perched on a bar stool.

I said, "A man working as a security guard for Ken Kurtz was murdered early this morning. He was shot in the head in the guardhouse."

Michael rotated his spoon, meaning *Get on with it.* "I heard that on the news. What does it have to do with you?"

I swallowed coffee and tried to think of a way to tell the story that didn't make me seem crazy.

"Ken Kurtz has an iguana I was hired to feed, so I had to go to his house."

Michael's eyes were getting brighter blue, a sure sign his patience was wearing thin. "So?"

"I went there twice, once to get out of the rain and once to feed the iguana. The first time, I saw the dead guard and I didn't report it. The second time, I went for the iguana, only I hadn't realized the first time that it was the iguana's house because I'd never been there before, because the man who hired me wasn't really Ken Kurtz, he just pretended to be. And there's a woman mixed up in it somehow. Two women, really, the nurse and the woman with a bulldog, but the nurse ran away and Kurtz claims the other woman is dead. But I think he's lying because he has her picture and I'm sure it's the same woman."

I couldn't bring myself to look higher than Michael's belt, but from the stiff way he stood, I was pretty sure I hadn't done a good job of telling the story like a sane person.

He said, "Anything else?"

My voice came out weak as a new kitten's. "A *Herald-Tribune* deliveryman called nine-one-one to report the guard was shot. He had seen me leaving as he drove in the driveway, and he reported that too, so Guidry has me as the only person seen leaving the crime site. The ME has put the time of death within the last few hours before it was reported. Guidry took my thirty-eight for ballistics testing."

Michael moved to the bar stool across from me. He had gone so pale I could see tiny freckles I'd never noticed before dotting his cheekbones.

"Are you saying you're a murder suspect?"

"Only because the *Herald-Tribune* guy saw me. When they do the ballistics test, they'll know it wasn't my gun."

I tried to make my voice sound positive, but the truth was that Guidry hadn't told me if they'd recovered an intact bullet or a casing. If they hadn't, a ballistics test on my gun wouldn't help me a bit.

When a bullet travels through a gun barrel, the bullet takes on marks unique to that particular barrel. Any bullet fired from a specific gun will show the same marks, unless there's been some intentional alteration between firings. Or unless the bullet itself is distorted because of hitting bone or passing through a body and hitting something else hard. Shell casings leave distinctive marks too, so the Forensics firearm examiner would be able to match a casing to the gun that fired it—unless no casing was found.

"But until then you're a suspect, right?"

I was surprised at how calm he sounded. Then I noticed the handle of his coffee cup lying on the bar. He had snapped it clean off.

Miserably, I said, "Michael, I try to stay out of these things, I really do. I don't know how I get involved."

"The important question," he said, "is how to get you uninvolved."

It was way too late for that and we both knew it, but for a few moments we pretended there was a way out and that I would find it.

I said, "By the way, I won't be here for dinner tonight. I have a date."

I tried for nonchalance, but my voice came out squeaky.

Michael's eyebrows climbed nearly to his hairline. He and Paco had been pushing me to get a man in my life for over two years.

Trying equally hard to sound like it was something I did every day, Michael said, "Actually, I won't be here either. One of the guys at the station needs to take the night off for his daughter's wedding, so I'm going to cover for him. A date with who?"

"Whom. Ethan Crane, the lawyer."

"Ahhh."

As I went out the door, I said, "This will all work out, Michael."

He said, "Yeah," and went back to laying out his pecan halves. I didn't look at his face, but he actually sounded a bit hopeful. Only thing was, I knew it was because I'd told him I had a date.

At Tom Hale's condo at the Sea Breeze, Tom stayed out of sight while I snapped on Billy Elliot's leash. Downstairs, we ran around the parking lot several times like demented dervishes. I was still wheezing when we got back to Tom's apartment, but Billy Elliot was grinning and calm. As I hung Billy's leash in the hall closet, Tom rolled into the living room with a smile that managed to be both smug and sheepish, one of those sexual reactions peculiar to men.

He said, "Sorry about this morning, Dixie. I would've introduced you to Frannie, but you left too soon."

"I didn't know you were involved with somebody. It sort of took me by surprise."

"Me too. I mean, I just recently decided to get involved. I figured I've been without love too long."

I gave him my best cynical look. "You decided to fall in love?"

"Sure. Not that I wasn't particular about the woman, but I'd made the choice to love before I met the person."

I must have looked unconvinced, because he gave me a somewhat pitying smile.

"Love is always a decision, Dixie. It's not something that descends on you like manna from heaven."

I thought about that remark for the rest of the afternoon, while I was walking the dogs on my list and while I was playing with the cats. At Muddy Cramer's urine-stinky house, I found him clinging to the top of the Cramers' silk velvet draperies, leaving shred marks with his claws and making heartrending cries of desperation. While I tried to coax him down, it occurred to me that humans are the only species that considers a house a shelter. Muddy had spent all his life in the open air, taking his chances with rain and wind and predators and traffic. While that's not what anybody wants for a domestic cat, it had been Muddy's life and he obviously didn't consider it a blessing that the Cramers had rescued him from it.

The sun sets early in December, around five-thirty, and it was almost seven when I headed home. What with changing clothes half a dozen times and changing my mind about my hair and makeup I don't know how many times, I barely had time to shower, dress, and leave for the Crab House by eight-fifteen. I'd finally settled on a pair of butt-hugging black leather pants with short high-heeled boots and a fuzzy pink sweater. Hair left hanging. No makeup except gloss and mascara. Sort of an innocent-whore look.

A full moon hung low on the fresh-washed horizon like a newly minted gold coin, bathing the key in such a flood of bright radiance that security lights were redundant. Driving past the Kurtz house, I looked toward the guardhouse and the palm hedge beyond it. In the bright moonlight, the place had a lost, forlorn look that gave me a guilty nudge. My angel self said it wouldn't kill me to pop in and check on Kurtz and Ziggy and give him the key to his back door. My selfish self said to shut up, I didn't have time, and anyway I didn't want to. My selfish self won.

The Crab House is at the southern tip of the key on the bay side. I thought it spoke well of Ethan that he'd suggested it, since it's one of my favorite places. The clientele is a good mix of straight/gay, young/old, rich/middle-class, some from boats tied up at the Crab House dock and some off shiny Vespas or Hogs. The food is good, the music is good, and those who are so inclined, which I never am, can dance on its tiny dance floor.

I parked the Bronco at the side of the parking lot next to a car with two teenagers making out in the backseat. From the sounds coming through the open windows, I got the distinct impression of an impending orgasm, maybe two. For their sakes, I hoped it would be two. For my own sake, I hoped I got away before it happened. It had been four years since I'd known that kind of mindless joy, and now that I'd sort of decided to maybe put myself in a possible situation which might conceivably one day lead to me having an orgasm with a new man left me feeling weak and stupid, as if I needed a diagram of how to do it, like *Insert Tab B into Slot A*. As I hurried toward the door, I heard the girl in the car howl like a cat in heat. So much for missing the sound of her orgasm.

When I opened the door, Ethan Crane was inside waiting for me, and when he saw me he got that look in his eyes that men get when they're interested in making you yowl like an alley cat.

Holy smoke, he was almost too good-looking.

# 11

Smooth man that he is, Ethan had already snagged us a table, and he steered me there with a couple of fingers light on my fuzzy pink shoulder. One of the most strikingly handsome men in the world, Ethan is an arresting combination of Seminole Indian and some other genes that produced shiny shoulder-length black hair, deep-set dark eyes, an engaging white-toothed grin, and a firm, nicely muscled body. A woman who didn't find him enticing would have to be either dead or hard-core lesbian. I'd noticed him even when I was almost numb, and it had scared me to death.

Now that I was thawing out and thinking I might want to live like a woman after all, I still got flustered when I was around him. I was also confused. How could I feel such a strong pull from Guidry and still have deliciously indecent thoughts about Ethan Crane?

I was acutely aware of the heat of his fingers through my sweater and relieved that our table was by the back glass wall. If we ran out of things to talk about, or if I became totally inarticulate, we could look out at the bay.

A waiter slid up as soon as we were seated, and I had the feeling Ethan had engineered that too, probably with money and the promise of more with excellent service. He was that kind of man.

I ordered a margarita—on ice, with salt—and Ethan ordered a beer. Somehow, that surprised me.

I said, "I'd have expected you to order something more sophisticated, like special scotch that's been filtered through oatmeal or something."

He shrugged. "You know how it is with us Injuns. We don't do well with strong firewater."

His voice had a bite to it, as if he resented the stereotype, even though he was invoking it himself and even though he was only a quarter Seminole.

I said, "Makes you crave more?"

"No, makes me puke in the parking lot. Plays hell with a date."

That made me remember we were on a date, and I instantly tensed.

He said, "You look terrific. I like that fuzzy stuff. What is it?"

"Mohair. It's mohair. Comes from a goat. I think it's a goat. Maybe it's a sheep. I'm not sure, goat or sheep."

Lord help me, my mouth wouldn't shut up.

His grin was a white slash in his bronze face. No doubt about it, he was one gorgeous Indian.

The waiter whipped back with our drinks and asked if we wanted to order yet.

Since I was suddenly famished, I nodded vigorously. Ethan allowed as how menus would be a good idea, and we spent the next few minutes deciding on what to eat. The waiter was at our side the instant we both decided on grilled grouper, which made me positive he'd been paid to shower us with attention.

When the waiter left, Ethan said, "I'm glad to see you again. When I saw your car at that house, I was concerned."

His voice had gone deep and throaty. I thought of the teenagers in the car. I thought of how Ethan Crane would sound having an orgasm. I thought of how I would sound having an orgasm with Ethan Crane. I was very warm in my pink fuzzy sweater.

To keep him from guessing my carnal thoughts, I said, "Do you happen to know anything about Ken Kurtz?"

"Who?"

"The guy who lives in that house where the guard was killed."

"I didn't know his name. The house was built by a corporation based on the Isle of Man."

"The Isle of what?"

"Man. It's in the Irish Sea off the northwest coast of England. It's a little tax-free island where people keep money they don't want traced."

"You mean Ken Kurtz doesn't own the place?"

"I don't know who owns it. He could be doing business as the corporation, although the corporation itself was a shell for another company."

Suddenly Ethan Crane didn't look so hot to me. For all I knew, he could be involved in whatever was going on with Ken Kurtz. Maybe his interest in me wasn't personal at all. Maybe he had given my name and number to the Irishman who had called me.

I said, "How do you know so much about who owns the Kurtz property?"

The chill in my voice made him look up with a question in his eyes. "I served as escrow agent for the shell company."

That was even more suspicious, because Ethan wasn't a real estate attorney.

He must have sensed my withdrawal, because he almost blurted out an explanation.

"I met an attorney in London a couple of years ago, and we exchanged business cards. You know, in case I ever needed a contact in London or in case he needed one in Sarasota, the kind of networking thing people do. I never expected anything to come of it, but he called me about this time last year and asked if I'd handle this transaction here on Siesta Key. His client wanted to buy an existing house to tear down and put up a new one, but they didn't want any public notice of the purchase. I filled him in on Florida realty laws, told him they'd have to retain thirty percent of the existing house to avoid zoning changes and public postings. To keep their name out of it during construction, the sale would have to be a land contract rather than the usual possession-at-funding deal. That way, the seller retains title until final payment is made."

"So you handled it?"

"Yeah, it was just a favor to the guy. I might need his help in London someday."

"When was final payment made?"

"It hasn't been made yet. It'll be finalized on January first."

"In two weeks?"

"Right."

All my nerve endings were standing up waving red flags, but I wasn't sure if it was because I was still a little suspicious of Ethan or because what he'd said pointed to something that was important.

I said, "How'd you know the company you dealt with was a shell company?"

"Because the check they sent was cut by BiZogen Research, and the company buying the property was Zogenetic Industries."

An icy trickle crawled down my spine. "Do you know anything about BiZogen Research?"

"Not a thing, do you?"

I shook my head. I didn't, but I intended to find out.

The waiter brought our salads, and for a few minutes we filled time nodding yes to an offer of fresh ground pepper and then watching with faked rapt attention while he turned the pepper mill. You would have thought we were aboriginal people who'd just newly arrived in America and had never seen such an astonishing thing before. That's when I realized that Ethan was just as nervous as I was, a realization that hit me like a thunderbolt. I'd known all along he was interested in me, but not that he was *that* interested. It was such a pleasant surprise that I smiled sweetly at him, the way you smile at a baby who's doing something especially cute. Nothing like knowing a man is nervous in her presence to make a woman feel powerful.

His shoulders relaxed and we both began to talk about safe things—the chill weather and wasn't it a shame that all those tourists weren't enjoying the beach, the salads and wasn't the house dressing just the best, the music playing and wasn't it smooth. The waiter whisked away our empty salad plates and replaced them with plates of grouper grilled exactly the way I like it, plain, with just a squeeze of lime and no yukky sauces to hide the fresh sea taste. With it we had what the menu had described as a "medley" of grilled vegetables—zucchini and snow peas and some broccoli flowerets. None of it was as good as what Michael makes on his prize grill, but then not many chefs cook as well as Michael.

I had long since polished off my margarita and switched to water, and I noticed that Ethan had done the same. I liked that in him. Too many men guzzle down alcohol like they have to have it in order to boost their spirits or their nerve or their egos. The fact that Ethan was cool without booze made him go up another notch in my estimation.

The musicians had moved from light listening music to dreamy dance music, and a few couples were on the dance floor.

Ethan said, "Care to dance?"

All my newfound feeling of female power went flying into space. "Dance?"

"You know, the thing where two people stand with their arms around each other and move to music."

I hadn't danced since a New Year's Eve party just before Todd and Christy were killed. I hadn't thought I'd ever dance again, hadn't thought I'd ever be in another man's arms again.

I felt the old familiar tug of loss and grief and hopelessness—and let it go. I do not honor my husband or my child by living as if I had died with them.

Ethan was looking at me with a dark shadow in his eyes. "Something wrong?"

"No, I just spaced out for a minute. I couldn't remember if I left water out for the last cat I saw today, but I did."

He nodded, eyes hooded, not believing me for one minute but letting his disbelief go to the same place I'd sent my sadness. Some things are better left unsaid. Some old wounds are better left under their scabs. I was glad we both understood that.

I said, "To tell the truth, I haven't danced in a long time. I'm pretty rusty."

"Then it's time you did it again."

I rubbed my sweaty palms on my black leather thighs and tried not to look terrified. I wanted to ask Ethan if I could have time to think about it. I wanted to tell him I couldn't get that close to him yet. I wanted to run to the ladies' room and sit on a toilet and cry.

In a bitsy voice that barely reached my own hearing, I said, "Okay."

He stood up and reached for my hand, and I allowed myself to be elevated to my feet and led to the dance floor, where Ethan took me in his arms and moved so gracefully that I forgot I was rusty at dancing and moved along with him. They say you can tell a lot about a man by the way he dances. Ethan danced like a man comfortable with taking the lead, like a man always mindful of where his partner was, both physically and mentally. Like a man who enjoyed his body. In a few minutes, my own body had learned him so it knew what he was going to do before he did it, knew by the flexing of his muscles when he was going to move this way or that, knew it was safe to let him lead me wherever he wanted me to go.

I was an astronaut floating in space with a disconnected tether, moving through vast potential without any control over my next move. Even in the midst of all the music and laughter and sounds of dishes clinking, I felt as if I were in an eternal quietness where the only sound was a cosmic heartbeat. Or was that my own heartbeat? Or perhaps his? If I turned my cheek to lay it against his chest, I couldn't be sure whose coursing blood sang under my ear. The only thing I could really be sure of was that I never wanted to move, never wanted to break this contact of flesh and breath and pulse beat. No doubt about it, I was in trouble.

He tightened his arm around my waist and drew me close. Leaning to nuzzle my hair above my ear, he said, "Could I lure you to my place, right now?"

Only God knows how much I wanted to say yes.

I pulled back and looked up at him. "Not tonight, Ethan."

He grinned. "Does that mean I can try again?"

I laid my finger on his lips to shush him, and he grabbed my hand and kissed it.

Oh, my, when a man as handsome as Ethan Crane kisses your hand, it makes you feel like a fairy princess who's just found a way out of the tower.

We went back to the table, where I got my purse and Ethan picked up the bill that had been left while we danced.

I said, "I think I'd better head home now." I didn't add *Before I throw you to the floor and have my way with you here in front of all these people*, but I thought it.

As if he read my mind, Ethan gave me a slow grin. "I'll walk you to your car."

I shook my head. "No, thanks. I enjoyed the evening, Ethan."

Before he could debate the issue, I turned on my stiletto boot heel and hightailed it out of there, breaking into a run when I got to the parking lot as if I were afraid he was after me. The only thing I really feared was that I would turn around and run back in and fling myself into his arms. It had been too long since I'd been with a man. I didn't know how to behave with one anymore.

I headed home in something of a stupor, sort of letting the car drive itself. Every time I thought about what had just happened, my whole body blushed. My back still remembered the touch of Ethan's hand. And that was nothing compared to what my front remembered—of feeling Ethan's hardness, of knowing he was as turned on as I was.

As I drove past the Kurtz house, I looked down the driveway and saw a dark sedan crisply illuminated by the full moon. I knew that sedan. It was the one the woman with the bulldog had driven. I made such a sharp turn that the car behind me went into a squealing skid and blasted me with its horn.

With my heart pounding and my fists clenched on the steering wheel, I pulled even with the sedan. I didn't see the woman or the dog, but I was certain it was the same car. Okay, dammit, this was proof that Kurtz had lied when he said he didn't know her. He and the woman had made me look like a paranoid fool—to Guidry, to Michael, to Cora, and even to myself. The woman was probably inside with Kurtz, telling him how she'd made sure I would show up at his house. They were probably planning their next clever move.

More than anything, I wanted to march up to the front door and confront Kurtz and his mysterious lady friend and force them to confess whatever their scheme was. But I'm not that dumb. I would call Guidry and let him handle it. Pulling my cell phone from my pocket, I got out of the Bronco and moved to the side of the sedan next to the guardhouse.

In the next instant, something hit the back of my head and the world went black.

# 12

I woke with a sickening headache, stretched on my back, both hands at my sides. I tried raising my head, but it stayed firmly fixed on the ground. My skin shuddered with sudden fear. Was I dead? Paralyzed? No, I could wiggle my toes, and I could flex my hands.

Slowly, memory came seeping back—for a nanosecond there had been a dull scuffling sound behind me, somebody coming up fast on the pavement, perhaps from behind the guardhouse. Before I'd had time to turn my head, something had hit me. Hard.

Willing my arms to move, I raised my hands and squinted at them. No blood, no mangled fingers. I pulled my knees up and extended my feet toward the sky. I was okay. Nothing was broken. I felt the back of my head and winced. I had a tennis-ball-sized lump, but it wasn't wet and I didn't feel any crusty dried blood. Okay, all I had was a concussion. Not my favorite way to end a day, but it wasn't life-threatening.

I managed to push myself up and sat swaying drunkenly for a few minutes while the surrounding landscape seesawed crazily. The air had an strange acrid smell and seemed oddly thick, as if I could cup it in my hand. I sat for a moment marveling at how it moved in pale gray swirls, ribboning around tree trunks and creeping along the ground.

Then my civilized cortex pulled itself together and shouted down to my old primitive brain, *Fool, that's smoke!*

With an audible groan, I fumbled my cell phone open. When the 911 dispatcher answered, I said, "There's a fire at a house on Midnight Pass Road. I imagine it's arson. There may be people inside."

I was almost surprised the dispatcher didn't recognize my voice and say, "Oh, hi, Dixie! Gee, it's been a couple of months since we've heard from you!"

Instead, he took the house number, told me to stay put, and promised somebody would be there shortly. As I stumbled to the Bronco, I could hear the fire engine's siren coming from the station at the corner of Midnight Pass and Beach Drive. My brother would be on that truck, and the knowledge that he would soon be risking his life to battle a fire set by an arsonist didn't do a thing for my headache.

Before the firefighters arrived, I pulled the Bronco out of the way behind the woman's sedan. Then I laid my cheek on the steering wheel and stayed very still because moving caused waves of nausea and chills. I raised my head when the fire truck careened into the driveway, but it sped by so fast that I couldn't tell which yellow-suited man was my brother. The truck swung around the areca palm hedge and stopped in front of the row of garages.

Within seconds, a fire marshal's vehicle and an unmarked county car swung into the driveway and came to a stop behind me. Officers piled out of the cars and ran toward the invisible house.

A fat column of black smoke was rising behind the hedge now, making my eyes and throat burn. I felt the back of my head again. There was definitely a large lump back there, but it wasn't oozing blood or brain fluid. Turning my head very carefully to keep the shapes of things within their boundaries, I scanned the area around me. The sedan was still there, but where was the woman? Maybe she'd been hit by the same person who'd conked me on the head and was lying dead or unconscious somewhere. The officers from the Fire Department didn't know about the woman. Boy, would they be surprised when I told them.

A sense of importance gave me a little boost of energy that helped push me out of the car. I would go find the fire marshal and tell him about the woman, which would sort of cancel out my failure to report the dead security guard. When I told him, I would not look at the firemen who were risking their lives to put out the fire, because that was my brother in there and I could not bear to think of what might happen to him. I would simply tell the officers about the woman so they could initiate a search for her. Then I would go home and take a shower. Maybe one of the officers would give me a ride home. Maybe I could even catch a quick nap after my shower and get rid of my headache.

My knees didn't want to hold themselves straight and my spiky boot heels caused my ankles to wobble, but I managed to shame my legs into walking down the driveway toward the privacy hedge. At the end of the hedge, I leaned against an areca palm frond because I felt very, very tired. Then I felt myself falling and couldn't do a thing about it.

Next thing I knew, I was on my back again, and Guidry was on his knees beside me.

"Dixie? Dixie? Wake up, Dixie. Come on, baby, wake up."

A little voice in my head said *Baby*?

I guess that's why I threw up. Hearing a man I lusted after call me *Baby* just naturally brought out my innate ability to show him my grossest side.

He handled it with his usual finesse, which made me feel even klutzier. With a clean white hanky that only Guidry would have, he mopped my face and helped me to his car. I pulled away and pointed toward my Bronco, but he shook his head.

"I'll have somebody drive your car home. I'm taking you to Sarasota Memorial."

Ignoring my protests, he stuffed me in the passenger seat and slammed the door. I could still smell the heavy odor of smoke, but I could see firefighters putting away their equipment, so the fire must be out. Guidry got in the driver's side and carefully backed down the driveway. I hadn't seen Michael, but all the way to the hospital, I fought back the tears I'd felt when I knew Michael was there suited up to face a fire. I didn't need a shrink to tell me it had brought back the pain I'd felt after our firefighting father had died.

At the ER, a roomful of people coddling various sprains and cuts and bruises watched as Guidry pulled rank and got me immediately into an examining room. An intern who looked about twelve years old examined me and pronounced me concussed, which I could have told him without the examination.

He said, "Any idea how long you were out?"

"Just a minute or two." I had no idea at all.

"Any amnesia?"

"No."

He recommended that I stay overnight in the hospital. When I refused, he didn't seem surprised.

He said, "Look, a concussion's not something to fool around with. It's especially important not to have another one anytime soon. I'm not kidding. A second impact syndrome can cause enough pressure in the brain to kill you."

"I don't plan on having another one."

"Nobody does, but once you've had one, you're four times more susceptible to another. Just be extra careful until this has had time to heal. Wait at least a month before you go skiing or bungee jumping or anything like that."

The kid actually thought I might leap off a bridge from a bungee. Made me feel about two hundred years old. I signed some papers, acknowledging that I was leaving against medical advice and absolving the hospital of any blame if I died during the night, and wobbled out to where Guidry waited.

The pubescent intern followed me. He said, "Somebody should stay with her tonight. Don't give her any anti-inflammatory drugs for her headache. They'll stop the pain in the short run, but in the long run they'll keep soft tissue from healing and create chronic pain. If her pain persists, bring her back for an MRI. Sometimes a concussion represses vasopressin, so if she experiences frequent urination in the next few weeks, she should see her doctor. It would be best if she didn't sleep for several hours tonight. If she falls asleep, wake her every thirty minutes and check her pupils. If they contract any more than they already are, bring her back."

Guidry nodded and shook the kid's hand, the way men do when they're signaling each other that their superior male wisdom is ensuring a woman's safety. For once, I didn't mind. I just wanted to go home and take a nap.

With one hand on my arm, Guidry steered me out to his car in the cop's reserved place outside the emergency room doors. I sank into the seat and leaned my aching head back on the headrest and didn't look up until the car stopped beside my carport. Without saying a word, Guidry swiveled out of the car and trotted around to my door. Tender as a mother, he helped me out and stayed so close behind me as we headed for the stairs to my apartment that I could feel his breath on my neck. When we got to my shuttered French doors, I stopped and groaned.

"The remote's in my purse. In the Bronco."

The metal storm shutters started rising anyway, folding into neat little accordion pleats and disappearing into the soffit over the door.

Guidry said, "I got your purse."

If I'd had all my faculties, I would have given him my grandmother's lecture about how you never, ever, under any circumstances, stick your paws into a woman's purse without her permission. But since my faculties seemed to be taking a sabbatical, I was just glad he could get us inside my apartment.

Guidry reached around me and unlocked the French doors, using the keys from my purse—the purse I hadn't given him permission to open. Then, with one arm around my fuzzy pink shoulders, he ushered me into my living room and steered me toward my grandmother's sofa with the green flower-printed slipcovers.

I said, "I want to take a shower."

"Not unless I'm in there with you."

I tried for indignant, but the most I could muster was a weak pout.

"My mouth is nasty."

"Okay, we'll go brush your teeth."

*We?*

"Guidry, you aren't going to the bathroom with me."

"Honey, you can pee without me, but only with the door unlocked. I know you. You'll push the limits and end up getting hurt."

I considered that while I tottered into the bedroom and kicked off my high-heeled boots.

I said, "I'm already hurt."

"Because you pushed the damn limits. What were you doing at the Kurtz house, anyway?"

Oh, God, I hadn't told anybody what had happened. In fact, I'd completely forgotten it. The thing about having amnesia is that you don't remember what you've forgotten.

Carefully, I turned around to face him. "Guidry, the woman was there. The woman with the dog."

His eyes narrowed. "The woman with the dog."

"Yes! Her car was there, but she was gone. That's her car parked in front of my Bronco. I was going around her car when somebody hit me."

"After you called nine-one-one about the fire?"

"No, before. Somebody hit me and knocked me out. I smelled smoke when I came to, and then I called nine-one-one."

"Dixie, you're confused. Somebody hit you after the firefighters arrived, not before. The chief thinks the arsonist must have been lurking on the grounds and attacked you because he thought you had spotted him. Did you?"

I shook my head and groaned at the pain the movement caused.

"No, no, I was hit before the firefighters came. When I came to, there was smoke in the air. I called nine-one-one, and then I moved my Bronco so the fire trucks could get past. I was on my way to tell the fire marshal about the woman when I fainted. She may be under the bushes, unconscious."

"You say her car is still there?"

I nodded and groaned again. God, I had to stop moving my head. "It's a Ford sedan. It's the same one she was driving the first time I met her."

Guidry had pulled out his cell phone and was punching in numbers with his thumb. I left him and started down the hall toward the bath-room.

As I stepped into the bathroom, I heard him behind me speaking to a deputy.

"Check out the plates on the Ford sedan in front of the Bronco. And start a search of the grounds around the house. You're looking for a woman. Maybe hurt."

I pushed the door, but Guidry's foot slid into the opening so it wouldn't close.

"That's far enough for modesty. I'll wait out here, but if I hear any thudding sounds, I'm coming in."

"Come on, Guidry, I have pet hair and grass and vomit and God knows what on me! Just a quick shower, okay?"

There was a pause on the other side of the door. "I'll make a deal. You get undressed and cover up with a towel. I'll turn on the water and help you in the shower. I'll give you two minutes, and then you turn off the water and I'll hand you a robe and help you step out."

I opened my mouth to yell *No!* Then I remembered the squishy feel of the areca palm frond just before I fainted, and the somber warnings of the adolescent emergency room doctor.

"It'll take me awhile to get undressed. I'm moving slow."

"I noticed."

Peeling off tight leather pants is tricky under the best of circum-stances. When it makes you woozy to lean over, it's a bitch to get them down to your ankles. By the time I'd stripped to my panties, I didn't have the strength to take the sweater off too.

Gingerly, I leaned over the sink to brush my teeth and splash my face. Leaning made my head feel like it might explode any minute. When I straightened up, the room began to spin, and I had to clutch the edge of the sink until it came to rest. Taking a shower suddenly seemed like climbing Mount Everest.

When I opened the door in my underpants and pink fuzzy sweater, Guidry took one look at me and scooped me into his arms like a daddy picking up a tired two-year-old.

I said, "I'll just stay dirty for a while."

"At least you don't have nasty teeth anymore."

"I'd like to take a nap now."

"We're going to talk awhile first."

"I need Extra Strength Excedrin for my headache."

"I have Extra Strength Tylenol, and I'll make you some coffee."

His cell rang as he lowered me into the green chair and tucked my grandmother's afghan around my legs. He answered as he started toward my little cubbyhole kitchen. At my bar, he stopped and grabbed a notepad and pencil.

"Spell the name. And the address? Okay, dust the car for prints and run them through IAFIS. Top priority. Like in the next hour."

He pronounced IAFIS as if it were one word, but anybody who's ever been in law enforcement is familiar with the FBI's Integrated Automated Fingerprint Identification System. IAFIS has a database of close to fifty million subjects in its criminal master file, and its computers hum twenty-four hours a day, seven days a week, screening ten-point prints electronically submitted by law enforcement agencies. Not too long ago, it could take weeks to get a positive match to a print. Now they can spit back identifications of ten-point prints—the ones taken of every finger—within two hours if they're criminal prints and twenty-four hours if they're civil prints.

Latent prints—the ones lifted at a crime scene—are not so easy to match. They're analyzed and classified and fed into the network, and then all possible matches are returned. It's up to the investigators to decide which, if any, most closely resembles the known ten-point print. If the latents are clear and complete, an identification is fairly certain. If they're fuzzy or incomplete, it can be like making a decision based on tea leaves.

I could hear squawking sounds from the other end of the line. Guidry didn't look impressed.

"Then you'd better get on it," he said. "Time is fleeting."

He hung up, shed his leather jacket, and draped it over the back of my bar stool. Then he moved around my kitchen in search of coffee and cups, his chest looking broad and strong in his black turtleneck.

I leaned my head back and wondered if I had ever heard a normal human being say *Time is fleeting* before. I decided I hadn't. Like everything else Guidry did, it had a slightly foreign flavor. At least he hadn't said it in a foreign language, which he probably spoke several of, including the French he'd once spoken to me when he called me a liar. But he'd said it softly, and not in a mean way.

With my head pounding like a son-of-a-bitch, I sat there quiet as a mouse and wished he would talk French to me again. Not that I would know what he was saying, I just wanted to hear it.

I had dozed off when he jostled my shoulder and set a cup of coffee on the table next to me. He took a seat on the sofa across from me.

"Drink up. The caffeine may help your headache."

With a start, I said, "I have to call Joe and Maria!"

"Who?"

Struggling to get to my feet, I said, "Joe and Maria. I have to call them and ask them to take care of my pets tomorrow."

Joe and Maria Molina have a housecleaning service on the key, and a lot of their clients are the same as mine. Our paths cross a lot and we give each other a hand when it's needed.

Guidry pushed me back in the chair. "You stay put. I'll bring the phone."

Right there in front of me, he picked up my shoulder bag—which he'd slung on the sofa—and plunged his hand in it as if he weren't committing a major offense. Without even a smidgen of embarrassment at having gone in my purse again without my permission, he handed my cell phone to me, sat down on the sofa, and picked up his coffee. I would have glared at him, but it made my head hurt worse to wrinkle my forehead.

Feeling like I should press the button gently since it was so late, I hit the speed-dial for Joe and Maria, and waited dully until Joe's sleep-addled voice answered.

Without going into detail, I told him I wasn't going to be able to keep my morning appointments and asked if he and Maria could cover for me.

Joe didn't even hesitate. "Sure, Dixie. Which houses?"

Leaving out Billy Elliot, I named them one by one while Joe mentally ran down his own list of places where he had keys or entrance codes.

"Okay, okay, okay, no problem. You want us to see to them in the afternoon too?"

I told him I would be okay for the afternoon visits and got off the phone before he woke up enough to ask what was wrong. Then I called Tom Hale, imagining him lying in bed with his new lady love.

When he answered, I said, "Tom, I can't explain now, but I won't be there in the morning. Can your friend run with Billy Elliot?"

Groggily, and with a little affronted burr, he said, "I guess so, Dixie."

"Thanks, Tom. I'll explain when I see you tomorrow afternoon."

I didn't even say goodbye, just closed the phone and laid it on the table, noting as I did that my hand was shaking. Across from me, Guidry's gray eyes were studying me as if I were a fingerprint.

"Guidry, what about the fire? Was Kurtz hurt?"

"It wasn't in the house, it was outside. Some kind of chemical fire, I think."

"In the courtyard?"

"No, behind the house entirely, on the east side."

That would make it behind Ken Kurtz's bedroom, behind the gym where Ziggy was.

I said, "Chemicals that could have blown up?"

"I'm not sure. I haven't spoken to the fire marshal yet."

"Guidry, you told me once that you'd been married. Did you love your wife?"

It's just amazing the things a person's mouth will say when they least expect it.

Surprised, Guidry put his cup down and rotated it on the coffee table, looking at the wet circles it was leaving as if they held the answer to my question.

"I loved her when we married, and I didn't love her when we divorced."

"Why not?"

A shadow flickered across his face. "We had both changed a lot, taken on different ideas. I didn't like hers and she didn't like mine."

For a moment there was pain in his eyes like a hurt animal's—raw and astonished.

He took a deep breath. "It all blew up when I found out she was having an affair with my best friend. I hated them both for a while, but I got over it."

"You forgave them?"

"It wasn't a matter of forgiveness, I just decided to stop reliving it every day. Every time I remembered it, I felt the same pain and anger all over again. So I let it go. It's done, over, in the past. If I go around resenting it, I keep it in the present."

I understood what he meant. That's why I've forgiven the old man who smashed his car into Todd and Christy in the supermarket parking lot and killed them. Forgiveness may be the most self-serving of all emotions because you do it for yourself, not for the one forgiven.

I said, "I'm sorry I asked. It's none of my business."

He gave me a keen look. "Maybe it is. You ready to start loving again?"

I leaned my huge head back against the chair and closed my burning eyes. "You sound like Tom Hale."

"Who?"

"A guy. He says love is a choice people make."

"Well, you sure as hell can't love if you choose not to."

I opened my eyelids a tiny bit and looked at him through the slit. I was tempted to say, *How can I help holding dear the memory of my first marriage?* but I knew that wasn't the issue. Nobody expected me to forget Todd.

The issue, plain and simple, was that Guidry was a cop. I didn't know if I could bear loving another man who left home every day with a chance of being gunned down by some jerk whose judgment had been stolen by fear or greed or drugs. On the other hand, it takes a particular kind of courage to go out every day to do a job that can get you killed, especially when half the population hates or fears you, and I was drawn to that kind of bravery.

But did I choose to love a cop, when there might be another man I could also love?

# 13

Guidry's cell phone rang, startling me so that I slopped coffee on my already stained mohair.

He answered while he walked to the kitchen to get me paper towels. When he handed them to me, his face had taken on his cop look—flinty-eyed, cool, objective—not the open face he'd had a few moments before. He went back to the bar and took notes while the person on the other end of the line talked. Then he spoke briefly and low and hung up. When he came back to the sofa, he was all cop.

"We have a tag ID for your mystery woman. The car she's driving was reported stolen three months ago in Langley, Virginia."

"Did they get latents from the car?"

"Surprisingly few, and what they got were poor quality."

Guidry sat down on the sofa and took his coffee cup in both hands, leaning over it with his elbows on his knees and looking into its dark depths as if he were trying to find the woman's identity there.

He said, "She look like a car thief to you?"

If my head hadn't been so full of wet wool, I would have said *Aha! So now you believe me about the woman!* Instead, I just thought it, but slowly.

I said, "She looked like a soldier."

He raised his head with a spark in his eyes that told me I'd said something that fit an idea he had.

"Talk to me, Dixie. Why did she look like a soldier?"

I squirmed down in the chair to find a more comfortable place for my head. "Her posture, I guess, and her shoulders were square, like somebody who's spent a lot of time standing at attention."

"Anything else?"

"Just a general feeling of authority, like she knew how to give orders. Deep, husky voice. She didn't smell like a heavy smoker, so I think the voice is more from expecting people to listen when she talks."

"So she could have been law enforcement too."

"My head hurts really bad, Guidry. The coffee's not helping and I need to take a nap."

He got up and extended his hand. "Let's go out on the porch. The fresh air will make you feel better."

Upright, I felt nauseated again, and I had to take a minute to let my brains settle down inside my skull. With the afghan around me like a sarong, I held Guidry's arm while we slow-walked to the French doors. Outside, we leaned on the porch railing under a star-sparked cobalt sky. Down at the shore, a moon-oiled sea whispered secrets to the pale sand, and somewhere in the treetops a nesting osprey whistled urgently for its mate.

Guidry said, "Somebody wiped down the inside of that car. Just like somebody wiped down the nurse's bathroom and bedroom, the washer and dryer, the kitchen counters. Both those women made deliberate efforts to erase fingerprints."

I put my hand over my eyes to shade them from the piercing starlight. "You checked the refrigerator door handle? From when Gilda opened it and took the bundles inside?"

He gave me a stern glare. "None there either, although yours would have obliterated them if there'd been any."

I said, "Probably the gloves."

"What?"

"Gilda was wearing latex gloves when she came to Kurtz's door. Not the colored things that people wear to clean house, but thin ones like nurses use. She kept them on, too. Maybe the mystery woman also wore them."

Guidry stood straighter and stared out toward the invisible horizon for a second, then whipped out his cell phone, hit a number, and barked at whomever answered.

"Did you find latex gloves in the sedan?"

A beat went by.

"Did you lift latents from inside them?"

I could tell from his face that the answer was no.

"Do it!"

He clicked off and stared out at the horizon again.

I said, "I've had enough fresh air. Can we go inside now?"

He looked startled, as if he'd forgotten why we were on the porch. "You want some pizza? I'm starving."

I waved vaguely at Michael's house. "Michael will make you something. I don't want delivery people coming here."

"Michael's on duty, Dixie. Remember? He was at the Kurtz fire."

Faster than an eyeblink, I was draped over the porch rail sobbing. "He's so brave! My brother is so brave!"

Guidry said, "Okay, concussion emotions. Sorry. Come on inside, I'll scramble us some eggs. You have eggs?"

Still bawling, I held up five fingers to show how many eggs I had. Grinning, he led me into the living room and gently shoved me back into the chair, where I continued to leak tears while he went in the kitchen. I heard the refrigerator open, I heard soft thumps of items being deposited on the countertop, I heard my microwave buzzing and a pan clank on the stovetop. I stopped crying and wiped my wet face with the paper towel Guidry had brought me to blot the coffee on my sweater. I also used it to wipe at some stains that I suspected were dried spit-up.

Guidry came back with the coffeepot and refilled my cup, gave me a searching look, and went back to the kitchen and got two plates, one of which he set on the table beside me. I knew I couldn't eat, but I looked at it anyway, curious to see what he had managed to put together from my meager supplies. Along with buttered toast, there was a mysterious mass of yellow and green stuff with some little chunks of something I couldn't identify. I took a tentative bite and did a mental groan. I should have known Guidry would be a good cook. Coming from New Orleans, he probably interned as a chef at Antoine's. He probably knew how to make beignets and crawfish étouffée and jambalaya, whatever that is. I took another bite and looked at him. The arrogant son-of-a-bitch was watching me with a slightly smug expression.

I said, "Not bad."

"Thanks."

"What's this green stuff?"

"You had a package of spinach in your freezer."

"Hunh. Where'd you find the mushrooms? I didn't have mushrooms."

"Yeah, you did, dried ones way back behind the year-old packages of rice cakes that have never been opened. At least you had real Parmesan, not that stuff in a can. It was so hard it must have been in your refrigerator for months, but it was real."

"I got those rice cakes when I thought I would go on a strict diet."

"Changed your mind?"

"Uh-hunh."

"Dixie, tell me again what the woman said to you this morning."

God, had it just been this morning? It seemed like eons ago when I'd met the woman with her bulldog.

I sipped coffee and tried to remember the woman's exact words. "She said her dog's name was Ziggy Stardust because she was a David Bowie fan. I said that was the second time I'd heard about a pet named Ziggy, but the other one was an iguana. Then she said, 'You've just heard about him? You haven't seen him?'"

Guidry was leaning forward as if he wanted to soak up every word. "Then what?"

"I said I was on my way to see him right then, and she said 'Good' and ran off. In a minute or two, I saw her driving away in a sedan."

"That's all?"

"Something about it seemed odd. I had the feeling she'd been watching for me. She was relieved when I said I was on my way to see the iguana. Then, when I saw her picture on Kurtz's table, I knew there was a connection."

"You said you asked Kurtz about it. How did he react?"

"That was odd too. For a second he looked excited, and then he said it was purely coincidence, that the woman in the photograph was dead. I'm almost positive it was the same woman."

Guidry sat back on the couch and gnawed on the inside of his cheek.

I said, "There's something about the name Ziggy that has meaning. Kurtz changed when I told him the man who called me said the iguana's name was Ziggy. I think it's some kind of code, a message of some kind."

As soon as I said the word *message,* I sat up straight. "Uh-oh."

"What?"

"I got a phone message this afternoon. It was the same man with the Irish accent who called me last night, the one claiming to be Kurtz. He apologized for lying to me and told me to give Kurtz a message."

"What message?"

"I wrote it down so I wouldn't forget it, but I remember it. *Ziggy is no longer an option. You must act now.*"

Guidry said, "Did you give Kurtz the message?"

"That's why I called you this afternoon, to tell you about it."

"But you didn't tell me."

"When you accused me of killing the guard, I forgot."

"Kurtz doesn't know about the call either?"

I shook my head and winced. "I should have told him. The message must have been a code about the fire. Somebody knew there was going to be a fire and wanted to warn him."

Another thought hit me, and I sat upright so fast I felt my brain slosh. "Guidry, the man said *Ziggy is no longer an option.* Did anybody check on Ziggy? Is he all right?"

"The fire marshal spoke to Kurtz, but I don't know if he specifically asked about the iguana."

I pushed myself up and stood swaying. "I have to go see about him."

Guidry got up and took my arm. "The only place you're going is to your bedroom."

My heart gulped, and I tried to think of a graceful way to say, "Sorry, but right now I'm having a concussion."

Then I realized by the way he was guiding me toward my bed that he hadn't meant it in a romantic way, which made me feel like weeping again.

Guidry said, "I think you can safely sleep now, but I'm going to stick around. I'll stretch out here on your couch."

He turned down my covers and waited until I crawled between the sheets, then tucked me in with surprising tenderness. I was too exhausted to do anything except clutch a pillow under my cheek and fall into the abyss of blessed sleep.

# 14

I woke up to birdsong and bright light and the worst headache of my life. My first thought was of Billy Elliot, who was surely waiting behind Tom Hale's door with all four legs crossed. So were the other dogs on my list. I had broken the first rule of professional pet sitters, which is to show up, no matter what.

Groaning, I swung my legs out of bed and stood up, only to sit right back down again. One thing for sure, I wasn't going to be running with Billy Elliot today. A movement at the bedroom door brought my head up—Paco, with a worried look in his eyes and a hopeful smile on his lips.

"Hey, Sleeping Beauty. How's your head?"

"Dire. Why are you here?"

"Guidry met me when I came home, told me what happened."

"I have to go see to my pets—"

"Guidry said you called somebody to do that."

Slowly, my brain crawled to the memory of talking to Tom Hale and Joe Molina.

"Oh, yeah, I did. I forgot. Does Michael know what happened yet?"

"I had to tell him. He'll be okay."

I winced, getting a mental image of Michael at the firehouse flinging a water hose around like a cowboy's lariat, practicing to capture the person who'd hit me.

Paco said, "Michael will be home tonight. Since he worked some-body else's shift last night, he has an extra twenty-four off."

I let out a pent-up breath I hadn't known I was holding. Until Guidry caught the person who'd killed Ramón and knocked me out, I would feel a lot safer knowing my brother was nearby.

Paco was watching me closely. "Guidry wants you to call him when you can."

I was afraid I would bawl if I tried to talk anymore, so I said, "I need a shower."

"Boy, I'll say. What's that on your sweater?"

I hauled myself to my feet and shuffled to the hall like an old woman. "You don't want to know."

Of all civilized inventions, hot water is the best. I stood under a steaming torrent for a long time and let its healing power work magic. When I finally stepped out, my head was still heavy, but I didn't feel like I had feathers for brains. I pulled my wet hair back into a ponytail, catch-ing it just below the sore spot where I'd been clobbered, and made a fast pass at my lips with rosy gloss. With a towel around me for modesty, I padded down the hall to my office-closet and shut myself inside. When I reached for a lacy bra and thong bikini, I knew I was going to live. Oth-erwise, I'd have settled for cotton Hanes. I listened to my messages while I pulled on clean jeans and a fresh T, holding my breath at each one for fear it was the same man who'd left the message about Ziggy.

One was from the night before. Ethan Crane, his voice warm and intimate. "Dixie, it's Ethan. I stayed behind at the Crab House for a while and listened to the music, and when I left there were fire trucks at the Kurtz house and a Bronco that looked like yours. Are you all right? I hope you're safe and sound in bed, but would you let me hear from you so I'll know whether to worry?"

Oh, shit, I'd completely forgotten about the evening with Ethan Crane. Even as I dialed his number, I wasn't sure if my memory failure had been because of the concussion or because my subconscious hadn't wanted to remember. Since I knew he could see the call was from me, I started talking when the line clicked open.

"Ethan, this is Dixie. I'm sorry you were worried about me last night. Actually, I wasn't in bed, I was at Sarasota Memorial. Somebody hit me in the head and I had a concussion."

"A concussion?"

"You know, swollen brains."

"I know what a concussion is, I'm just . . . how do you get mixed up in these things, anyway?"

His voice sounded a bit aggrieved, which was all I needed to blow up. "I sure as hell don't try to get mixed up in them, Ethan. I'm sorry you were worried, sorry I didn't call sooner, but this is the best I can do."

I slammed down the receiver and laced up clean white Keds, ignoring the ringing phone and not listening to the recording because I'd had all of Ethan Crane I could take for the morning.

I found Paco standing in front of my refrigerator looking morosely into its innards.

"Don't you keep any food here?"

"Guidry ate it all."

"Is that why there were dishes in your drain?"

"He washed dishes?"

"Come on, we need sustenance."

Since Michael was still on duty at the firehouse, that meant going to the Village Diner on Beach Drive, where I have breakfast almost every day of the year.

When we went out on my porch, a flock of robins who'd been having a committee meeting on the railing fluttered away. Funny thing about robins, while they're visiting us in the winter they form cooperative flocks and happily feast on berries and seeds and ripening fruit. As soon as they fly back north, they revert to their old ways, squabbling over earthworms and chasing away any other robin that comes into their self-assigned domain. Human snowbirds do the same thing. Here in Sarasota, their diet is heavy on oranges, mangoes, papayas, strawberries, avocados, and guavas, and they're as friendly with one another as a bunch of wintering robins. But in the spring, they head back home, shut themselves up in their respective houses, and go back to meat and potatoes.

Downstairs, I saw Guidry had kept his word and had my Bronco driven home. It was parked in the carport with the keys in the ignition.

Moving toward it, I said, "I'll meet you at the diner. I'll have to go see to the cats after we eat."

Paco hesitated a bit and then nodded. That's the great thing about Paco. He protects, but he doesn't hover.

When I passed the Kurtz house, I slowed to stare at a chubby man dressed in a long brown caftan that looked like it was made with feed-sack burlap. He had a giant cross hanging from a rough chain around his neck, and he was wagging a sign at passing traffic. The sign had a Bible verse in red lettering—Revelation 13:15–18. Not being one who knows Bible verses, I didn't know what it referred to, but I wasn't surprised to see him. Murders bring out crazies of every stripe. It's simply something that law-enforcement people accept as part of the terrain.

When I got out of the Bronco at the diner, I dropped my car keys into my shoulder bag and heard them clink on metal. A prim little voice in my aching head said, *Dixie, you still have that man's door keys.* In no mood for a lecture from my conscience, I said the F-word to the prim little voice and trudged into the diner.

Inside, the windows were sprayed with fake snow, and somebody had draped a string of Christmas lights around a miniature tree at the cashier's stand. They had also put little pots of fake poinsettias on each table, which made me remember we were a day closer to Christmas.

*Bleh!*

I'm such a regular at the diner that Tanisha, the cook, starts making two eggs over easy with extra-crisp home fries and a biscuit when she sees me come in the door. Today she did a double-take and rolled her eyes when she saw me with Paco. He has that effect on women. Makes them go all swoony.

Judy, the waitress who's been at the diner for as long as I've been going there, grabbed two mugs and trotted to my usual booth with her coffeepot at the ready. When Paco turned to slide into the seat across from me, she surreptitiously eyed his butt, which is understandable, since Paco may have the best butt in the Western Hemisphere. Paco ordered a Denver omelet, fries, bacon, and biscuits. Judy wrote it down as if he were Moses handing down holy commandments and swished off, fanning her bosom with her order pad.

From the booth behind us, a woman's nasal voice floated over the partition. "Ed don't understand me one bit," she said. "We can go to a movie, and I swear to God when we come home you'd think we'd gone to two different shows. We just don't see things the same way. He's not my soul mate."

A second woman's voice said, "Honey, a soul mate is just a man you haven't heard fart yet."

There was laughter, and three women stood up to leave. One of them said, "You want a soul mate, get a dog."

They walked out grinning at their own cleverness, and Paco and I exchanged a pained smile. Love may not make the world go around, but it certainly occupies a lot of people's thoughts—both the best and the worst of it.

He said, "What's up with the iguana thing?"

I sighed, weary with telling it. "Some guy called me and asked me to go feed an iguana named Ziggy. When I got there, it turned out the owner of the iguana, a man named Kurtz, hadn't called me and didn't know who had. He also didn't know somebody had put Ziggy in a cold wine room, which is bad for iguanas. I got him out and warmed him up and fed him. But before that, somebody had shot Kurtz's security guard. And before *that,* a woman with a miniature bulldog named Ziggy had stopped me, and later I saw her photo on Kurtz's nightstand. Then his nurse disappeared. Nobody knows where she went, and she had wiped away all her prints. Wore latex gloves while I was there. Last night on the way home, I saw the woman's car in the driveway—the woman with the bulldog—and went to check on it. Somebody hit the back of my head and gave me a concussion, and while I was out a fire was started. Behind the house, not in the house itself. Guidry thinks it was a chemical fire of some kind. The woman was gone. Guidry checked the car's tags, and it was stolen in Virginia. I guess that's all, except I got a message to give to Kurtz. I'm supposed to tell him that Ziggy is no longer an option and to act now."

Paco said, "The iguana and the dog are both named Ziggy?"

"That's what I mean! How strange is that? Oh, and I forgot that Kurtz has blue skin, like an all-over bruise. Has something seriously wrong, and now he doesn't have a nurse to take care of him."

Judy came with our orders lined up on both arms, a talent so impressive to me that it seems second only to discovering DNA. She got everything settled without dropping anything, which also seems amazing to me. I love watching people do their work well. While she hustled away to get her coffeepot to give us refills, I salted everything in sight and inhaled the wonderful fried fat odor of Paco's bacon. It was cooked just right, stiff and brittle, with no icky white spots.

Paco said, "Want some of my bacon?"

"I never eat bacon."

"Yeah, like I never drink beer."

He slid half his bacon onto my plate just as Judy came back with the coffee.

She said, "She conned you into giving her bacon, didn't she? She does that with everybody. Girl gets more bacon off other people's plates than a sneaky dog."

She sashayed away with her pot while I shamelessly nibbled at Paco's bacon.

Paco said, "Why's the guy blue?"

"I don't know. He's really sick, though. Lots of pain."

"Silver nitrate poisoning causes your skin to turn blue, but I don't think it causes pain or serious illness."

"His skin is covered with dimples that jerk and quiver."

"Jesus, poor guy. Where'd he come from? What kind of work did he do before he came here?"

"I just went there to feed his iguana. I don't know anything else."

"The man who called you, how'd he sound?"

"Muffled, like he was talking through cotton. He had an Irish accent."

Paco grimaced. "Oldest trick in the book, Dixie. Use a foreign accent, and that's all anybody remembers. You sure it was a man?"

I hadn't even considered that the speaker wasn't really a man or really Irish, but of course an undercover agent like Paco would think of that first thing.

Uncertainly, I said, "Sounded like a man to me."

Paco chewed for a moment while his dark eyes sparked with speculation.

He said, "Any idea why they chose you to call?"

"My guess is that they saw me on the news when . . . you know."

"That still bothering you?"

I shrugged. "Sometimes I feel like killing somebody caused me to slip over the line that separates good and evil. You ever feel like that?"

"I don't know about good and evil, Dixie. Those are subjective terms. But if you mean do I feel a kinship with the criminals I catch, sure. Criminals and cops are the same kind of people, we're just on different sides."

"But you always know you're on the good side."

"Depends on how you look at it. When I bust a guy for selling drugs, and selling drugs is the only way he can feed his family, which one of us is good and which one evil?"

"He could find another job."

"No, *you* could find another job, and *I* could find another job, but maybe he can't, or maybe he doesn't know he can. I don't make those judgments. Criminals choose their lifestyle, and I choose mine. If I have to take a criminal out when I'm doing my job, that's just how it is. You did what you had to do. It wasn't good and it wasn't evil. Given the choice the guy had made, it was inevitable. It doesn't have to be a defining point in your life unless you make it one."

I said, "Bottom line, killing is wrong, no matter what."

Paco's dark eyes were calm. "There's a story in the Mahabharata about a civil war between cousins. One of the warriors went to an avatar named Krishna, who by the way was dark indigo blue, and said he couldn't kill his own relatives. Krishna told him that if he thought he actually killed anybody or that anybody actually died, he just didn't understand life. In essence, he said that life is eternal and that a warrior's job was to go to war and kill other warriors, and to just get on with it."

I spread jelly on my biscuit and wondered what the odds were that any other woman in the world was sitting in a diner eating bacon with a drop-dead gorgeous undercover cop who knew the Mahabharata, something I didn't even know how to pronounce.

I said, "Why was Krishna blue?"

He grinned. "Don't know, but I doubt it was for the same reason your guy is blue."

"You think I should give him the message? About Ziggy not being an option?"

"How would you feel if you didn't, and the iguana died of some condition that Kurtz could have treated him for?"

Ziggy seemed about ten or twelve years old to me, not terribly old for a healthy iguana, but maybe he wasn't healthy. Maybe the caller knew something about Ziggy's health that made it imperative that Kurtz take some sort of action before it was too late.

I said, "You think that's what the message means?"

"Hell, Dixie, I don't know what it means. I also don't see why they can't just call Kurtz and tell him directly. They've got some kind of game going, and sending mysterious messages must be part of it."

I said, "Iguanas and chickens have the same digestive and respiratory systems, did you know that? If Ziggy's sick, he could take medicine made for sick chickens."

"Son-of-a-gun, I didn't know that."

I sat back with a little sigh of satisfaction. We all have our areas of expertise. Paco knew law enforcement and Hindu scripture, and I knew that iguanas and chickens have the same kind of systems. That may not have made us exactly even, but at least I knew *something* he didn't.

# 15

As we left the diner, I picked up a discarded copy of the morning's *Herald-Tribune* from a table by the door. Paco gave me a pat on the butt and got in his car to drive off to whatever secret job he was working at the time. Michael and I don't ask Paco for details about what he does. He wouldn't tell us anyway, and if he did the details would make us take up nail-biting as a hobby.

I sat in the Bronco for a minute to scan the *Tribune*'s lead story about the latest horror in the world. Everybody claimed the other side was responsible, everybody lied, everybody postured, children died. All our realities are dramatic plots intersecting, each with its own creator and climax and theme. I suppose the conflict is the energy that keeps the universe together, but couldn't it be conflict of man against hunger, man against disease, man against ignorance, man against despair, instead of man against man?

The guard's murder and the subsequent fire were all over the front page too, with an article full of "no comment" quotes from Guidry and the fire marshal. There was also a photograph of the grieving widow taken on her front porch. The photographer had caught two street signs over her shoulder. Even though the address wasn't given, anybody familiar with Siesta Key would recognize where it was.

The guard's wife was a softly pretty dark-haired woman who had lashed out angrily at the female interviewer in what was described as broken English. Without fully understanding what she'd said, the reporter had rather loftily concluded that the widow blamed American society for her husband's death.

I doubted that a woman who had just lost the man she loved and the father of her children would take such an abstract view of death. Maybe later, but not when her grief was still raw and red. Fresh grief is always personal, and the fury it generates isn't directed toward a nameless society but toward specific people. For the first year after Todd and Christy were killed, I funneled all my rage toward the half-blind man who had smashed into them in the parking lot, and only later toward a state that routinely allows people to renew their driver's licenses for a total of eighteen years without a vision test.

I studied the photograph, feeling a kinship with this woman whose husband had been killed in a senseless act of violence. So far as I knew, I was the only suspect in the murder, and I wanted to talk to her. I wanted to know what her husband had told her about Ziggy. I wanted to know if she had any idea who had called me to go to the Kurtz house.

I found the house easily enough, and as I pulled into the driveway I wondered how many other people had identified its location from the newspaper photograph. As I had expected, it was a weather-beaten Florida cracker house, with a front porch wide enough for a swing and chairs for visiting. A new red tricycle with plastic streamers on the handlebars sat on the cracked sidewalk, and an equally new girl's pink two-wheeler leaned against the porch railing.

As I went up the steps to the porch, I saw a little girl who looked to be about six years old sitting with her legs spread apart to make a nest of her skirt. A calico kitten was in the nest, and the child was tickling the kitten's nose with a fluff of yarn. The kitten was probably a Persian mix, and definitely a true calico, not a tabby or tortoiseshell that often get mislabeled as calicoes. From the alert way it was leaping at the yarn, I could tell right away it was healthy and intelligent.

The little girl was so intent on the kitten that she barely gave me a glance. Being a fool for kittens, especially calicoes, I went over to kneel beside the child and make the *aaahing* sounds that probably originated with someone who was kitten-smitten.

I said, "What's her name?"

The child gave me a level dark-eyed stare. "How'd you know it was a girl?"

"All calicoes are girls. Well, every now and then there's a boy, but mostly they're girls."

She nodded slowly, and I recognized the look I'd always given people when I was her age and didn't have a clue what they were talking about.

I said, "Calico means she has three colors, black, orange, and white, and the colors are in big separate patches, not striped or swirled together."

"You wanta hold her?"

That's the neat thing about kids. They don't really care about their pets' official names, and they don't think it's weird that a grown woman would want to hold a bit of fluffy kitten just for the pure pleasure of it.

Gracious as a hostess at a tea party, she tenderly scooped the kitten up in both hands and handed her to me. Surprised and offended at the yarn game ending so abruptly, the kitten stretched its little needle claws into my palms.

When I winced, the child said, "Hurts, don't it? We're going to get her fingernails taken out so she can't do that."

I said, "Oh, no—"

The front door flew open and a Hispanic man stepped out with a furious frown on his face and his stiffened arm palm up like a traffic cop.

"Get away from here! Leave us alone! This is a house of mourning, and you people are . . . are . . . you are without shame!"

That pretty much answered the question of whether anyone else had been led to the house by the photograph.

I disengaged the kitten's claws from my hand, set it back on the girl's skirt, and got to my feet.

"I'm not a reporter, sir. I'm Dixie Hemingway."

The little girl was watching us, so I stepped closer to him and lowered my voice almost to a whisper.

"The same person who killed Ramón Gutierrez tricked me into going to the house to take care of the iguana that lives there."

He dropped his hand and peered at me suspiciously. "You take care of the iguana?"

"Just since yesterday. I'm a pet sitter. I don't know who called me to go there, but I know it's tied in somehow with . . . what happened." Assuming the child was the murdered man's daughter, I tilted my head toward her to signal that I didn't want to talk about the murder in front of her. "I got to the house shortly after . . . you know. I was hoping I might speak to Mrs. Gutierrez. Maybe her husband told her something."

"My sister knows nothing."

He sounded so bitter that I didn't think he was referring solely to the murder.

The little girl went back to playing with the kitten, but I knew she was listening.

I said, "I lost a husband and a daughter a few years ago. When it happened, people tried to keep me from knowing certain details about how . . . about the end, but I needed to know everything. Perhaps there are things I could tell your sister that would help her now."

His face softened, and he looked over his shoulder as if consulting somebody inside.

Low and urgently, I said, "Look, I'm not a cop. I don't have any authority and I don't have anything to do with the police investigation, but somebody involved me, and the killer is still out there. I need to have some facts to protect myself."

A thin young woman appeared beside him, looking anxiously first at the little girl and then at me. Her dark eyes were so surrounded by sorrow's purple shadows that she looked as if she'd been beaten.

She said, "You are not from the paper? Or the TV?"

"I promise."

She and her brother exchanged a look, and he stepped aside and gestured me in. He closed the door behind me with a soft finality, and I understood he didn't want the little girl to listen to our conversation. Adults try to protect children from the realities of death, even though children usually handle it as if it were no more mysterious than any of the other realities they're learning about.

With some notable exceptions, the living room was a typical young family's—a beige sectional sofa curved to offer an entire family viewing angles of the TV, a couple of homemade afghans of the dark brown and cream variety draped over sofa arms, throw pillows showing signs of jelly smears and spilled soda, and a big cedar chest doubling as a coffee table littered with remotes for the TV, coffee cups, a clumsily formed ceramic Santa, a cell phone, a plate with half a sandwich and some chips, a small poinsettia plant in a foil-wrapped pot, a Barbie doll with no clothes on, and several notepads and pens. The out-of-the-ordinary thing was a plasma TV with tall freestanding speakers and a screen big as some multiplex movie screens. Pretty pricey for a rent-a-cop.

As I perched at the end of the sofa, the woman murmured something under her breath to her brother.

He said, "I am Jochim. This is my sister, Paloma. Would you like some coffee?"

"If it's already made. Don't go to any trouble, please."

He said, "No problem," and hurried from the room.

Paloma sat down at the opposite end of the curved sofa, so that we were facing each other. She was much younger than her brother and her husband, with an immature mix of shyness and defiance. For a second, we looked silently at one another, checking each other out the way women do.

I said, "I'm very sorry for your loss."

"He knew," she whispered. "Why didn't he tell? He didn't need to die."

So far, I hadn't heard any of the "broken English" the reporter had described. From my own experience with news reporters, I thought it was more likely that Paloma had been so furious she'd been incoherent.

Cautiously, so as not to frighten her, I said, "Can you tell me what he knew?"

From the doorway, her brother said, "Paloma!"

Jochim bustled forward with a mug of coffee, and Paloma wearily settled back against the sofa.

Taking a seat between us, Jochim looked uneasy. He said, "These things you can tell us about Ramón's death, what are they?"

I took a sip of coffee and wondered what it was that Jochim hadn't wanted Paloma to tell me.

I said, "It's just that I know a little bit about how the Kurtz household works, so I might be able to answer questions she may have."

Paloma spoke to her brother in Spanish, so rapidly that I only caught a few words. She ended with "*¡Pregúntele! ¡Pregúntele!*"

He swallowed so hard his Adam's apple bobbled. With a nervous smile, he said, "My sister insists that I ask you about the nurse in the house. She has always wondered if her husband and the nurse were . . . you know."

It must be a trait peculiar to women that even when their husbands are lying in the morgue, they want to know if they were unfaithful while they were alive. She was obviously able to ask me herself, but I supposed she couldn't bring herself to say the words.

I rotated my coffee mug on the table, careful not to make eye contact with Paloma. To tell the truth, I'd wondered about the nurse and Ramón myself.

I said, "I only talked to the nurse for a few minutes before she left."

Paloma sat forward, ashen-faced. "She left? The nurse left?"

"Soon after I arrived. Nobody knows where she went."

Okay, so this was probably information Guidry didn't want noised around, but Paloma's husband had just been killed, and I figured she had a right to know.

She buried her face in her hands, and the keening noise she made sent icicles up my spine. In some corner of my mind I remembered making that sound myself after Todd and Christy were killed.

I said, "The fact that she left doesn't mean she and Ramón had anything going on."

Paloma jerked her head up and shouted, "It means she killed him! That's what it means! And he knew! He knew!"

"Knew what?"

Jochim jerked his head around to stare reproachfully at me.

He said, "My sister has suffered enough. She has children to protect, and I've got a wife and kids of my own. We can't get involved in anything. You understand?"

I understood that Paloma and Jochim knew something they hadn't told Guidry.

I said, "If Ramón's killers think you can identify them, they'll have to get rid of you for their own protection. Help put them away, and you have a chance."

"It was *her*," said Paloma. "She killed him!"

"I was there when the nurse learned he was dead. I think she was genuinely shocked when she learned it. Personally, I think she ran away because she was afraid she'd be killed too."

"Then they were together," said Paloma. "She tricked him, but he could have quit when he knew what she was like. He stayed even after he knew."

"Please, what do you mean? What did he know?"

Jochim said, "Enough! You have told my sister something she needed to know. We are grateful for that, but now you must go."

In an involuntary plea, my hand opened toward Paloma, and I saw the pinpricks from the kitten's claws.

I said, "Is that your little girl on the porch? The one with the kitten?"

"*Sí.*"

"She said you planned to have the kitten's claws removed. Is that true?"

"Oh, *sí*, it scratches everything."

"Please don't. Kittens outgrow their scratching, and if you remove its claws, it will be crippled. Its balance will be off, and it won't be able to defend itself."

Both Paloma and Jochim gave me incredulous looks.

I said, "I know it sounds crazy to talk about a kitten at a time like this, but I can't stand to hear about kittens being declawed. It's too cruel."

Paloma rose to her feet, stiff and creaky as an old woman. "Please go now."

When somebody tells me to get out of their house, I obey. But first I pulled a dog-eared business card from my pocket and laid it on the coffee table with all the other stuff.

I said, "I wish I weren't involved in this mess, but I got tricked into it, and now my own life may be in danger. There's something odd going on in that house. I don't know what it is, but I believe it has to do with the iguana. Please, if you decide later that you can tell me something without causing danger for yourselves, call me."

At the door, I stopped and turned to look squarely at Paloma.

"I lost my husband too, and I know the pain you feel. But it's a mistake to torture yourself with suspicion about him and the nurse. You had a life together, children together. It's bad enough that you've lost him. Don't make it worse by forgetting that he loved you."

I pulled the door open and almost made it out without opening my mouth again. But I had to give it one last shot.

I turned back and said, "Please, please don't mutilate that kitten."

I left them then, looking toward the little girl and the kitten as I fled down the steps. Both child and kitten had fallen asleep in a pool of sunshine on the porch floor, the kitten cuddled in the curve of the child's body, both innocently unaware of how their lives were about to change.

As abruptly as we had briefly plunged into winter, temperatures had soared into summer again. It was almost 80 degrees when I left Paloma's house, causing me to regret wearing long pants instead of my usual shorts. I made quick visits to the pets on my list to make sure Joe and Maria had tended to all of them. At the beagle's house, I scanned the neighborhood for the miniature bulldog and the mystery woman, but I didn't really expect to see them again. I brushed the beagle, gave her a doggy treat for being such a good sport about staying alone while her owners were gone, and promised I'd be back in the evening. When I backed out of the driveway, I could see her face in the living room window, dolefully watching me leave. People say "It's a dog's life" to mean a life of contentment, but dogs frequently live with boredom and loneliness.

Billy Elliot didn't seem bored when I got to his condo, he seemed nervous and agitated, which meant he hadn't got a good hard run that morning. He looked highly disappointed when he realized I was there for a social call and not to run with him. I took a bit of nasty pleasure in knowing that Tom's new girlfriend hadn't been able to satisfy him—the dog, I mean, not Tom. From the way Tom looked, he was plenty satisfied.

Tom wanted to know all the details about how I'd been conked on the head and what the cops were doing about it.

After I filled him in, he said, "The murder was on the news, but nothing about a fire or about you getting hit."

"Good. I don't want reporters nosing around me again."

"Dixie, you need to take it easy for a few days, give your head a chance to heal. Don't worry about Billy Elliot, Frannie can walk him."

The little hard knot of jealousy in my chest nudged. "Tell her she has to run hard with him, two or three times around the parking lot."

Two little worry lines appeared between Tom's eyebrows, but Billy Elliot came over to grin and whip my legs with his wagging tail, his way of confirming what I'd just said. I stroked the top of his head and tried hard to believe he loved me more than he loved the unknown Frannie. But in my heart of hearts I knew he loved running, Tom, and anybody who fed him, in that order.

I said, "Tom, would you mind looking up something on the internet for me? I want to know about a company named BiZogen Research."

In one smooth move, Tom wheeled himself backward and pulled a slim gray case from the kitchen counter behind him. Pushing the tax returns he was working on aside, he laid the case on the table and opened it. He hit some keys while I tried to act like I'd known all along that it was a computer.

He looked intently at the screen for a moment, and said, "There's a bunch of stuff about BiZogen Research. What exactly do you want to know?"

I moved to peer over his shoulder and read a list of titles and sentences that contained the words *BiZogen Research*.

"Gosh, that's a lot."

"That's only the first page. There are three more pages. You see anything that looks like what you're looking for?"

When I hesitated, he clicked on the first thing on the list, and in a few seconds the screen was filled with an article from *The New York Times*. The article began:

BiZogen Research Labs announced today that it has developed a vaccine against the four viruses that cause dengue fever, a mosquito-borne infection of international concern. Predominantly in tropical and subtropical regions of the world, dengue fever and its potentially lethal complication, dengue hemorrhagic fever, affects most Asian countries and is a leading cause of hospitalization and death among children.

I shook my head. "That doesn't mean anything to me. Try something else."

He made the article disappear and clicked on the next thing on the list. It was a similar article from *The Wall Street Journal.* So were the next three entries. I relaxed. BiZogen Research was exactly what it sounded like, a research company. And it did good things, like creating vaccines to save lives. I couldn't imagine why it had a shell company that had built a house for Ken Kurtz to live in, but for all I knew Ken Kurtz was the chairman and CEO of BiZogen.

I was about to tell Tom to forget it when he pulled up another article, also from *The New York Times.*

An intellectual property lawsuit was filed today in federal court against BiZogen Research Labs by Genomics Unlimited of Switzerland. The suit charges that spies from BiZogen infiltrated Genomics' research department and stole records on their development of a vaccine for dengue fever. BiZogen announced that it patented a vaccine for dengue fever three months ago, but Genomics contends that the patent was obtained fraudulently. The patent is worth billions of dollars over the ten years it will be in effect.

Tom said, "That mean anything to you?"

I didn't answer. I was too busy reading that 85 percent of espionage crimes were perpetrated by employees.

On suddenly weak knees, I walked around the table and sat down opposite Tom.

I said, "Ken Kurtz must be a scientist wanted for espionage. That's why he's hiding out. Maybe that's what's wrong with him. Dengue fever, I mean." I stood up. "I have to tell Guidry about this."

Tom looked worried. "Dixie, you be careful. Don't go getting yourself involved in something dangerous again."

I gave him a grateful smile. Tom really was a good friend, even if he hadn't told me he had a new girlfriend.

I said, "I'll be back in a couple of days. If your girlfriend just walks briskly with Billy Elliot, that'll be good enough."

Tom looked immensely relieved, and I ducked out before Billy Elliot realized I had sold him out.

# 16

As I got in the Bronco, I remembered that I hadn't called Guidry earlier in the morning. A concussion not only makes your brain feel like it's stuffed with chewed-up paper bags, it makes you forgetful. He didn't answer his cell, so I left a message saying I was okay, in case he cared, and that I had more information for him.

With their indoor potties, cats are about a million times easier than dogs because they're more self-sufficient. And since Joe and Maria had fed them, I knew they weren't hungry. Even so, I went into every cat's house apologizing for not coming earlier to groom them and play with them.

Most of them gave me a supercilious look that said, Oh, is that you? I'd forgotten you were coming.

Cats never let you forget that they were considered divine by ancient Egyptians. So far as they're concerned, the Egyptians were right. Even divine Egyptians can't resist being petted, though, so by the time I got out my grooming equipment, they were rubbing their scent glands on my ankles and vowing to be my best friend forever.

Since the weather had warmed up, I took them out to their lanais for their grooming session, because cats need fresh air the same way humans do. Besides, they like to watch birds and squirrels in the trees. At Muddy Cramer's house, I found him in the kitchen sitting like a jug facing his food bowl. He looked over his shoulder at me with a CEO's indignant scowl. Joe and Maria hadn't known to add chicken livers to his dry organic food, and he was sulking.

I said, "Sorry, Muddy. I had a little accident last night."

He lowered his eyebrows and peered at me with accusing black eyes while I got out a bag of individually frozen livers from the freezer. When I put one in the microwave to thaw, he whirled around and leaped atop the refrigerator, where he hunkered on his front paws and peered down at me as if I were a bug he might pounce on.

I put the thawed liver in his bowl and left him while I made my house inspection, and by the time I said goodbye, Muddy had calmed down. But his behavior rattled me. Muddy was neurotic, but he was also a cat with a cat's keen intuition. He knew something was wrong, and he wasn't sure he trusted me anymore. When a pet doesn't trust you, it means you've lost your emotional equilibrium, that you need to get back to your central self. The question was, Where had my central self gone?

I was backing out of Muddy's driveway when Guidry called.

"We got a match from IAFIS. Since I gave you a hard time about your woman, I thought I owed you the results. Her name is Jessica Ballantyne. Born in upstate New York, Ph.D.s in both zoology and biogenetics from the University of Maryland. Did fifteen years of germ-warfare research, most of it for the army." He paused for a nanosecond and added, "Last known address was in London, five years ago."

Something about that little pause made my inner ears rise. I said, "What is it you're not telling me?"

I could almost see him doing that inner-mouth chewing thing that people do when they're not sure they should let their lips say the words that want to be spoken.

"A woman named Jessica Ballantyne died two years ago. Her ashes are buried in the family plot in New York. Her mother says she died on an obscure island in the Indian Ocean where she was doing some kind of secret research for the government."

"Our government?"

"Yeah, that one. The one that puts people in identity protection programs when there's been some kind of security breach. The mother sounded bitter, said nobody had ever come clean with the family about the exact nature of Jessica's death. All they were told is that she contracted a fatal disease and died swiftly. She was cremated on the island and her ashes returned to the family. Or at least somebody's ashes were."

"You think—"

"I don't know what I think, Dixie. This whole case seems like somebody's idea of a joke. I'm just not sure who the joke's being played on."

I said, "Did she ever work for BiZogen Research?"

"Why?"

"Because the house Kurtz lives in is owned by a shell company formed by BiZogen Research."

There was a long pause. "How do you know this?"

"Ethan Crane told me last night that BiZogen Research built the house. He knows because he was the escrow agent. Tom Hale looked up BiZogen on the internet for me a little while ago."

Another long pause. "Dixie, it would have been really nice if you'd told me about the BiZogen angle and let me research it." Guidry's voice had gone cool and annoyed. "Is there anything else you haven't told me?"

"Nope, that's it."

"Thank God."

Without even a perfunctory goodbye, he left me holding a silent phone.

Into the air, I said, "But what about the ballistics report on my gun?"

My head hurt. It was full of ideas banging around in it like a crazed pinball machine. I kept thinking about the calico kitten and wishing there was something I could do to prevent Paloma from having it declawed. I wished I had made a stronger case against it. I even considered going back to her house and talking to her again. Not about her husband's murder, but about her kitten's claws. Some might say I had a problem with priorities, but that's how it was. A lot of people don't realize that declawing a cat is like amputating a human's toes, with the same destruction of balance and psyche. Even cats who don't show any effects, cats who seem perfectly fine without their claws, would be a lot more sure-footed with them. People who know that and get their cats declawed anyway because they value their furniture more than their cats should be ashamed of themselves. Veterinarians know better, but a lot of them do the surgery anyway because they don't want to lose clients who demand it. They should be especially ashamed of themselves.

Probably the only thing that kept me from making a U-turn and following through on the save-the-kitten idea right that minute was that I badly needed to go home and take a nap. Sometime I would go back to Paloma's house and talk to her again about the kitten. But not now. Now I had to go home.

On the drive home, I slowed at the Kurtz house, where three more sign-carrying marchers had joined the ersatz monk. Two of the signs carried Bible numbers from Revelation in runny red paint. One said, 666—MARK OF THE BEAST.

Under my breath, I said, "Oh, doodles, now I get it. They think the devil lives there."

I hadn't given it any thought before, but the street number of Ken Kurtz's house was 666. In Southwest Florida, where people have been known to run screaming from a store if their purchases total $6.66, that's a number guaranteed to bring out the loonies.

Behind the marchers, the crime-scene tape was still up, but I didn't see any cars. I also didn't see a replacement guard. That meant Ken Kurtz was alone, with only Ziggy for solace and comfort.

Well, tough titty. Kurtz was an intelligent adult with money, and he could call a nursing service if he needed one. He could call the police. He could call friends or relatives. It wasn't my fault the man was blue and in pain. It wasn't my fault he was weird or that his guard had been killed or that his nurse had run away or that he had nuts marching in front of his house.

Besides, Paco had been right. If the person who'd called me had an important message for Ken Kurtz, why didn't he just call him and tell him? All the cloak-and-dagger secrecy was silly, and so was I if I got sucked into it. I had promised to look in on Kurtz and Ziggy once a day, and that was all I was going to do. I would go see Kurtz later and give him the ominous message about Ziggy.

With one last look at the pickets, I drove on, shaking my head. They were too sad to be funny and too funny to be taken seriously.

At the lane leading home, I stopped at the mailbox to scoop out the day's assortment of pizza ads and offers for discounted lanai cages and haircuts. As I slammed the mailbox door shut, a woman's firm hand clamped on my wrist.

A husky, authoritative voice said, "I have to talk to you."

I knew who it was even before my head whipped around and sent stabbing pain down my spine. Without waiting for an invitation, the mystery woman opened the back door and got in.

She said, "Drive," and from the way she said it, I could almost feel the barrel of a gun pointed at me.

I said, "I'm not taking you to any private place. You want to talk to me, it'll have to be someplace where there are people."

"You think I might kill you?"

"Damn right! I think you may have already killed one person, and maybe two."

In the side rearview mirror, I saw a look of resigned sadness move across her face. "Just don't go where we can be overheard."

Feeling like a robot with bad wiring, I pulled back out onto Midnight Pass Road and headed north toward Crescent Beach. We didn't speak for the entire drive. When I parked by the stairs, we climbed from the parking lot to the pavilion area, where blissful tourists were eating sandwiches and watching the sun sparkle on the waves. I chose a table under the canopied area and took a seat. Swinging her thick dark hair back so it fell behind her shoulders, she sat down opposite me.

I said, "Are you the one who hit me last night?"

Her eyes closed for a moment as if she couldn't face me. "No, that wasn't me."

"But you were there."

"I set the fire behind the house. It was contained and harmless. I wanted to draw attention, to bring fire trucks and police to the house."

My head was throbbing in rhythm with the waves lapping at the shore.

"So who hit me?"

"The same person who would have killed Ken Kurtz if I hadn't interfered with his plans."

"What a load of melodramatic crap! If you know who hit me, you have an obligation to tell me. Or at least tell the police."

"I can't tell you anything more. I've already told you too much. If they ever find out I set that fire—"

She broke off and looked down at her clenched hands.

"They? They who?"

"I can't tell you that. All I can tell you is that it's not a simple matter of two opposing sides in conflict."

I said, "I told him I'd seen you."

Her jaw firmed. "And what did he say?"

"He said you were dead, that you died two years ago."

She looked startled. "He abandoned me! Ran off and left me to die."

"He has your picture next to his bed."

All the color drained from her face, and her eyes glazed with shock. I was almost moved to feel sorrier for her than I felt for myself.

Softly, she said, "There was a time when I loved him more than I ever thought it possible to love another human being."

It's the damnedest thing, but ever since I became more loosely put together, people have started spilling things to me that they shouldn't. Maybe they sense how close to the outer borders of sanity I've been, so they know I'm in no position to judge anybody else's lapses of good sense. This woman had brought me here practically at gunpoint, but now she was talking as if we were having drinks together and discussing old loves.

"Is that why you wanted to talk to me? To tell me you and Kurtz used to be lovers?"

Her eyes met mine and she made a little moue of embarrassment. "I know somebody phoned you with a message to give to Ken. Have you given it to him?"

The bitch had a nerve. The only way she would know the Irishman had called me was if she was in cahoots with him.

"Why don't *you* give him the message? Why don't you just call him yourself?"

"They have his phone tapped. And if they knew I was trying to help him, I would be in as much danger as he is. Maybe more."

There was that *they* again.

I said, "What's Ken Kurtz's connection with BiZogen Research?"

Her eyes widened. "Your reputation is correct. You're quick."

"I'm also the prime suspect in the murder of Ken Kurtz's guard, I have a concussion from being hit in the head at his house, and I resent the hell out of the way you've used me."

Her eyelids fluttered for an instant, and I could feel her fatigue. "I can't tell you about BiZogen, but I can tell you that Ken is in grave danger. It's imperative that you give the message to him."

The woman had to be either a complete wacko or something like the head of Army Intelligence. Maybe both. In either case, I felt like a slippery avocado seed skewered with toothpicks and set to hang in a cup of water.

I said, "I'm planning to do that tonight. But how do I know *they* won't come after me?"

"They know you go there to take care of the iguana. They'd never suspect that you had any information for Ken."

I said, "The homicide detective traced your car's tags. Did you steal it?"

She smiled suddenly, and the smile made her look softer.

"I'm not a car thief," she said. "I just took what was provided."

"By *them*?"

She smiled again and got up. "Thank you, Dixie. I'll see you again.

Oh, and one other thing. I'm sure you'll tell the homicide detective that we've met, and that's okay. But if anybody else should ask, please don't give me away."

Sweet Jesus, the woman seemed to think we were friends and that I would protect her secrets.

She walked away rapidly, breaking into a jog as she went toward the steps to the parking lot. By the time I got to the Bronco, she had completely disappeared and my head was threatening to blow up.

I called Guidry again and left another message, then made the drive home and dragged myself upstairs to my apartment. I immediately fell into bed and unnaturally hard sleep.

I dreamed that Ken Kurtz and I were having tea in his red-dimmed wine room, drinking from Cora's cups and eating her chocolate bread with our tea. The wine bottles seemed to be leaning in to listen, and the room was so cold I was shivering, but Kurtz didn't seem to be bothered. The calico kitten was nestled in my lap, kneading at me with its sharp little claws, and I was afraid Ken would see it and rip out the kitten's fingertips.

I said, "You're very hearty, aren't you?"

He said, "You mean hardy. I'm very hardy."

I hadn't meant hardy at all, but I said I did because I was afraid of him.

My racing heart woke me up, and for a few seconds I had to remind myself it was just a dream. Then I came fully awake and began to wonder why I'd had the dream at all. I believe in dreams. I believe they're messages from our unconscious that we should pay attention to. But I couldn't find a meaning in this one, and after a while I turned over and went back to sleep.

I slept until my inner clock told me it was time to get ready for my afternoon visits. A hot shower helped me get oriented and ready for the rest of the day, and I took a little more care when I got myself presentable. Put on a little blush to counteract my concussion pallor, brushed my eyelashes with mascara, left my hair hanging to my shoulders, and made sure my faded jeans were the ones that brought out the best in my butt. When I backed the Bronco out of the carport, I headed for the key's business district. Since I wasn't going to run with Billy Elliot, I had some extra time, and I wanted to see Ethan Crane before I got covered in cat hair.

# 17

iesta Key's business district is known to locals as the Village. On the front side of the Village, real estate offices squeeze between ice cream parlors and boutiques, and upscale cafés share parking spaces with funky tourist shops selling plastic flamingos and Siesta Key T-shirts. Ethan's office is in a dingy stucco building on an unfashionable side street. I parked at the curb and nodded hello to a man sitting on the sidewalk nursing a ragged military duffel bag. He looked homeless, but Christmas-wrapped packages poked through the holes of his bag as mute testimony to connections to somebody somewhere.

The building's corners looked even more chipped than the last time I'd been there, and when I pulled open the the glass-topped entrance door, I saw it was still etched with his grandfather's name, ETHAN CRANE, ESQ. Ethan apparently had seen no reason either to change the sign or spruce up the building when he inherited it.

A small vestibule inside the door led to a flight of stairs whose every step had been worn slightly lower in the center from decades of climbing feet. At the top of the stairs, a broad corridor stretched toward Ethan's office, with another office to the left where a plump secretary with white-streaked hair sat at a desk facing the door. Christmas cards hung on a string in a drooping line across the front of her desk, and a miniature Christmas tree with miniature electric lights glowed on her windowsill. She looked up with raised eyebrows when she saw me, but Ethan's door was open and I headed straight back without giving her a chance to stop me.

Ethan was standing in front of a bookcase holding a book in his hands, and when he turned and saw me his face registered surprise, annoyance, and pleasure all at one time.

I said, "I wanted to come in person and apologize for being so bitchy this morning."

Some of the annoyance drained out of his face, but all he said was, "That wasn't necessary."

I said, "It was the concussion. A concussion causes mood swings."

My ears flamed with embarrassment when they heard my mouth make such a whiny, victimized statement. It practically bore a banner demanding that he feel guilty for even a moment of irritation because I'd been so nasty to him.

Quickly, I added, "I don't mean that as an excuse, it's just an explanation."

He grinned. "Does that mean we can try again?"

Okay, that was better. He wasn't being so reserved now, and I'd got the megawatt smile. I absolutely hate it when people are disappointed in me. I can live with people not liking me from the get-go, but I always feel challenged when they start out liking me and then something happens that makes them think less of me.

His face took on stern lines again and he motioned toward one of the rump-sprung leather chairs facing his desk. "Dixie, tell me again what happened to you."

"There's not much to tell, really. I stopped at Kurtz's house on my way home last night, and when I got out of the car somebody conked me on the back of the head and knocked me out. When I came to, there was smoke in the air and I called nine-one-one. A chemical fire had been set behind the house, and the fire marshal thinks the arsonist hit me to keep me from seeing him. The homicide detective took me to the emergency room and then stayed with me until Paco came home."

Okay, so I wasn't telling the whole truth, but the fact of Jessica Ballantyne setting that fire was something I would only tell Guidry.

Ethan said, "Homicide detective?"

"Somebody was murdered at Kurtz's house yesterday morning. The arson is probably connected somehow, so the detective went to his house."

Ethan's dark eyes flashed with some emotion I couldn't decipher. "Would that be Lieutenant Guidry? The one who investigated the other murders you were involved in?"

I felt my face flame again. "I haven't been *involved* in any murders, Ethan, I just happened to get caught in their backlash. But yes, Guidry is the investigating detective. Now, of course, there's also an arson investigation, but the fire marshal is handling that."

"You could have called me. I would have stayed with you."

"I wasn't up to calling anybody, to tell the truth. I was sort of dazed for most of the night."

"How's your head now?"

"I still have a headache, but it's a lot better."

"Think you'll be up to having supper at my place Saturday night? Just the two of us."

As he scribbled his address on a notepad, time suddenly swirled backward, and for a stricken second I remembered that Saturday nights were reserved for Christy. This year she would be old enough for the two of us to make dough with flour and salt and oil for Christmas ornaments. We might make bells and candy canes and wreaths, bake them until they were like concrete, and then Todd would help us paint them. We would string popcorn and cranberries, too, for our Christmas tree, and on Sunday the three of us would go choose a tree to put all our handiwork on.

Those time warps are always so vivid that when reality snaps into place I feel disoriented. Silent as a rock, I came back to the present, where there were no Christmas ornaments or Christmas cookies or Christmas tree, no Todd or Christy, and when Christmas would merely be a day my heart would break again because they weren't there with me.

I got up and stuffed Ethan's address in my pocket. "I have cats and dogs waiting."

Giving him a parody of a smile, I scurried away, catching a glimpse of the secretary's curious gaze as I rushed past her office. I wanted to turn around and tell Ethan I had been mistaken, I couldn't spend Saturday night with him. But I knew if I spoke I would burst into tears, so I hurried down the stairs and out the door instead.

As I ran to the Bronco, the man sitting on the sidewalk with his bag of gifts raised his hand like a beauty-pageant winner and called, "Merry Christmas, pretty lady!"

I managed not to cry until I was in traffic, and the tears had stopped by the time I got to the first traffic light. I considered that a sign of progress. There had been a time when an onset of memories and tears would last for days. Maybe someday they won't come at all, just an ache in the heart.

On a sudden impulse, I turned toward the cemetery where my grandparents are buried. I don't believe in planting people, but my grandparents were not the kind of people to be cremated—too much possibility that the fundamentalists might turn out to be right and they'd wake up on Judgment Day with no bodies to reconnect.

The cemetery is a morbidly pretty place with evenly manicured green grass. Except for the flat stone markers, it could be a golf course. Several people were decorating their loved ones' graves with fake poinsettias and plastic holly wreaths. The best I could do was kneel and scrape a blob of dried bird shit from my grandmother's marker.

"Gran, I wish you were here. I could use some wise advice. Somebody got killed, and they think I might have done it. And there's this kitten I'm worried about. They want to declaw it, and you know how awful that is. And then a man has invited me to supper at his house Saturday night, and it's bound to get romantic. Sexy romantic. I know it's time for me to start living like a normal woman, but the sex part scares me. If I have sex with a man, I'm afraid it'll blot out my memories of Todd. If I do that, I'll be somebody else."

An egret flew overhead making low gargling noises, but I didn't think it was channeling my grandmother. She lay in her grave as silent as my grandfather in their double-bed burial site.

I looked out at all the graves and their plastic flowers and wondered if this was what my grandparents had intended as their final statement. I doubted it. They had been too vital, too busy living and loving to want a vast synthetic silence to mark their wisdom.

A little voice in my head said, *There's your answer, Dixie. Don't be a coward. Throw yourself into life and it will meet you halfway.*

Maybe I was really just talking to myself, but I felt lighter when I left.

Considering that my head still weighed about ten tons and a muffled drumbeat sounded every time I put a foot down, the afternoon pet visits went smoothly. I slow-walked my sedate dogs and slow-played with my cats, all the time thinking about the calico kitten and hoping it would grow up to be as graceful and sure on its feet as the cats I played with, and not like a ballerina surgically consigned to wearing clogs.

I moved so slowly that it was an hour past sunset when I finished with the last cat. I stored my equipment in the back of the Bronco and drove to a street off Avenida del Norte where Joe and Maria Molina live in organized chaos with their children, Joe's parents, and whichever relative is in need of a place at the moment.

The Molina house is a rambling turquoise stucco that Joe's father, Antonio Molina, bought fifty years ago for thirty thousand dollars. He had come from Mexico with nothing but the clothes on his back, a sharp mind, and a strong body. Now he has one of the area's most successful lawn services, and the house is worth a couple of million. Joe grew up watching his father come home every day burnt dark as cork by the sun and decided to make his living some other way. He and his industrious wife, Maria, own a business that keeps half the houses on the key clean, and they do it in air-conditioned coolness.

Tony Molina thinks grass is for suckers, so the Molina yard is landscaped with shell and beach-hardy plants. I parked in the wide paved driveway that curved around a thick clump of royal palms planted in redwood mulch. Strings of tiny white lights outlined the palm trunks, and near the front door a herd of dwarf reindeer stood in various poses.

They were outlined in lights too, and methodically turned their heads side to side. Behind them, an inflated plastic Santa bathed in the beam of a floodlight waved his ballooned arms, while winged angels looked down from the rooftop. The Molina family had all Christmas bases covered.

Joe and Maria's eleven-year-old daughter, Lila, opened the gift-wrapped door when I rang. She had a new thick-haired russet dog with her that looked like a chow mix. The dog yipped sharply and Lila bent to him.

Solemnly, she said, "This is our friend Dixie. Never bark at her."

The dog woofed one more time to save face and then grinned at me.

Lila said, "I'm teaching him who is a friend and who it's okay to scare."

I said, "That's a good thing to know. Sometimes I scare people who might want to be my friends."

Lila smiled and motioned me toward the kitchen, where delicious odors beckoned.

"We got him at the animal shelter. He was so scared at first, he thought we might not keep him."

Passing a table holding a large crèche scene with fuzzy sheep and a holy family dressed in velvet, I stopped in the kitchen doorway and felt a momentary pang of envy for the dog. Papa Tony sat at the round oak table in the middle of the room drinking a Tecate and reading the *Herald-Tribune*. Maria was at the sink chopping an onion on a wooden board, and Joe's mother, who had become everybody's *Abuela* Rosa the minute her first grandchild was born, was stirring an aromatic something on the range. A young woman I didn't know leaned on a counter with a chubby baby balanced on her hip, and Joe knelt in the corner talking eye-to-eye to his two-year-old son.

When they saw me, everybody turned with such welcoming smiles that I was afraid I might get sloppy and cry again. I guess I still had concussion emotions.

Joe introduced the young woman, one of Maria's sisters, and picked the little boy up.

"Say hello to Miz Dixie," he told the kid, to which the child gave me a dimpled smile and hid his face in his father's neck.

Joe laughed and handed off the boy to Maria's sister, who left the room with a kid on each hip, their chubby legs gripping her backside like little monkeys. Nature's designs are infinitely practical—a woman's round hips attract men, result in babies, and then provide transport for them.

Maria said, "What happened to you, Dixie?"

I fingered the knot on my head. "Somebody hit me on the head and gave me a concussion. Thanks for helping me out this morning. I want to pay you."

In unison, Joe and Maria shook their heads. Maria said, "You've helped us plenty of times. Don't even talk about money."

At the stove, *Abuela* Rosa spoke to the ceiling. "You see? God spoke to me this morning and said, *Make menudo, Rosa.* I thought, *Why must I make menudo?* But I do not argue with God, so I made menudo. Now I know why. It is because you have a concussion. The menudo is for you. God always has a reason for everything."

With the same look Joan of Arc probably had when she rode off to do God's bidding, *Abuela* Rosa bustled to a cabinet and got out a wide soup bowl.

Joe said, "It's true. Menudo cures everything."

Papa Tony folded his paper and said, "Sit, sit."

I didn't need to be invited twice. I sat.

Menudo is a wonderful Mexican soup of tripe, hominy, and chili in a rich, red, garlicky broth. Stewed for hours and eaten steaming and fiery, it is reputed to soothe the stomach, clear the head, and eliminate hangovers. The stuff works too. Just the steam from the big bowl *Abuela* Rosa set in front of me immediately tunneled through my sinuses to my bruised brain and made me feel more alert.

Maria said, "What do you mean, somebody hit you on the head?"

"I mean somebody hit me on the head. I stopped late last night at a house where I'm taking care of an iguana, and when I got out of my car somebody conked me on the head." I spooned up more menudo and said, "I guess I should tell you it's the same place where the guard was killed yesterday morning."

Immediately, every spine in the room stiffened, every face took on a guarded look.

Papa Tony said, "The Kurtz house."

"You know him?"

"I never saw him, but I took care of his grounds for a while."

I said, "I was wondering about that. How did you get inside the courtyard?"

"The nurse would open the last garage door and we went in that way. There's a storage room at the back of that garage, with a door to the courtyard."

"So you know Gilda? The nurse?"

He shook his head, looking as if he wished he hadn't said anything. "I just went there a few times, then she fired me. Said we made too much noise and upset her boss."

"Did you know the guard?"

"Ramón Gutierrez. Yes, I knew him."

Joe said, "They go to our church, he and his wife."

Maria said, "She belongs to some weird religious group too." With a wary look at her mother-in-law, she said, "The kind that's always worried about the devil. She has too much time on her hands. Thinks she's too good to work, just wants her husband to take care of her."

I said, "Well, he won't be taking care of her now."

*Abuela* Rosa crossed herself and shook her head sadly. *"Pobrecita."*

Joe said, "Do you know if the cops have caught the killer?"

I took several slurps of menudo before I answered. Just in case they snatched the bowl away when I told them.

"No, but I'm one of the suspects."

*Abuela* Rosa crossed herself again.

I said, "I saw Ramón dead in the guardhouse just before the *Herald-Tribune* man came and found him. I knew he would call and report it, so I didn't."

They all nodded vigorously. People with brown skin—including law-abiding citizens—understand all too well the wisdom of avoiding attention from the police when a crime has been committed.

"The *Herald-Tribune* guy told them he'd seen me leaving the scene of the crime, so now I'm a suspect."

*Abuela* Rosa pressed both hands to her bosom and sighed.

Joe said, "They can't think you did that!"

Papa Tony got up from the table with his face set in hard, stern lines. He stalked toward the door with an angry set to his shoulders. At the door he turned to me.

"You know those cops, right? You tell them to look closer to home. *Much* closer to home."

He left the room before I could ask him what he meant, but not before I caught a look passing between Joe and Maria.

I left the Molina house with a jar of menudo from *Abuela* Rosa and the knowledge that the Mexican community knew something about Ramón's murder that they weren't telling.

# 18

Thanks to the menudo, my head was only doing a muffled roll when I got to the Kurtz house, not big bass drumming like before. Good thing, too, because a small sign-toting crowd was now gathered on the sidewalk. A few women were on their knees, eyes cast toward the sky, hands folded under their chins. Some others were blocking the driveway. I pulled to a stop and put down my window so I could ask them to move, but they were all concentrating on a man in a cowled brown robe who seemed to be giving a sermon.

He shouted, "It is written that a vial was poured upon the earth and there fell a grievous sore upon the man who had the mark of the beast. The Bible tells us that the one with the mark of the beast has a number, and his number is six hundred threescore and six. Six hundred sixty-six, brothers and sisters! The number of this house! And hear this, brethren, it is also written that the beast worked miracles that deceived them that worshipped his image, and they were all cast into a lake of fire."

The crowd murmured approvingly, and several people seemed ready to go cast somebody into a lake of fire right then.

I leaned out my window. "Excuse me, I need to drive through here."

A woman in a shiny black dress glared at me and waved her sign, but a man at the side called, "Let the car through!"

The people parted to let me pass, but they all gave me hellfire looks.

I parked in front of the garages and walked down the palm-screened path to the front door. When I reached the expanse of living room windows, something felt wrong, and it took a second to realize that it was the distance from the garage door. Now that I knew the wine room was behind the first garage, I had unconsciously stepped off the length of an average garage and added the ten feet or so of the wine room's depth, which should have put me at the beginning of the living room's glass wall. Instead, it was a good fifteen feet farther ahead. Ken Kurtz evidently had a garage about forty feet deep. Maybe he kept a stretch limo or a yacht in there.

A helicopter flew over with a droning *whap-whap!* sound, and I wondered if there were surveillance cameras in it pointed at me. I thought about waving up at them, but the thought was only for my own entertainment. A little sick humor to jolly me along.

The living room wasn't lit, but through the glass wall I could see flames leaping in the fireplace. It was almost eighty degrees outside, and he had a fire. Somehow, I wasn't surprised. Ken Kurtz seemed almost as cold-blooded as Ziggy. While I waited for him to come to the door, I remembered there had been a basket of firewood by the fireplace. Fire must be important to Kurtz.

His shadowy form moved past the window toward the door faster than he had moved before. Perhaps all the excitement of the guard's murder and Gilda's disappearance had given him a spurt of new energy. Or maybe it was the food I'd brought him from Anna's. Maybe real food had cured the guy, the way menudo had cured my concussion.

He opened the door in the same bedraggled bathrobe he'd worn before and stepped aside to let me in without speaking. The house was like an oven.

I said, "Hello, Mr. Kurtz."

I didn't see any point in telling him his house was being picketed by religious fanatics. The man had enough problems without knowing that.

Ziggy had left the dry sauna and was running up and down the corridors. Iguanas only poop once every three or four days, and from the hint of desperation in his scurrying, I had a feeling this was the day.

I said, "It's eighty degrees outside. Shall I put Ziggy out?"

Kurtz flapped his blue hands. "Take him out. He needs the fresh air."

I opened one of the sliders to the courtyard and went to Ziggy's side. Kurtz seemed to lose interest and shuffled down the corridor toward the living room. Keeping a wary eye on Ziggy's tail, I got ready to slip my arms under his body and grab his legs to lift him. But he stuck out his tongue and tasted fresh air from the open slider and scampered out, heading straight for a clump of hibiscus bushes.

Remembering that my grandfather's iguana had also preferred to poop on the roots of hibiscus, I grinned and went to the hospital-white kitchen to gather Ziggy's fruits and vegetables for the day. Most of the leftovers from Anna's were still in the fridge, so Kurtz wasn't in danger of starving. For Ziggy, I sliced zucchini and yellow squash, bananas and pineapple, added romaine and swiss chard, and carried them outside in a big wooden bowl.

I said, "Hey, Zig, I brought you some goodies."

With an extra-satisfied smile on his face, he bobbed his head and sniffed me with his tongue. He was beginning to associate me with food, so I smelled good to him.

I knelt to set the bowl on the ground, and Ziggy raised himself on his front legs and flicked out his tongue to smell it. That's when I saw the telltale evidence of an indwelling tunneled catheter low on his chest wall—not like Kurtz's ordinary PICC line that any good nurse can insert, but one like my grandfather had in the months before he died—the kind that is surgically inserted directly into the large vein that enters the heart.

Somebody had been giving Ziggy transfusions or withdrawing blood, and on a regular basis. But why? And what was the connection to the catheter in Kurtz's arm?

The implications made me dizzy, but so did everything else in this weird house.

I left Ziggy eating his dinner and went looking for Kurtz. He was in the wine room, moving slowly down the line of bottles as if he were taking inventory. In the eerie red light, his bluish skin looked faintly puce.

He said, "Did you feed the iguana?"

It was another moment when I had a choice. I could keep my mouth shut and walk out the front door and go home. Or I could open my big mouth and then walk out the front door and go home.

I said, "I promised Jessica Ballantyne that I'd give you this message—*Ziggy is no longer an option. You must act now.*"

I turned and almost made it across the living room before Kurtz shouted at me. "Dixie! For the love of God, please!"

Sap that I am, I turned to look back at him. In the red-lit door to the wine room, he stood with both arms pressed overhead against the door frame. With his arms raised like that, his bathrobe sleeves had drooped over his sinewy arms, exposing the gauze dressing on the inside of one elbow.

"Jessie's alive?"

"She said you abandoned her."

He pulled his arms down and sagged against the doorway. "How does she look?"

"As opposed to what? She looked okay to me, but then I don't know her from Adam's off ox, so I really can't say if she looked unusually good or not. All I know is that somebody she called *they* are tapping your phone and that you're in danger. She's the one who set the fire last night, at which time, by the way, somebody hit me on the head and gave me a concussion. So thank you very much for involving me in your life, Mr. Kurtz. So far it's been a real pleasure."

"Jessie was here last night?"

"She said you ran out on her, that you left her to die. Evidently she loves you anyway, because she wants to warn you about *them*, whoever *they* are."

"I wouldn't have left her there! I thought she was dead. They said she was dead."

"Would these *they* be the same *they* who are watching you now?"

He wiped his hand against his face. "Jesus. I have to see her."

"I don't think so. From what she said, she can get in a whole lot of trouble from *them* if they find out she's trying to help you."

"Of course. Good God."

I said, "Okay, I've delivered the message, and I've told you everything she told me. That's all I'm going to do. It's all I can do. You people have used me sixteen ways from Thursday, and I'm going home now and leave you to whatever it is that you're doing. There's just one thing—I saw the catheter in Ziggy. If you're hurting him, I won't be so nice and cooperative. You understand?"

He gestured toward the chairs in front of the fireplace. "Please, I'd like to explain."

Okay, now we were getting somewhere. I dropped into a chair and waited until Kurtz had shuffled to a chair across from me. The fireplace was unpleasantly warm, but in its flickering amber light Kurtz didn't look so sick.

He said, "Not that it makes what I'm going to tell you any more palatable but I'm a veterinary microbiologist and pathologist with a long list of degrees and appointments."

I raised an eyebrow, meaning *What the heck does that have to do with anything?*

"I just want you to know that I'm not a mad scientist, never have been."

"Okay, so you're a professional."

"Jessica and I were both bizogenetic researchers for the army."

"Our army?"

He smiled. "I'm not a foreign terrorist, Dixie."

Maybe not, but I had a feeling he might be a native terrorist, which in some ways is even worse.

"In the beginning, we were trying to develop vaccines or antidotes for a host of animal diseases that we expect to see in humans in the future. Some of them have already popped up here and there, like the outbreak of SARS, which originated in an obscure wild animal in China, or the West Nile virus, which originates in horses. A disease that's benign in animals can be fatal to humans, and when a disease leaps from animals to humans, it can become highly contagious. Look at what happened with the bubonic plague. It spread from rats to humans via fleas, and in five years it wiped out a third of the European population. The next plague will probably come from poultry in Southeast Asia."

His eyes had taken on the shine of enthusiasm that people have when they talk about something that gets their juices flowing. Even his voice seemed stronger and more confident.

I hated to be the ant at his picnic, but I said, "And then what happened?"

"Excuse me?"

"You said you were developing vaccines in the beginning. What happened after the beginning?"

He took a deep breath, and the shine left his eyes.

"Then somebody in a position of power decided that a disease that began in animals and was fatal to humans could be a useful weapon. If we could find a way to create and disseminate an interspecies disease in a controlled way, we could wipe out an entire nest of terrorists or an entire population that we believed posed a threat to world peace."

Hearing somebody talk about widespread killing in order to bring about world peace always makes me want to projectile vomit, but I kept quiet.

He said, "The army contracted with a civilian company to take responsibility for the work, but basically the same researchers continued doing what we had always been doing. We just had different employers. Our assignment was to develop a fatal disease that we could test on an isolated island in Southeast Asia." Looking quickly at my face, he said, "Fewer than a thousand inhabitants, virtually no outside contact. It was an ideal testing locale, especially in the event that biocontainment was breached. That happens sooner or later in any animal disease lab, but in our location any accidentally released virus would disperse over the ocean."

With a bitter grimace, he added, "We never expected the ocean to turn on us."

"You lived there, on the island?"

"Yes, we lived among the people we planned to kill."

"And did you? Did you kill them?"

A ripple of pain moved across his face. "We were just doing our job, Dixie. But no, we didn't kill them. We killed our fellow researchers instead. Not by intent, of course—it was purely accidental. I imagine you find a poetic justice in that."

I shrugged. "What's the quotation, *He who lives by the sword dies by the sword*? I suppose that applies to those who live by diabolical research too."

"You call it diabolical. We thought of it as exploring the limits of genetic engineering."

"Okay. So what happened?"

Wearily, he said, "Our biocontainment lab was in a secret underground installation under a concrete complex that housed legitimate biotechnology laboratories. Our basement lab was divided into zones separated by heavy air-lock doors that opened and closed by a computer code known only to the senior researchers. The air pressure steadily decreased toward the central zone, where we kept freezers full of frozen viruses. That way, any stray pathogens would flow inward and up through a large particulate filter."

He fell silent for a moment, as if he had to summon the courage to tell the rest of what he intended to say. I didn't pressure him. I know all too well that some memories are too awful to tell all in one burst.

He said, "From the beginning, those of us in charge of the project were concerned about the fact that the air locks couldn't be opened manually. We wanted a manual option in case of a power failure, but every time we complained, we got a runaround about the expense, or the possibility of losing our secrecy, or some other bureaucratic crap."

As he talked, his arms began to cross over his chest until he was hugging himself against some chilling memory.

"The same tsunami that killed hundreds of thousands of people in Southeast Asia hit the island. The thing came out of nowhere, a wall of water that destroyed everything in its path, including the concrete building above the lab. Water flooded every zone of the basement and knocked out the backup generators that allowed the air locks to open. Without manual controls, everybody in the innermost chambers drowned, along with the infected animals in their holding chambers."

He put a quivery hand to the side of his face and held it there for a moment, either to calm the twitching tremors under his skin or to calm his own obvious fury at a company whose negligence had cost lives.

"If the goddamned company had listened to us and put in manual controls, they could have survived. Rescuers had to push their way through contaminated water to reach the dead, and many of the rescuers sickened and died too. My own theory is that they either had open sores or accidentally ingested some of the water. They all died within twenty-four hours."

He turned his tortured gaze to meet my eyes.

"Jessie was supposed to be on duty in the biocontainment lab when the tsunami hit, and she was listed as one of the dead. I have always believed she died there."

I felt like Alice after she ate the cookie that made her become enormous. The overheated room seemed to be shrinking, and Kurtz was beginning to look like somebody seen through the wrong end of a telescope.

"Why not you? Why not Ziggy?"

His face took on a sly, crafty look. "I was using that particular iguana for some special research. I had taken him to my private residence that was farther inland."

"And when the tsunami hit?"

"Near the shoreline, it was pure chaos. But higher up, where I was, some people weren't even aware it had happened. I heard the news on the radio and knew our lab would have been destroyed, along with all our work. I knew if any of the researchers survived, they would do what they could to keep the work secret. I did the only thing I could do. I put the iguana in the helicopter the army provided and got the hell out of there."

As delicately as I could, under the circumstances, I said, "That doesn't explain what caused your—"

He gave that braying pseudo-laugh again. "Funny thing about creating diseases to use for espionage. We can manipulate cells to cause blood to boil or bones to crumble or the brain to implode. But we never consider the long-range consequences to the creators. One careless moment, and you can be seeing a death mask in the mirror for the rest of your life."

"I'm just guessing here, but does that mean you were careless?"

"You get so familiar with the animals, you know? You sort of forget why they're there and why you're there. Sometimes you're too tired to do things exactly the right way. You don't put on gloves or you accidentally stick yourself with a contaminated needle or you inhale particulate in the air after an animal sneezes or coughs. In the early days we used silver nitrate to attenuate the viruses we were working with, and I was exposed to so much of it that my skin was beginning to turn bluish even before the tsunami. It's become a lot more pronounced in the past few months. The neural spasms and the episodes of debilitating pain didn't appear until after I left the island. That's why I need heat too. My body's temperature regulator has been destroyed."

"If you created your condition, can't you create an antidote for it?"

His face was blank for a moment, and then a light seemed to switch on in his eyes.

"Smart girl, Dixie. That's exactly what I think. That's why the vials Gilda took are so important."

I was a hundred and eighty degrees past exhaustion, but I knew Kurtz had just told a gigantic lie.

Dully, I said, "Those packages in the refrigerator were vials of an antidote?"

"Exactly! It's somewhat the same principle as homeopathy, to treat an illness with minute amounts of the the same toxins that caused it. Gilda gives me the injections. She's dedicated to seeing me returned to health."

"Then why did she run off with the vials?"

He shrugged, flicked his eyes upward, and found another lie.

"I think she was scared, Dixie. She didn't understand what had happened to Ramón, and she was afraid. But she'll be back when she thinks about it. She wouldn't abandon me."

I thought of Jessica saying, *He abandoned me,* and knew Ken Kurtz was hiding something I would probably be better off never finding out.

Before I left, I asked him if he wanted me to bring Ziggy inside for the night.

He shook his head. "Leave him out. He's happier outside."

His voice had an unaccustomed hint of affection. Maybe Kurtz wasn't as cold as he seemed. Whatever he was, I left him there in his house with the number that instilled fear in the hearts of the marchers outside.

As I drove past them, they didn't look as loony as they'd looked before.

# 19

When I got home, I went straight to Michael's kitchen, where he and Paco were busy putting dinner together.

Michael's face was grim. "Are you okay?"

"I'm fine. A headache, but it's better."

"Tell me what happened."

I did a mental groan. If I had to tell it one more time, I might start making stuff up to make it more interesting.

"When I was passing the Kurtz house on my way home last night, I saw the woman's car I told you about, the one with the dog named Ziggy. It was parked in the driveway by the guard's house, so I pulled in."

Michael gave me a big-brother disapproving look, and I hurried to justify myself.

"I wanted to catch her and Kurtz together because he'd lied to me, said she died two years ago, so it couldn't have been her that I talked to. But I was going to call Guidry to check it out, I swear I was. I drove in and got out of my car, and that's when somebody hit me on the head. When I woke up, I smelled smoke and called nine-one-one."

"The fire marshal said you passed out while you were there."

I rubbed my forehead, not unlike the way Kurtz touched his face before he lied. All the questions were taxing my brain.

I said, "I fainted on the way to tell your guys about the woman. Guidry found me and took me to the emergency room at Sarasota Memorial."

Michael rubbed his own temples with his forefingers, rotating his fingertips like giving himself a shiatzu massage. I had a feeling his head hurt almost as bad as mine.

He said, "That fire was set by somebody who knows chemicals and has access to them. The stuff they used doesn't explode, but it burns for a long time and puts out lots of dark smoke that looks like a major fire. Whoever set it meant to draw attention."

I didn't want to tell him I knew the arsonist. That was information still reserved for Guidry. Besides, as much as I resented her, I was beginning to feel a sort of female bond to Jessica.

I said, "Other than getting a concussion, I had a great evening. My date with Ethan, I mean."

He raised his head and quirked an eyebrow. "Yeah?"

"I really did. We danced."

Michael allowed his mouth to twitch in an almost-smile.

Paco said, "You danced? For real?"

"Honest to God, and I didn't step on his feet or trip him or do anything embarrassing."

In unison, they said, "Good girl!"

Then they beamed at me like mothers hearing a five-year-old's report of the first day of kindergarten.

Michael was so pleased he lost the worry wrinkles on his forehead. "I've got spareribs for supper. Sweet potatoes. Corn bread. I'm talking real soul food."

Two seconds ago, I'd intended to crawl in bed without dinner, but now I licked my lips like a feral cat offered a warm mouse.

As a kid, I thought soul food was something God dispensed, like a Mardi Gras king tossing trinkets down to clamoring humans. I imagined it as fluffy and insubstantial, maybe pink as carnival cotton candy. It was Michael who told me it meant basic down-to-earth things like collard greens and ham hocks and corn bread. Now, inhaling exquisite smells coming from a sizzling rack of ribs hot off Michael's prize smoker, I was glad soul food was real instead of ethereal.

He said, "So tell me more about your lawyer."

"He's not my lawyer, and I just went out to dinner with him. There's nothing *exclusive* about it."

Michael raised his face with such a look of shock that I laughed. For the last two years, Michael and Paco had been after me to start seeing men and I had refused with the chaste prudishness of a cloistered nun. Now all of a sudden I sounded like a woman ready to play the field.

Paco twirled an imaginary mustache. "Ah so, my little chickadee."

I got a stack of napkins and tossed them around on the butcher-block island, but my mind was playing a tape of Granddad patting Gran on the rump and saying, "My little chickadee," while she made pretend push-away motions and cut her eyes warningly at Michael and me.

He would grin and say, "Kids, why don't you go outside and see if you can count the stars. The one who gets the number right gets a hot fudge sundae at Dairy Queen."

Michael and I would edge out of the room, trying not to giggle, and wait until Granddad came out to see if we'd counted the stars correctly. We knew it didn't matter what number we came up with, he'd say we were right. Then we'd all pile in his Chevrolet Impala with the pelican hood ornament and the personalized license plates that said SIESTA-1 and drive to Dairy Queen and give ourselves tummy aches on too much ice cream. When we got home, our grandmother would be in her shiny satin robe that she reserved for special occasions, and she'd have a soft smile on her face. I was grown before I learned that the word *chickadee* belonged to a bird and not to my grandmother.

Paco said, "When are you going to see that Stork guy again?"

"His name is Crane, not Stork, and I'm having dinner at his place Saturday night."

"Awriiiiight!!"

While we ate, they made an obvious effort to get my mind off being a suspect in a bizarre murder case, so obvious that I wanted to squeeze them and plant grateful kisses on them. But I couldn't, because then we'd be acknowledging the spot I was in and they'd know their efforts to keep me from thinking about it had failed. I left them early, didn't even stay to help with the dishes. I knew that was okay because they knew my head still hurt from the concussion and they didn't expect me to help, which was something else we couldn't discuss because it would throw us into the *really* big thing none of us wanted to talk about.

Loving people is complicated.

As I crossed the deck to my stairs, I looked up at a violet-blue sky sparked by an infinity of icy lights zillions of miles away. Some of them might have men and women on them, people going about their daily lives without a clue that I existed. I found that an oddly comforting thought.

Guidry still hadn't returned my call, and I was glad. I needed a break from talking about it. Also, I wasn't sure how much of what I'd learned I was going to tell him, and that made me skittery. There shouldn't have been any question about what I'd tell him. I was a responsible citizen, and I should give him every scrap of information I had, no matter how queasy it made me.

I took a long shower, and when I was drying off I found a big blister on my right heel. Wars were breaking out in remote spots on the globe, loggers in the Amazon were destroying a large part of the earth's supply of oxygen, emaciated babies in African villages were dying of AIDS, and I had a blister on my heel. The blister was the only thing I could do anything about. I could not feel sad enough for the world's condition to change it, but I could put a Band-Aid on my heel.

I sat on the edge of the tub and stared at the square tiles on the floor. Funny how I'd never noticed how they were connected but still solitary in their surrounding lines of grout. I thought about how I'd felt dancing with Ethan. Was the blister worth the fun I'd had?

Damn right it was. I'd have tolerated blisters on both heels to do that again.

I thought of how I felt every time I was in the same room with Guidry, all warm and soft and ready to follow him home like a stray puppy. I put my face in my hands and whimpered. How could I have gone from expecting and planning to be alone for the rest of my life to being in love with two men?

I wondered if I had blisters on my brain to match my feet.

# 20

J essica was waiting for me outside the beagle's house next morning. The sun wasn't fully up yet, and she startled me when she stepped away from an oak tree beside the driveway. This time she hadn't bothered with the ploy of walking a dog.

She said, "Did you give Ken the message?"

"I did."

"And?"

"He told me what happened on the island, about the tsunami flooding everything. They told him you had been killed along with the others. He's pretty bitter about the company not providing a way for people to get out."

"I thought it might be something like that. Bitterness about our friends dying, I mean."

"He wants to see you."

"I hope you told him that's impossible."

"I told him his phone is tapped and the mysterious *they* are watching him."

"Thank you, Dixie."

"He's very sick, you know. I think he's in pain most of the time. A lot of pain. And he's blue."

As if she were consoling me, she said, "I'm sorry."

"I just thought you might not know that."

"I had heard. What do you mean, he's blue?"

"I mean he's blue. His skin is gray-blue."

She frowned. "But he couldn't have got that much . . . that doesn't make any sense."

I shrugged. "He said it had got worse in the last few months. His skin jumps and twitches too, and he said that started after he left the island."

She took a deep breath, the way people do when they need strength. "I didn't know it was that bad."

"He looks awful. Freakish, even."

Her hand covered her mouth for a moment, as if she feared the words that might come out, and she started to turn away. I thought she couldn't stand to hear any more, and I regretted telling her how bad Kurtz was. I certainly didn't intend to tell her any more, but my fool mouth opened without my planning it.

"The iguana has an indwelling catheter in his chest wall. Ken Kurtz has one in his arm. You have any idea why?"

She pulled herself sharply erect. "Dixie, don't be stupid. Don't ask questions like that. Not of me or of anybody else."

I said, "I know who you are. Your name is Jessica Ballantyne. And in spite of my better judgment, I sort of like you. But there are a lot of things that make me think you're not a nice person. Your parents think you're dead, for one thing, same way Ken Kurtz did. They've even buried your ashes, which is a pretty crappy thing to do to your parents, if you ask me. Are you wanted for some crime?"

She gave a short laugh. "It's the other way around, actually."

"What the hell does that mean?"

Sounding a little desperate, she said, "I'm trying to . . . you can't imagine what it's like to have . . . you don't understand how biomedical corporations work, you don't know their cutthroat rivalry."

"Come on. You're not going to tell me this is all about corporate rivalry?"

"You asked what Ken's connection was to BiZogen. Okay, try to understand this: Ken and I worked for BiZogen in the lab that was destroyed by the tsunami. Ken took his research with him when he left the island, and he contacted a rival company—the Zoological Interspecies-Genetic Institute—and offered to sell them his research. That research will be worth billions to the company that patents it, so ZIGI agreed. But then the FBI began investigating ZIGI over another patent they had fraudulently obtained, and ZIGI thought it prudent to report Ken's offer. That's when I was recruited."

I squinted at her as if that would help bring what she'd said into focus, but my mind had snagged on the word *Ziggy*.

Stupidly, I said, "Ziggy?"

She gave me a half-pitying smile. "Z-I-G-I is the acronym of Zoological Interspecies-Genetic Institute."

Feeling like a total idiot, I said, "I guess that's why Kurtz didn't know what I was talking about when I said I was there to take care of Ziggy. That's not his name, is it?"

She laughed lightly. "Scientists are careful not to become attached to the pets they use for research. They're more apt to assign them numbers rather than names. It makes it less uncomfortable for them if the animal is killed or hurt."

I clamped my back teeth together to keep from mentioning that nobody seemed to worry about making it uncomfortable for the animal, and forced my mind back to the BiZogen–ZIGI competition.

"Let me get this straight. Ken Kurtz double-crossed BiZogen by going to Zoological-Whatever and offering his research to them. They agreed, and now they're double-crossing him."

"That's about it."

"And you've been hired to catch him or trap him, and you're double-crossing whoever hired you."

She frowned. "No, that's not the way it is. Not at all." She began walking backward, then turned and jogged away. Over her shoulder, she called, "I'm only trying to help Ken get a fair shake." Then she disappeared into the shadows under the trees.

For the rest of the morning, I wondered who had recruited her after Ken contacted the Zoological-Whatever company. BiZogen? The FBI? Some other biomedical research company? Whoever it was, she clearly was divided in her loyalties, and anytime somebody's loyalties are going in two directions, the end result is always bad.

The entire situation was too complicated to even begin to figure out. It was a lot easier to think about the calico kitten and the awful possibility that Paloma might have her claws removed. That was a situation I could easily figure out. I could even do something about it.

Paloma had seemed a gentle soul, so she probably thought declawing a cat was like giving it a manicure. If she knew the facts, I was sure she wouldn't want to harm a helpless kitten. I was also sure that a woman grieving her murdered husband wouldn't want to talk about her kitten's claws and that my compulsion to go see her was a black mark on my road toward complete sanity.

But Paloma might have already made an appointment with a veterinarian to do the surgery. Even if she weren't up to it herself, one of Paloma's friends might take the kitten to be declawed. If that happened, I'd never forgive myself for not trying to stop it.

After I finished grooming the last cat, I crossed the bridge into Sarasota and swung by Nate Tillman's house. Nate's a retiree who lives in one of the few communities that haven't formed a homeowners' association to make rules about what people can do with their own property, so his neighborhood still has personality. Nate himself has hung old CDs from the boughs of a spreading oak in his front yard as year-round sparkly tree ornaments. If you don't look too hard, they look good.

I parked in the driveway, where I could hear the whine of a band saw from Nate's workshop in a backyard shed. Moving through flurries of yellow butterflies intent on wildly growing oregano edging the path, I walked toward the shed where Nate turns out everything from hokey yard whirligigs to beautiful Adirondack porch chairs.

Nate saw me through the open door and turned off the saw.

"Well now, Dixie, what brings you over here to the poor side of town?"

"I'm hoping you have a scratching post I can buy. I'm on a campaign to save a kitten from being declawed."

He winced. "Damn fool thing, pulling out a cat's claws. What size you want?"

"It's for a kitten, but she'll grow. But I don't think she'll be a big cat."

He went over to a shelf and took down a post about two feet tall. Securely attached to a sturdy square base, it was simply an upright log about six inches in diameter, but its heavy bark made it perfect for a cat to scratch or stick its claws in and stretch its muscles.

He said, "You can bring it back and I'll trade it for a taller one when the cat grows up."

"That's perfect. What do I owe you?"

"Aw, five bucks oughta do it. It's just a piece of wood. You doin' okay, Dixie?"

He had such kind brown eyes that I was tempted to tell him all about the iguana and the murder and how I was a suspect and all the other sordid details of my life at the moment. But I didn't.

I gave him a twenty-dollar bill and said, "I'm fine, Nate. Tell your better half I said Hi. I'd stop in and tell her myself, but I'm in a rush."

"She's not home anyway. Gone off shopping with a neighbor. That's her favorite hobby now, spending money."

He was trying for grouch, but his smile spoiled it. Nate and his wife are stuck so hard together it would take one of his saws to separate them. It was good to be reminded there are people who love one another blindly even after umpteen years together. I felt better about the world as I drove away.

There were cars in Paloma's driveway, and more cars parked at the curb. I parked a couple of houses away and went to the back of the Bronco for my supplies. Along with the scratching post, I got out my nail-grooming kit and a dime bag of catnip.

The front door was open when I went up Paloma's steps, and I could hear several people inside talking. Paloma suddenly appeared in the doorway as if she had rushed to meet me. She looked frazzled and tired.

I said, "I'm sorry, Paloma. I know this is a terrible time to come, and I know you don't want to see me anyway, but I'm so concerned about the kitten that I—"

"The kitten?"

"I'll trim the kitten's claws so she won't scratch people. I brought her a scratching post too, so she can exercise. Cats need to stretch their leg muscles, and the only way they can do that is to stick their claws in something and pull. But if I could just have five minutes with her, her claws won't be a problem anymore."

Paloma stared at me with round astonished eyes. Behind her, somebody called her name, but she ignored them. Her brother came to stand beside her, and when he saw it was me, he frowned.

"It's all right," Paloma said. "She has come to cut the kitten's claws."

Incredibly, Paloma seemed to find my uninvited presence as a kitty manicurist not only acceptable but welcome. I got the feeling she welcomed me as a diversion from all the talk inside more than as a kitten rescuer, but it didn't matter. After several shouts toward the back of the house that other people took up and repeated, the little girl came to the door with the kitten in her hands. She smiled shyly at me and stepped out on the porch. Paloma hesitated a second, as if she wanted to come outside too, and then went back to join the people in the house. After a moment, her brother left the doorway, leaving me alone with the child and her kitten.

As if it were our accustomed spot, the child and I went to the corner where I'd found her the day before. We sat down and I put the scratching post on the floor in front of us.

I said, "Kittens need to scratch things, but we have to teach them what is good to scratch and what isn't."

I took the kitten and gently pulled her paws down the post a few times to give her the idea. She was a smart kitten. In no time, she was digging her sharp little daggers into the bark so deeply that she got stuck and I had to disengage her paws.

I said, "I've brought my nail clippers with me, and I'm going to trim the kitty's claws so she'll be able to scratch the wood but they won't stick in your skin."

She nodded solemnly, but her eyes were apprehensive.

I said, "I promise I won't hurt her."

When the kitten seemed to have had her fill of scratching and stretching on the post and was nicely relaxed, I lifted her into my lap and stroked her, rhythmically running my fingers down her throat, the place where cats most love to be stroked, then on down her chest to her front legs and the ends of her paws. When she was strongly purring and half asleep, I got my clippers ready and pressed gently on one paw until she extended its claws. Quickly, careful not to clip into the quick, I clipped off the hooked end of her claws, then stroked her some more before I repeated the process on the other paw.

The whole process went so fast that it was over before she realized anything was happening. But to make her associate pleasure with having her nails trimmed, I opened the bag of catnip, pinched a bit between my fingers, and sprinkled it on the floor in front of my crossed knees. This was the iffy part of my plan because not all cats respond to catnip. Even those who do have to be about three months old before they like it. But for cats who are sensitive to catnip, it's the most exciting thing they've ever had, and they will bless you in their kitty prayers for giving it to them.

This kitten turned out to be both sensitive and old enough. When I put her on the floor next to the herb sprinkle, she had the typical catnip response, leaping and rolling and swaying in an ecstatic dance.

The little girl giggled so hard watching her that Paloma came to the door again. The kitten was going nuts with euphoric joy and the little girl was laughing with the cheek-jiggling glee that children can have even when their house is full of people mourning a father's death. Paloma stood a moment, watching them, and then gave me a long speculative look before she went back inside.

I gathered up my clippers and stood.

I said, "The kitten will get bored with the catnip in a few minutes, but if you leave it on the floor, she'll come back to it later and like it again."

The little girl looked disappointed. "Are you leaving?"

"I'll come back one day and trim your kitty's nails again. Don't try to do it yourself. And I'm going to leave you this little bag of catnip. Just give her a tiny pinch, and don't do it very often. Once a week is enough. That way, she won't get tired of it."

She blinked at me, and I remembered that kids don't think in terms of weeks or months.

I said, "How about every Sunday after church?"

She smiled and nodded vigorously, already seeing herself coming home from church and watching the kitten roll around in catnip.

Paloma materialized at the door again, which gave me the feeling she'd been nearby listening.

I said, "I trimmed the kitten's nails, and I'll come back and do it again when she's older."

She didn't answer, just stood silently in the door watching me.

Certain that I'd reached the end of my welcome, I said, "Okay, 'bye now. Call me if you need me."

She looked so sad and lost that I left as fast as I could. I couldn't do anything about her sadness. My expertise was limited to trimming kittens' claws, not taking away the numb despair of a woman whose husband had been murdered.

# 21

amón Gutierrez's funeral was held Friday noon at St. Martha's Catholic Church at the corner of Orange and Fruitville on the mainland. The church's chin rests on the sidewalk on Orange, and a surprisingly large crowd was climbing the steps to the front door when I got there. Some were probably there because they were members of the church or the Spanish community and wanted to show their support for Paloma, and some were probably drawn by the aura of mystery and violence surrounding her husband's death.

I sat at the back and watched mourners speak to Paloma and Jochim with the pitying and slightly fearful look that people save for those whose lives have been touched by unspeakable tragedy. Before the service began, Paloma stood up and surveyed the crowd face by face, as if she wanted to burn us all into her memory. She looked surprised when she saw me, then gave me a tremulous smile and raised her hand in a tiny wave.

Mercifully, the priest spoke of Ramón's life and not of how he died. When the service ended, half the crowd got in line to view the remains, while the other half, including me, headed for the exits. Two or three people ahead of me, a woman in a long dark dress with black hair hanging loose over her shoulders caught my attention. The square line of her shoulders and her rigid spine were so like Jessica Ballantyne's that I watched her move toward the front door. As if she felt my gaze, she turned and looked straight at me. It was Jessica, and her eyes rounded in surprise when she saw me. It didn't look like pleasant surprise. She quickly turned away and hurried out the front door and down the steps.

I pushed through the people in front of me in time to see her run down the sidewalk and disappear around the Fruitville corner. At the curb, a thin young man in a dark suit stood watching her too. As I came down the steps, he looked over his shoulder toward me. Even with his dark glasses, I could see him register the same surprise I'd got from Jessica. In a flash, he slipped through the crowd and disappeared too, leaving me rooted to the spot with a vague sense that I knew him.

Since I was in downtown Sarasota, I drove a block to Lemon—we like to name our streets after as many local fruits as possible—where we now have our very own Whole Foods market. Wandering the aisles in that organic emporium, I am always like a newly arrived immigrant made woozy by glorious abundance. The sight of bright-eyed fish caught hours ago in Alaska, red radish globes so recently pulled from the earth that the leaves are still crisp, and creamy cheeses and rich chocolate just off the plane from France never fails to make me thankful that I live in a country where such things are possible. I ended up buying an enormous bunch of yellow freesia, a Mediterranean dip of feta, sun-ripened tomatoes, and Greek olives, and a package of miniature pita for the dip.

Leaving the market, I caught myself watching for another glimpse of Jessica Ballantyne. What was she doing at Ramón's funeral? For that matter, who was that skinny man who'd been watching her, and why did he look so familiar?

I thought about it all the way home, and I was still thinking about it when I put the freesia in a big blue vase and set it in the middle of my kitchen bar where I could see it from just about every spot in my apartment. I did some laundry, spiffed up the kitchen a bit and deep-cleaned my bathroom until I was a little high on chlorine fumes, then got the Mediterranean dip and the pita and went to my office-closet to catch up on business.

I'm a stickler for detail about my pet-sitting duties. I keep a record for every pet, with every pill given, every bath, every flea or tick treatment administered, and any unusual things the pet did that might signal an infection or some other health problem. When the owners come back, I give them a note of all those things along with my bill. That way, they don't duplicate treatments, and if there's the possibility of a problem, they can watch for more symptoms.

Before I had a chance to even taste the Mediterranean dip, the phone rang. Holding a torn triangle of pita at the ready, I waited for the machine to tell me who was calling.

It was a woman's voice, thin and uncertain. "My name is Paloma Gutierrez. I wish to speak to—"

I dropped the pita and snagged the phone. "This is Dixie, Paloma."

"Oh." She laughed nervously, the way people do when they've been speaking to an electronic voice that's suddenly replaced by the human original. "I . . . um . . . I have been thinking about what you said."

"About the kitten?"

There was a pause, as if she were shocked, and I mentally slapped myself.

She said, "No, but it was because of the kitten that I decided to call you. I mean, I saw how much you cared about it, and that made me think about how you said I should remember that Ramón loved me. And he did, you know? He truly did, even though . . ."

Her voice trailed away, and I swallowed the dry grit of anxiety. I was glad she'd lost some of the bitter jealousy she'd had when we first spoke, but had she called just to tell me that she knew her husband had loved her?

"Paloma, could we meet someplace and talk?"

"Jochim doesn't want me to tell you anything."

"Jochim has a man's fear of the truth. Women know it's the only power we have."

I heard a sharp little intake of breath. "Yes. That is true."

I waited, clamping my teeth together to keep from bellowing *Please tell me what you know!*

She said, "Do you know the Sweet Pea Café? I will meet you there in thirty minutes. I can't stay long."

I said, "Bless you, Paloma," and really meant it.

Sarasota has a large Amish community. The men wear traditional beards and denim overalls, the women wear modest cotton dresses and little lacy bun covers over their upswept hair. Young Amish men and women zoom through the streets on bicycles, while their parents and grandparents opt for more sedate three-wheelers, some of them with seats wide enough for husband and wife together. Either because they are naturally entrepreneurial or because they can only indulge their love for sugary desserts if they make them, a lot of Amish operate restaurants serving the kind of hearty fare they ate before they left the farm and retired to Sarasota for an easier life.

The Sweet Pea is a cheery little Amish café with ruffled yellow curtains on the windows and religious music playing in the background. At this in-between hour—early for the dinner crowd and late for the lunch bunch—only a few tables and booths were occupied, mostly by elderly Amish couples who had parked their trikes on the sidewalk outside the door.

When I got there, "The First Noel" was playing too loud on the sound system, and Paloma was already seated in a booth at the back, a wan little figure looking like an exhausted teenager who needed a good night's sleep.

# 22

I slid in the booth opposite Paloma, and a sweet-faced waitress in an obviously homemade dress brought me a mug of hot coffee without being told.

Raising her voice to speak over the music, the waitress said, "Our special today is meat loaf and mashed potatoes. Would you like that, or would you like to see a menu?"

Out of consideration for Paloma's grief, I hesitated. I remembered what it was like to be unable to swallow anything other than tears, and I didn't want to seem crass. On the other hand, it had been a long time since breakfast, and I love the unabashed over-buttered, over-creamed, deep-fried, gooey, over-sugared excessiveness of Amish food, even if most Amish cafés consider canned green beans a vegetable.

I said, "The meat loaf, please, with a side of fried okra."

The waitress and I both looked questioningly at Paloma.

I said, "You'll have more energy to cope with things if you eat." I sounded like my grandmother, but she looked so beaten and over-whelmed that I couldn't help myself.

She managed a wan smile and nodded. "Okay. I'll have what she has."

The waitress swished away, her hair tidy in its prim little Amish bun cover, her butt cheeks so firm from riding a bicycle they could have cracked walnuts.

I said, "I'm very grateful that you called, Paloma."

"I can't stay long. Jochim would kill me if he knew I left. . . . There are people at my house, you know, people with food who have come to pay their respects."

Of course there were. People always bring food to the bereaved because they don't know what else to do and because they know grief makes people forget to eat.

I said, "It was brave of you to meet me."

"I always knew it was wrong . . . I just never thought it would get my husband killed."

Her eyes darted around the room as if she were making sure nobody recognized her, and I was glad the music was so loud. Maybe it would give Paloma the feeling that she couldn't be heard.

She leaned over the table toward me. "They are devil worshippers in that house. That woman, that nurse, does awful things with the blood of that animal, the what-you-call-it."

"The iguana?"

"Yes, the iguana. They use it for devil ceremonies."

I felt like a hot-air balloon that has just been shot full of holes while hovering above a bottomless abyss. Paloma didn't really have any information for me, she only had superstitious silliness, beliefs and fears carried over from centuries-old ignorance.

She must have seen my face sag, because her voice rose urgently. "She made Ramón carry the animal in the house for their devil rites. He told me, but he would not tell me exactly what they did, the nurse and the man and of course Ramón too, because they made him join in what they did. Evil, nasty things! He came home with whip marks on his body, scratches too. He was ashamed, I know . . . they had an unnatural hold on him. Jochim has told me there are people who play torture games. . . ."

Her voice broke and she grabbed a napkin to cover her face, hiding behind it like a child who thinks she's invisible if she can't see you.

The waitress came with a heaping plate in each hand and a basket of hot rolls and corn bread in the crook of one arm. When she spun away to get us fresh coffee, Paloma lowered the napkin from her face and looked suspiciously at her food.

The piped music changed to "O Come, All Ye Faithful," but there was nobody in our booth feeling joyful and triumphant. For a couple of minutes I was so disappointed that all I could do was fork up meat loaf and mashed potatoes. A few bites of crisp fried okra revived me enough to venture one remark.

"The whip and claw marks on Ramón probably came from the iguana. If you carry an iguana wrong, it will lash you with its tail and scratch you with its claws. Unless Ramón was experienced with iguanas, he probably didn't know the right way to carry them."

"He once worked in a zoo. In the reptile house."

"Did the zoo have iguanas?"

"No, only snakes."

"Well, there you go. Not the same thing."

With a slightly lighter expression, she took a few bites of mashed potato. "You really think it was the animal that made those marks on Ramón?"

"I'm certain of it."

I thought of the lash mark on Ramón's face when I'd seen him in the guardhouse, but I didn't think it would make Paloma feel any better if she knew I'd seen her husband dead.

"It doesn't matter. They were still performing devil ceremonies with the animal's blood."

I buttered a square of hot corn bread and looked bleakly at her. I suppose it will take several more millennia before some human beings stop scaring themselves with fables about a cosmic devil or believing that other human beings regularly consort with it.

Dully, I said, "What makes you think they did something with the iguana's blood?"

"Ramón told me himself. He watched them take blood from the animal. Straight from the heart, not like when they stick your finger, but right from the heart. *She* did it, not the man, but the man was present every time, waiting for the blood. It was for *him*. Ramón said he has drunk so much of the animal's blood that he has turned blue. Is that true? Is the man blue?"

Well, she had me there. No doubt about it, the man was decidedly blue.

I said, "Mr. Kurtz has a blue cast to his skin, but I don't believe he has drunk iguana blood. That wouldn't turn him blue, it would kill him."

Paloma waved her fork at me. "He is very sick, no?"

"Not from drinking iguana blood."

"Then why?"

She had me again.

"I don't know why, but I know that humans can't mix their chemistry with animals' chemistry."

Even as I said it, I thought of the legendary Bill Haast, a Florida serpent expert who injects himself once a week with the venom from thirty-two species of poisonous reptiles. His system has such powerful snakebite antibodies that his blood once saved a snakebite victim's life. Perhaps Paloma was telling the truth. Even though iguanas aren't poisonous, and even though no possible good could come of it, perhaps in some twisted way Ken Kurtz was trying to emulate Bill Haast.

I said, "Did Ramón actually watch any devil ceremonies?"

She lowered her eyes and patted at her mashed potatoes with the tines of her fork, making little railroad tracks in them.

"When I asked him what they did, he yelled at me to shut up. He didn't want to tell me what he saw."

"How can you be sure he saw anything?"

"He had to. He was there. He saw and he was ashamed, but he did not leave."

I felt a surge of irritation for this pretty woman who was so angry at her dead husband.

"Paloma, was your husband paid well?"

"Sure, they paid him a lot to keep quiet about what he saw."

"Maybe that's why he didn't leave. The money was for his family."

"That is true. He always brought his pay to me."

"What will you do now?"

She lowered her eyes again. "We will go home now. All of us, Jochim and his family too. Maybe we will start a business together."

Something furtive and sly in her expression made me sit up straighter. "A business?"

She gave a little toss of her head. "Jochim is smart. We could do that."

Keeping my eyes fixed on my meat loaf, I said, "Takes a lot of money to start a business."

In a proud rush, she said, "That won't be a problem now."

"Ramón had insurance?"

"I shouldn't tell you—Jochim will kill me if he knows I told—but it's the way you said, Ramón did love me. He had to, or he wouldn't have provided for us so well. With the insurance money, we can go home and have a good life."

Her eyes sparkled with happy anticipation, for a moment forgetting the source of her new wealth.

I said, "I take it you've already contacted the insurance company."

"No, I didn't even know about the insurance until the man came."

"The man?"

"The man who brought the money. He came late last night."

"Let me get this straight. A man came late last night with a check from an insurance company."

"Not a check, real money. That's where Jochim is now—he's putting it in a safe box at the bank."

"Did the man give you his name?"

She shrugged. "I don't think so. He was a skinny Anglo in a suit. He gave me an envelope with the money and said now I could take my children and go home. He said that was what Ramón told him he wanted, for us to go home."

The music changed to "O Holy Night," and I looked down at my arms to see if my goose bumps were visible. "Do you mind telling me how much money he gave you?"

She leaned forward and in a proud girlish whisper said, "A hundred thousand dollars!"

The likelihood that somebody from an insurance company had hand-delivered a hundred thousand in cash to Paloma was so remote that it boggled my mind that she believed it. On the other hand, it wasn't much of a jump from believing Gilda had performed satanic rites with Ziggy.

I swallowed the last morsel of meat loaf and said, "I suppose your brother is pleased for you."

"And for himself too. To tell the truth, Jochim has not been himself here. He has been influenced by bad friends, I think. Now he can start over again."

I wondered if Jochim was as naive as Paloma or if he was simply taking advantage of a chance to take his family and go home. In either case, I had a feeling that he and Paloma would be a lot safer once they were well away.

Feeling like somebody who's already seen what's behind Doors Number One and Two, I said, "Paloma, the man who gave you the money—did he have an Irish accent?"

She looked confused. "He sounded like any Anglo to me."

I thought about Paco saying people always remember an accent instead of anything else. But maybe Paloma lumped all non-Spanish accents together and just heard Anglo.

"Thank you for meeting with me, Paloma. It has been a big help."

She smiled shyly, caught in a flood of new self-importance that almost overshadowed her grief.

I couldn't help myself. I said, "What about the kitten?"

As if she were reprimanding a child, she said, "We can't take a kitten all that way. We will give it to somebody."

I said, "You should leave as soon as you can. Whoever killed Ramón may think you know whatever he knew. You could be in danger too."

She turned her head in slow motion, as if she were afraid her cells would fly away if she moved too fast.

"We are good people! Ramón was a good man! Why has this happened to us?"

I didn't have any answers. Her questions would be with her forever. They're the real legacy survivors are left with—the endless questions of *why*.

In the Bronco, I sat for a second before I pulled out of the parking place. It wasn't true that meeting with Paloma had been a big help. All it had done was give me a bit of information about the man who had called me to take care of Ziggy. He was either rich enough to pass out envelopes containing a hundred thousand dollars in cash, or he worked for somebody who was.

As I drove away, my mind played hide-and-seek with itself. At least Paloma seemed to have dropped the plan to declaw the kitten, so I could stop worrying about that. She had been so positive about Gilda taking blood from Ziggy that I had almost believed her. At least I believed that she believed it, and that Ramón had told her he'd seen Gilda do it. But I drew the line at the idea that Ken Kurtz had drunk Ziggy's blood. No way, José. Kurtz might be a weird duck, but he wasn't weird enough to drink iguana blood.

A little voice in my head said, *Maybe he didn't know he drank iguana blood. Maybe Gilda slipped it to him in one of his health drinks.*

"Hunh," I said, because when my little voice makes a good point, I give it credit.

Ken Kurtz had made a big point of saying Gilda kept him on a strict diet, saying she gave him special drinks she concocted. It seemed too bizarre to credit, but maybe Ramón had actually seen Gilda mix the drinks. Maybe he and Gilda had indulged in a few good laughs at how she was turning old Ken blue with her blood cocktails.

I thought of the missing packages from the refrigerator and said, "Hunh," again. Could those packages have been vials of blood? Ziggy's blood? Was that why Gilda had taken them and run, because she was afraid Guidry would find them and know she was playing at being Dr. Jekyll?

Out loud, I said, "Come on, Dixie, get a grip. That's as nutty as Paloma's devil rites."

When I made the rounds to my pet clients, I found that Muddy's owners had returned early to the rank odor of cat urine and the sight of Muddy on top of their baby grand piano. He had been systematically making deep scratches on the lid.

I didn't know whether I felt more sympathetic toward them or toward Muddy. He was far too old to be trained not to scratch, and even the most dedicated cat love can lose its hold in the presence of claw marks on the furniture.

I said, "You know, Muddy lived outside for such a long time, he may never make the adjustment to living in a house."

Mark Cramer said, "It's too dangerous outside."

"Here in the city, yes. But maybe you could find a family in the country where he could sleep in a barn or on a porch."

With her nose wrinkled against the acrid urine odor, Mrs. Cramer eyed the grooves cut into her piano. "He'd be safe from traffic in the country, wouldn't he?"

I said, "And he could chase moles and rabbits."

Mark said, "Do you know any farmers who'd like a cat?"

I didn't but said I'd check with the vets I knew with an offer of a free mouser to a good country home. I left them with my blessings and a bottle of Anti-Icky-Poo spray.

It may have been my imagination, but Muddy's yellow eyes seemed full of gratitude when I told him goodbye.

I was still in the Cramers' driveway when my cell phone rang. Not very many people have my cell phone number, so I thought it might be Guidry. But it wasn't Guidry, and the voice was loud and abrupt in the way of people more comfortable speaking face-to-face.

"Dixie? Antonio Molina—Tony."

I had always called him Papa Tony, but his clipped tone made me abrupt too.

"Yes?"

"I had Joe give me your number. People are saying Ramón Gutierrez was shot by his wife's brother. That's what is going around, and you should know this."

"Jochim?"

"*Sí*, Jochim. I have spoken to him, and I want you to hear what he has to say. Private, you understand?"

My heart fluttered, but I said, "I understand."

"We will be at the Flores Cantina on Three-oh-one at five o'clock today."

"Okay, I'll be there."

He rang off without saying goodbye, leaving me knowing that I had just agreed to keep anything I learned from Tony or Jochim to myself.

# 23

U.S. Highway 301 branches off Tamiami Trail, cuts through the middle of Sarasota's municipal district, and continues as Washington Boulevard through a welter of dingy strip malls and stand-alone businesses. The cantina was on the west side, wedged between a run-down print shop and a take-out pizza place. The pot-holed asphalt parking lot was filled with pickups pulling metal mesh-sided trailers holding landscaping tools. Inside, recorded mariachi was blaring over Hispanic men washing down grit and grass clippings with cold cervezas.

Tony and Jochim were in a booth at the back, Jochim's face taut with humiliation and resentment. Tony's was stern and hard, the visage of a proud man made ashamed by one of his own.

Tony said, "Draw up a chair, Dixie," which meant that both men were too macho to scoot over to make room for me.

I pulled a chair from a table behind me and sat at the end of the booth between them. Jochim hadn't looked at me yet, but stared at a sugar packet in his square hands that he was tearing into fragments.

Tony gave Jochim a disdainful glare. "Tell the lady what you told me."

Like a petulant child, Jochim shot me a hostile glance and remained silent.

Tony sighed. "*Hijo,* you have two choices. You can tell the truth to Dixie or you can go with me to the cops and surrender."

"But I didn't do anything!"

Jochim's voice held such panic that several men heard him over the music and turned to stare.

Tony said, "I believe you, Jochim. If I did not, I would not provide you the chance to be a man."

The sugar packet demolished, Jochim reached in his shirt pocket and pulled out a book of matches. He flipped the cover and began tearing the matches out one by one as if they were a smoker's abacus.

He said, "The woman in that house, the nurse, asked Ramón if he would find somebody to get rid of her boss."

I said, "You mean Mr. Kurtz?"

His eyes flicked to the side in a bloodshot glance. "Ramón just called him the boss."

I took a deep, careful breath. "So Gilda asked Ramón to find a hit man to kill Kurtz."

Jochim winced as if he couldn't bear to hear it put so bluntly, but Tony nodded sternly.

Jochim said, "She told him she would pay a hundred thousand dollars for the job. That's a lot of money, you know?"

Trying to keep my voice smooth and neutral, I said, "It would be tempting."

He nodded eagerly. "With that much, we could go home, start a business, be with people we know."

Tony slashed the air with his hand. "Tell her what happened."

Jochim looked glumly at the matches and tore off another one. "Ramón and I decided I would go into the house while the man slept. He was sick, weak, I could smother him in his bed. Then I would strike Ramón on the head and knock him out."

He paused and frowned. "I did not want to hurt my brother-in-law, but it was the only way to make him innocent. When he woke up, he would run to the house and alert the nurse, who would go to the boss's room and find him dead."

"But wouldn't she already know you had killed him?"

"No, she told us to do it without telling her when. That was so she could be innocent too."

These people not only approached murder with the klutziness of the Three Stooges, they had a strange definition of the word *innocent.*

"So what happened? How was Ramón killed?"

"I went there at the time Ramón said, a little after midnight. Ramón was supposed to take me to the door and let me in, but he wasn't in the guardhouse. I went around the line of bushes to the front of the house, where I could see inside. Ramón was in the room carrying the iguana. The woman was there, and also the man. The woman was making hurry-up signs with her hands. The man was watching Ramón."

He fell silent and pulled more matches out, tossing them on the table with quick, nervous motions.

"What happened then?"

He looked ashamed. "I ran away. I could not kill a man I had seen, you know? And he was not asleep. If he had been asleep in the dark, I could have put a pillow over his head and pressed hard until he stopped moving."

Tony and I exchanged a look, both of us hearing not a fantasy of smothering a sleeping man but most likely a memory.

Jochim said, "I saw his face too. I would not touch a man with that face. Anyway, he did not look so sick or weak as Ramón said he was."

I felt deflated, as if I'd expected Jochim to confess to killing Ramón and then in a burst of guilt accompany me to the sheriff's office.

I said, "That doesn't explain how Ramón got killed."

"She killed him! It had to be her. I don't know how it happened, but she had murder on her mind, you know? I'm sure it was her."

Carefully, so I wouldn't give away that Paloma had told me about the money, I said, "I'm sure you were disappointed not to get the hundred grand."

"Very disappointed, but we are going home anyway, my sister and my wife and I."

So much for hoping he might mention the man who had delivered the money.

I didn't know what good the meeting had done, but when I stood up, I said, "Thank you for telling me this, Jochim."

Then I met Tony's eyes and tilted my head a bit to show gratitude without embarrassing him with anything gushy.

Gravely, Tony said, "I will talk to you later, Dixie," by which I knew he meant that he expected me to keep my promise and that he was my good friend.

At the Kurtz house, I eased to a stop a few feet in front of a line of people stretched across the driveway. They still carried the same signs with quotes from Revelation. I was tired of them and their ancient fears, but with every intention of being polite, I put down my window and leaned my head out.

A tall man in a rough brown robe detached himself from the crowd, came to my window, and leaned his hands against it. His long fingers on my window were pale, marking him an import brought in for this current craze. His eyes were intelligent and watchful, without whites all around the pupils like most fanatics.

I smiled politely. I swear I did.

At the top of his voice, he hollered, "Harlot of Satan! Have you come to lie with the beast? To worship the man with Satan's mark?"

All my polite juices dried up.

I hollered back, "No, numb nuts! I'm here to take food to a pet in the yard! You have a problem with that?"

A light flared in his blue eyes, and his hands tightened on the edge of my window.

"The wages of sin are death, daughter. Woe be unto those who consort with the beast or those who bear the mark of the beast."

"Yeah, well, woe be unto those who block traffic and harass those entering private property. Move your people out of the way or I'll have the cops move them."

He let a beat go by, then raised his palms in a gesture of conciliation and stepped back from the car. "Go in peace, daughter."

He waved to the people stretched across the driveway.

"Let her pass."

He said it with such authority that they sulkily moved to the edge of the driveway, where they looked mournfully at me as I drove through. But I wasn't paying much attention to them. I was too shaken by what I'd seen on the man's wrist. What kind of religious fanatic wears an ultra-thin Movado wristwatch? Now that I thought of it, I realized he'd had manicured nails too. I had a feeling I'd just talked to one of Jessica Ballantyne's FBI agents in disguise.

When Kurtz answered the door, he was almost as nasty to me as the phony monk had been.

He grunted and flapped his hand toward the kitchen. "Just take care of the iguana's food, please. I'm busy now."

I squeezed my lips shut before my tongue managed to tell him what I thought about his attitude, and watched his back move through the darkened living room toward the open door to the wine room. The dim red light in the room reminded me of my dream and of how frightened I'd been of Kurtz. He didn't seem threatening now, just rude.

It took me all of three minutes to slice banana and yellow squash and zucchini and mix it with some chard and romaine leaves for Ziggy, another two minutes to take it out to him. I didn't look to see if Kurtz had any leftovers to eat. I didn't tell him goodbye, either, just got in the Bronco and zipped out. As I passed the marchers, I didn't see the man I'd talked to. Maybe he'd become bored with the whole thing and gone home. Or maybe he was making a report to Jessica Ballantyne.

It was past sunset when I got home. A congregation of snowy egrets and great blue herons had gathered on the beach to pick at goodies washed ashore on slow-rolling wavelets. Seagulls circled overhead, making rude noises to announce their prior claim to beach flotsam. On the horizon, sailboats glided toward harbor bathed in the fading amber glow of a submerged sun. My dejection had lifted on the way home, and now I felt oddly expectant, as if I were waiting for a signal of some kind. I even scanned the sea the way wives of old whalers probably watched for some clue that the long and harrowing wait was over and their men were coming home to them safe and sound.

I didn't notice Guidry's car parked by Michael's deck until I came out of the carport and started up the stairs to my apartment. He was on my porch, sitting at the round table looking out at the Gulf. As usual, he looked like an Italian playboy.

I said, "Why haven't you returned my call?"

"I saw you at the Gutierrez funeral. I was surprised you were there."

I dropped my shoulder bag on the table and heard a metallic clink that reminded me I hadn't returned Ken Kurtz's keys. Damn.

I sat down opposite Guidry. "I wanted to support Paloma."

"Paloma?"

"Mrs. Gutierrez."

"You know the guard's wife?"

"I went to see her and talked to her and her brother. His name is Jochim. I trimmed her kitten's claws too. She was going to have them surgically removed, but now I don't think she will. It's a cute little calico."

Guidry pressed his fingertips to his closed eyelids. "I don't suppose there's anything I can say that will make you stop talking to people, is there?"

"Not really."

"What the hell kind of breed is a calico?"

"It's not a breed, it's a coloring. It happens every now and then in every breed. It's when a kitten has three distinct colors. If it's a true calico the colors are pure white, inky black, and bright orange. If it's a diluted calico, the colors will be pale and creamy. Paloma's kitten is a true calico. It's really cute."

I heard the wistful note in my voice and shut up.

"This is why you called me? To tell me about a cute kitten?"

I narrowed my eyes at the smug bastard and considered exactly how much to tell him. I had promised Tony not to tell about meeting with Jochim, but I figured my meeting with Paloma was fair game.

I said, "Paloma told me a man brought her a hundred thousand dollars in cash. He told her it was insurance money. Then he told her Ramón would have wanted her to use it to go home to Mexico. I think they'll leave soon."

"She never told me that."

I shrugged. We both knew people told me a lot more than they told him.

He said, "Did she get the man's name?"

"No, and I don't imagine he left a card. She said he was a skinny Anglo, but that's all she remembered. Today at the funeral, I saw a skinny man in a suit outside on the sidewalk. He looked familiar somehow, but I couldn't place him. Maybe that was the skinny Anglo who gave Paloma money."

"She still have the money?"

"Jochim took it to the bank to put in a safe deposit box."

Guidry reached inside his thin leather jacket and pulled out a notepad. He flipped some pages and said, "That would be Jochim Manuel Torres?"

I shrugged. "I don't know his full name."

"He's a small-time hood, part of a ring selling stolen cars, mostly to illegal aliens."

That answered the question of whether Jochim was as naive as his sister. What he was doing was a particularly cruel trick in which a stolen car is sold to a person with bad credit. The buyer agrees to pay exorbitant interest because it's the only way to get wheels, and he doesn't get title to the car until final payment. The title is a fake, so if he ever manages to pay the thing off, he's driving a stolen car with a false title.

"Paloma said Jochim has been influenced by bad friends. She thinks he will get a new start with the insurance money, said they might start their own business in Mexico."

Guidry raised an eyebrow, but put his notepad back in his jacket without saying what he thought about Paloma's plans.

I hesitated, then went ahead and said it. "I also saw Jessica Ballantyne at the funeral. She ran away when she saw me and I lost her."

"Did you give Kurtz the message?"

"I did. He said they worked together on a secret project for the government. They were to create a virus that would jump from animals to humans. For espionage purposes, he said. But a tsunami hit and all the researchers drowned. He thought Jessica Ballantyne drowned with them. He seemed genuinely shocked to hear she's alive."

"What else did he say?"

"He said the packages that Gilda took from the refrigerator were vials of antidote for whatever his condition is. But he was lying."

"How do you know?"

"I don't know, Guidry, I can just tell when people lie. Probably because I had to know when my mother was lying when I was a kid. It's something I developed to protect myself."

I doubted that Guidry's mother had ever lied to him. He probably had a perfect mother who was always there for him, a beautiful mother who let servants do all the hard work so she could be pleasantly, lovingly available to her son.

"Guidry, what about the ballistics test?"

"Inconclusive. They don't have a bullet, they don't have a casing. The best they can do is give an educated guess that the bullet was a thirty-eight caliber."

I shivered. The absence of a casing could mean the killer had used a revolver or a single-shot rifle. But a thirty-eight caliber was more likely a semiautomatic with an attached brass-catcher—the way of a hired gun. Or somebody had collected the casing and pocketed it.

"Am I still your prime suspect?"

"Dixie, I know you didn't kill Gutierrez. Everybody except our new hotshot DA knows you didn't kill Gutierrez. If it should go to trial, it would all be circumstantial evidence. Don't worry about it."

It has been my experience that when people say, "Don't worry about it," worrying about it is exactly what you *should* be doing.

People are convicted of murder every day on circumstantial evidence. Half the people on death row have been found guilty because of circumstantial evidence, and a lot of them are innocent. I knew that.

Guidry knew that. God knew that, and unless the new DA was an imbecile, she knew that.

I said, "I'm not feeling very good, Guidry. I'm going inside."

He stood up while I raised the shutters with the remote. I unlocked the French doors and turned to tell him good night. The next thing I knew he was enfolding me in a tight hug and I was snuggling into it like a puppy searching for a warm nipple.

Against the top of my head, he said, "I'm sorry, Dixie. You deserve a lot better than this."

I didn't say anything, just stood there for a long time clinging to him while my eyes leaked all over my face. Guidry took a deep breath and tilted my chin up and kissed me. A gentle, sweet kiss that made me tremble for something more, that made my lips open with an urgent hunger. He ran his hands down my back to my butt and pulled me closer, and the kiss deepened just long enough to leave me gasping when he stopped.

"Good night, Dixie."

He left me standing there and took the stairs two at a time. Then he got into his car and pulled out without looking back at me.

Weakly, I stepping into my living room and dropped to the sofa. My mouth still vibrated from the kiss, as if my lips had been touched with an electric charge and all the taste buds of my tongue had been inflamed. Guidry's taste was still with me, a clean, healthy, liquid taste, a little salty, a little tart. I covered my face with both hands and let out a small moan that was half whimper of despair and half satisfaction.

I had crossed a line from which there was no turning back, and I wasn't at all sure I knew what the hell I was going to do about it.

# 24

When the alarm went off at 4 A.M. Saturday morning, I came awake with the gluey memory that I was having supper with Ethan that night, that it would probably get sexy, and that I was still a suspect in the murder of Ramón Gutierrez. I weighed about three hundred tons as I went down the hall to the bathroom. After I'd brushed my teeth and splashed water on my face, I was almost surprised that my reflection in the mirror over the sink looked normal. I twisted my hair into a scrunchy and slogged to the office-closet to pull on underpants, shorts, and a T-shirt. Laced up clean white Keds, grabbed my shoulder bag and all my pet-sitting stuff, and squared my shoulders. Once again, ladies and gentlemen, Dixie Hemingway is going forth into the world to act the part of premier pet sitter. She may feel like shit, she may have a few loose cogs in her machinery, but by God nobody can say she doesn't do her job!

Downstairs in the carport, a grumpy pelican on the Bronco's hood gave me a yellow-eyed glare before he went off to find a more hospitable roosting place. If the parakeets in the trees noticed my passing, they decided it was too early for pretend histrionics and closed their eyes again.

My brain was still too sore to try a hard run with Billy Elliot, but I looked into the parking lot as I drove past the Sea Breeze to see if he might be taking Tom's new girlfriend for a fast-stepping walk. All I saw in the dark lot were sleeping cars. I had to fight the impulse to pull in. Billy Elliot was probably upstairs waiting for me, all nervous and twitchy, but the adolescent ER doctor had done a good job of impressing me with the fact that a concussion wasn't something to take lightly. I'd give my brains until Monday to finish healing, and then I'd make it up to Billy Elliot with an extra-long run.

I finished the morning dog routine early and headed south to see to the cats. It was still that waking-up time of day, when the only people on the streets are dog walkers, delivery people, and a few enterprising early risers getting a head start on the day. Starbucks was doing a brisk business dispensing hot coffee to a line of caffeine-needy drivers, and I swerved into the turn-in to get my share. Next door, Dr. Phyllis Layton pulled into her empty parking lot and went inside her office. Dr. Layton is an African-American veterinarian of uncommon courtesy to her animal clients. She would never declaw a cat.

Once I'd got my cup of hot jolt juice, I pulled into Dr. Layton's lot and parked next to her car. She was behind a holly-circled receptionist's window when I went in, and for a second her face showed a trace of wariness at having such an early morning visitor. Then she saw it was me and smiled.

We exchanged good-mornings and I said, "I have a formerly feral cat client who hates being inside, and he's spraying and clawing everything in sight. Do you know anybody who lives in the country and would like a good mouser? A kind family with maybe an enclosed porch where he could sleep?"

"And give him lots of affection and protect him from dogs and see that he gets his shots every year?"

"Yeah, that too."

She laughed. "You can add him to the list."

She handed me an index card and pointed toward a bulletin board on the waiting room wall where cards were arranged in neat rows.

I said, "I guess you get a lot of requests like this."

"I do, but the surprising thing is that people read those cards and take in pets that need new homes. Pet lovers are generous."

I wrote the particulars of Muddy, stressing that he was a nice cat, he just didn't like being cooped up in a house, and gave my number to call.

I said, "Muddy can get cantankerous. What if somebody takes him and it doesn't work out?"

"Then they'll bring him back. A couple of days ago a woman took a miniature bulldog who'd been orphaned when his owner died. He was such a sweet little guy that I'd put a FREE TO GOOD HOME notice out front. She came in late in the afternoon, acted like she loved him, and took him home with her. Brought him back the very next morning. Didn't even keep him twenty-four hours! Said, being Irish, she hadn't felt right with such a wee dog. Took me a minute to get what *wee* meant. I don't think it was because she was Irish, I think she just changed her mind."

My head felt as if it needed air holes drilled in it to keep my brains from expanding wider than my skull. I think rage does that to a brain—makes it heat up and swell. I knew before I asked the question what the answer would be.

"Was she a tall dark-haired woman?"

"You know her?"

"I met a woman like that Tuesday morning with a miniature bull-dog."

"Well, I found another home for the wee dog, so it worked out okay."

I pinned Muddy's card to Dr. Layton's board and left her going through pet files.

My cell rang, and I barked "Hello!" without looking at the ID tag.

Mildly, Guidry said, "You get up on the wrong side of the bed this morning?"

"I just found out who the Irishman was who called me. It was Jessica Ballantyne faking an Irish accent."

"My, my, imagine that. One would almost think she wasn't an open and aboveboard person."

I made mocking faces at the phone. "Did you call me because you felt like being an ass, or was there some other reason?"

"We got a call from a neighbor of Kurtz's last night. He heard gunshots he thought came from Kurtz's house and wanted us to investigate. The officers who went out found Kurtz in the driveway. He'd been chasing an intruder and collapsed out there."

"Ken Kurtz was chasing somebody?"

"Probably more like inching along wanting to chase somebody, but he did shoot at somebody. Or at least that's what he claimed. He said he heard a rumbling noise during the night that he recognized as the sound of one of his garage doors going up. He got up to investigate and saw a man in the courtyard carrying his iguana. The iguana was fighting pretty hard, I guess, because the guy was having trouble holding him. Kurtz fired a shot in the air and the guy dropped the iguana and ran through a garage to the driveway. Kurtz tried to follow him and collapsed. The deputy helped him back to bed and secured the garage. He looked around, but he didn't see any intruder or evidence of one. Do you think Kurtz hallucinates?"

My heart was racing and I could feel my face growing hot.

I said, "The yard people go through the last garage to get to the courtyard. There's a storage room in it with an access door to the courtyard."

"You think it was a yardman?"

I shook my head. "I don't know who it was."

That wasn't altogether true. I had a pretty good idea who it had been. In my head, I heard my own voice telling the crazy fanatic with the sane eyes and the manicure and the Movado wristwatch that I was going to take food outside to a pet. I remembered the little flare of light in the man's eyes when he'd heard it.

That's how he'd known where to find Ziggy. I had told him.

I was ashamed to let Guidry know that I'd been played so easily. Instead, I bitched about the religious fanatics gathered outside the Kurtz house.

"Can't you make them disperse?"

"Not unless they're blocking traffic or harassing people."

"They blocked the driveway and they harassed me."

"I'll have somebody stop by and talk to them."

I rang off wondering why a man who only pretended to be afraid of the number 666 would want to steal Ziggy.

Rage at Jessica and chagrin at having been used by the fake monk stayed with me all morning, sitting between my ears and humming like a power line beside a country road. The cats all sensed it and stayed clear of me, which made me feel bad, but there wasn't anything I could do about it. I was like a vibrating magnet, just waiting for the moment when Jessica Ballantyne or the man in the robe would pop up again so I could yell at them.

When I finished with the last cat, I took my rage and hunger to the Village Diner and slammed myself into my regular booth. Judy was immediately there with her coffeepot and a mug for me.

She said, "Why are you frowning? Did you lose that gorgeous guy that was with you Wednesday?"

"I didn't lose him. He's a close friend."

"If I had a friend like that, I'd tie him down and molest him."

She turned to give a woman across the aisle a coffee refill and left me to cuddle my mug in peace. The woman across the aisle was reading the *Herald-Tribune* with the front page held in front of her face, so only her short blond hair was visible. My grandfather used to hold the paper like that, sort of screening out the world with newsprint. I always fold a newspaper and look down at it. Maybe it makes me feel more in control of what's going on in the world if I'm hovering over it.

Judy returned with my usual two eggs over easy with extra-crisp home fries and a biscuit. As if she knew I was on my last nerve, she put the plate down and refilled my mug without comment.

I thanked her and fell on the food like a ravenous wolf. In the midst of mopping up egg yolk with my biscuit, I suddenly remembered my date with Ethan, which was now several hours closer than it had been the last time I thought of it. I guzzled the last drop of coffee and looked around for Judy, who was coming toward me with her pot held out like a rescue lamp.

She said, "Good grief, girl, when's the last time you ate?"

"I know. It's awful, isn't it?"

"I wouldn't exactly say it's awful. More like a substitute for sex. If you were getting any, you wouldn't be eating like there's no tomorrow. That's what I always think when I see those big fat women putting away another helping of mashed potatoes. Poor things probably haven't had good sex in years. Maybe never. All those diet books people read, that's a lot of hooey. Women having good sex don't gain weight, and you can put that in your pipe and smoke it."

With an emphatic nod, she turned away to slap down a check on the table across the aisle. I held my mug with both hands and wondered what she would say if I told her I was probably going to have sex to-night. Good, bad, or mediocre, it was probably going to happen. I tried not to groan out loud at the thought. I hoped I didn't make a complete fool of myself. I hoped I remembered how to act in bed.

The blonde across the aisle stood up and gathered her folded news-paper. Then in one smooth motion, she pivoted and sat in the seat across from me. I blinked at her a couple of times and then slammed my mug on the table.

"Bitch, you're the one who called me!"

"I couldn't think of anything else. I had to bring attention to that house. Besides, I knew if you showed up talking about an iguana named ZIGI, he would know he was in danger."

"Anything else I can do for you? Polish your shoes? Fluff your blond wig?"

"I understand your anger."

"Oh, great! Now you're going to play shrink."

She folded the edge of her newspaper into a triangle. "I have to know something. The woman who lived with him, were they lovers?"

"Does it matter?"

She sighed. "I suppose you've guessed that I'm new to this. I don't imagine I'll ever do it again."

"Do what? Impersonate Irishmen?"

"Work as an undercover investigator."

"For BiZogen?"

"No, the FBI. They knew Ken and I had worked together. They thought I would be able to track him down before ZIGI's people did."

"No offense, Jessica, but that has to mean they didn't think it was important enough to put one of their real investigators on it."

She nodded meekly. "It's the war on terrorism. All the agents who know what they're doing are looking for men with wires coming out of their shoes."

"You suck as an undercover investigator. I have pets that could do better."

"Ken is right about BiZogen causing our friends to die. They drowned because of BiZogen's negligence. I'm sure that's why he contacted ZIGI. I find that somewhat endearing, don't you?"

I leaned closer to her and spoke very slowly. "I don't find any of this endearing. What about the murdered guard?"

"I don't know who did that, Dixie, and it's not part of my job. That's something for the local law-enforcement people to handle."

"What about Gilda?"

"That's what I'd like to know. What about Gilda? Who is she? What is she to Ken? You say Ken kept my photograph beside his bed, but he apparently took another woman into it."

"Well, to be fair, he did think you were dead."

"I would not have taken a lover so soon if I'd thought he had died."

Neither would I, obviously.

I said, "How did you find him?"

She looked smug. "It wasn't hard, actually. Ken is a dedicated wine collector, and he always ordered wine from the same company. I simply went there and told them Ken had sent me to select wine to be shipped to him. Then I had them verify the address for me."

I wasn't surprised. Criminal investigators maintain that half their arrests are due to criminals doing something stupid. Bank robbers write demand notes on the back of personalized deposit slips. People on the lam use their credit cards at hotels and restaurants. Hardened killers survive bullets and barbed wire and snarling dogs to escape from maximum-security prisons and then head straight to their mothers' kitchens. It's like we all have a fatal flaw that trips us up, and if we turn to the dark side we take our fatal flaw with us.

Ken Kurtz was a scientific genius, but his persistence in a known habit had allowed Jessica to trace him to Siesta Key, which was dumb. Furthermore, a man who claimed to subsist on Gilda's health shakes surely couldn't drink the wine he collected, which made having it even dumber.

Just as I was congratulating myself on being smarter than Kurtz, a little doubt crept into my mind. The wine could be a deliberate ploy. Kurtz might want people to concentrate on his wine so they wouldn't notice something more important.

The smart-ass voice in my head said, *Which would be what?*

I didn't have an answer, but I wasn't sure anymore that I was so smart.

I said, "And the stolen car?"

"My employer provided the car. I don't know if they knew it was stolen."

"Your heart isn't in this job, is it?"

"It's just that I feel the same way Ken does about what happened at the lab."

"But you took a job for the FBI."

"It's complicated."

"Seems pretty simple to me. You're pissed at Ken Kurtz because you think he abandoned you to die, so you're working to help the FBI arrest him for industrial espionage. But for old times' sake, you're giving him advance warning so he can run away or hide the research or somehow save himself before the Feds with the big guns move in. That about it?"

"What he's doing is wrong, but I understand why he's doing it."

I leaned back against the booth seat and let a moment of silence pass.

"Jessica, this isn't just about Ken Kurtz and his research. A man was murdered. Whoever killed the guard may have been there to kill Kurtz. You said yourself that the rivalry between BiZogen and ZIGI was cutthroat. With or without the FBI's involvement, BiZogen is probably out to kill him."

"If they get his research back, they won't kill him."

"Because they're such warm, fuzzy people."

"No, because Ken is such a brilliant researcher. They'd rather hire him back than kill him."

I said, "Kurtz seems certain that Gilda will return, but he didn't say why. He claims the packages she took from the refrigerator were vials of antidote for whatever it is that has turned him blue and given him nerve damage. But anybody in as bad shape as he is would be more concerned about losing his antidote, so I don't believe him. Do you have any idea what was in those vials, or why he's so sure she'll be back?"

"If they're lovers—"

I banged the table with my fist. "Forget the lover crap! Come on, you're a researcher too. What would have been stored in the refrigerator in wrapped packages? It must be something that has to be replaced. Otherwise he wouldn't be so sure Gilda was coming back."

She shook her head. "I have no idea."

"What are you going to do, Jessica? Seems to me you've pretty much blown your cover and lost all your effectiveness as an FBI agent. Why don't you just go whole hog and quit? Go see Kurtz. You love him, he loves you, you're both brilliant scientists—maybe you can figure out a way to give the research back to BiZogen and keep Ken out of prison."

"I could end up in prison myself if I tip him off that he's under investigation."

"*If* you tip him off? Hell, you've done everything but hire the Goodyear blimp to fly over his house blinking a sign. It's too late to get skittish, you've already crossed the line."

I stood up and tossed money on the table.

"If I'm arrested for Ramón Gutierrez's murder, I will sing like a prize Roller Canary about a certain FBI agent who was working both sides of the street. So keep that in your wee fake-Irish head while you think about what you're going to do."

# 25

I went home after talking to Jessica. I couldn't think of anything else to do. I mean, what can you do to follow up something like that? The Bronco sort of guided itself down Midnight Pass Road and onto the meandering drive to the carport. I got out and went up the stairs to my porch, where a cat's cardboard travel case sat on my glass-top table, with faint mewing sounds coming from it.

Even before I peered through an air hole, I knew what was inside. The calico kitten was crouched in a bunny pose with her ears flattened and her eyes wide with anxiety. A note had been taped to the case, written in round girlish script on paper torn from a child's school tablet.

*Dixie,*
*I know you wanted the kitten so it is yours.*
*Your friend, Paloma.*

I groaned. I didn't want a kitten! I had merely been concerned about the kitten, not covetous about it. I opened the carrying case and lifted the kitten out. She really was cute.

"It's okay, kitty, don't be scared."

Some stroking and soft talk make the kitten retract her little trimmed claws, and a bowl of cool water in the kitchen and more smoochy talk made her hunched shoulders relax. Then, knowing I would really need to pee if I'd been confined in a box and carried to a strange place, I carried her down to the big sandbox by the sea. She seemed to believe me when I told her the waves and seagulls wouldn't hurt her. After she made a silver-dollar-sized puddle, I took her back upstairs, explaining as I went that while I thought she was the smartest and cutest kitten I'd ever seen in my life, I couldn't keep her.

I said, "It's just not in my life plan right now to have a pet."

She licked my thumb with her little sandpapery tongue and purred.

I lay down in the hammock with the kitten on my stomach. She sat up with her front legs straight and looked around. A seagull flew by with a loud squawking sound and she raised one hairy eyebrow and made a little firping sound that made me laugh.

I said, "You know, I don't even know your name."

She made some more firping sounds.

I said, "You sound like Ella Fitzgerald when she does that skatting thing. If you were my kitty, I'd name you Ella Fitzgerald."

She yawned and curled into a contented ball and fell asleep. I lay there with both hands cupped around the calico kitten and told myself I should get up and call Guidry and tell him what I'd learned. But the kitten was sleeping so peacefully I didn't want to disturb her.

Besides, Jessica Ballantyne's predicament was so stupid and so *human* that I wanted to give her more time. While my fingers lay warm in the kitten's fur, I thought about all the significant world events that have been instigated or foiled or screwed up by love. Napoleon and Josephine. Abelard and Héloïse. King Edward and Wallis Simpson. Princess Diana and Prince Charles and Camilla. Funny how those supposedly stiff Europeans are the ones willing to give up all they have for love, while supposedly less repressed Americans—think Bill Clinton with Monica, Gary Hart with Donna Rice, Wilbur Mills with Fanne Foxe—give up all they have for sex. Not even grown-up sex either, but immature, trivial, banal sex.

Ken Kurtz wasn't a national leader, but he had developed something of international significance, something worth the FBI's interest, something that had caused a man's murder. Jessica Ballantyne had been a respected scientist, a woman who had been tapped by the United States government first as a researcher and then as an undercover investigator. These two people had awesome intellects, and yet both of them were acting like high school kids blowing their SATs because love was turning their brains to mush. Maybe it was all that time they'd spent in Europe and Southeast Asia. If they'd stayed in the United States, they might be focused on sex instead of love.

And what about me? What was I focused on?

I was thirty-two years old, a healthy, normal woman with a healthy body and healthy desires, and cuddling this kitten was the closest thing I'd come to real intimacy with another living being in over three years. Ethan Crane was the answer to any woman's best sex dream, but was that the way I wanted to go? When I decided to live again and love again, was it so I could go to a man's house and have sex?

While my mind agonized over the question, my body rolled out of the hammock, causing Ella to wake up and wiggle in my hands.

I said, "It's okay. We're going inside now. There are some things I have to do. See, I have this date tonight." She raised an eyebrow again, and I said, "A date is something humans do when they're in heat. You cats just go ahead and do it—*wham, bam, thank you, ma'am*—but we humans can't do that until we have dinner and talk first. That's what a date is. Dumb, isn't it?"

Inside, I left Ella exploring the apartment while I took a shower. I shaved my legs. I put a deep conditioner on my hair. I used an exfoliant to make my skin smooth. I decided to call Ethan and cancel the date. I thought I would use the kitten as an excuse—*Somebody left this cat with me, and I have to take it to the SPCA.* I was an astronaut on the liftoff pad having a genuine crisis of conscience or a bad case of first-time jitters.

I crawled into bed. Ella came crying for me, and I took her into bed with me. She was soft and warm against my side, and we slept for a couple of hours. When I woke up, the headache was gone. Was that a go-ahead sign from God? Or just a sign that my concussion was healed? Maybe both?

The evening with Ethan was now only seven hours away.

Naked, I carried Ella to my office-closet and put on a terry-cloth robe. I put on a Patsy Cline CD and sat down at my desk to enter information in my pet records. Ella came to my side and tried to jump up. I picked her up and let her sit in my lap for a few minutes while I worked, but then I put her down and stomped to the CD player and turned Patsy off. Sometimes innocent love is too sweet to stomach.

Somebody rapped on my French doors, and I pulled the robe closed and padded into the living room. Guidry was leaning with one hand on the door, looking calmly through the glass into my life. As if he had a right to drop by in the middle of the afternoon without calling. As if it didn't matter that some people might like a little advance notice so they could dress before they had company.

I jerked open the door and scowled at him. He ignored me and sauntered inside, leaving me with the doorknob in my hand. He went to my refrigerator and opened it and took out a bottle of water. While he uncapped the bottle and drank half of it, I closed the door and went to stand at my bar. The soft back sides of my knees tingled. I wished he would kiss me again.

I said, "How nice to see you, Lieutenant. Could I offer you something to drink? Water, maybe?"

"Thanks, I already have some."

He carried the bottle into the living room and set it on the coffee table, then dropped onto my green-printed couch. After a moment, I sat in the chair. Too late, I realized I was squeezing my knees together like a schoolgirl on her first make-out date. Only we weren't making out and we weren't going to, and I had to make that crystal clear before Guidry got the wrong idea. If he hadn't already.

The kitten trotted into the living room and mewed at Guidry.

He said, "You have a kitten?"

I shook my head. "It's just temporary. Somebody left it here. I named her Ella. Or that's what I would name her if I were going to keep her."

"Ella Fitzgerald?"

"Sure."

"It bothers me that I knew it would be Fitzgerald."

He took a sip of water while he eyed me.

He said, "We took Jochim Torres in today. None too soon, either. His car was packed to the roof and he was ready to leave town."

When my mouth dropped, he shrugged. "The hundred grand was obviously a payoff."

"But it was to Paloma."

"That's what Jochim said. But when I calmly pointed out to him that he had a record, and that we had good reason to believe he would take money to knock somebody off, he understood where I was coming from."

"You didn't tell him I'd told you about the money, did you?"

"I told him somebody at the bank reported it."

"You lie to people you pick up?"

"All the time. It's called being a homicide cop."

I wondered if he had lied to me too.

As if he knew what I was thinking, Guidry's lip tugged at the side in an almost-smile.

"According to Jochim, he was at home with his wife and kids and several grown cousins the night Ramón was killed, and he has no idea why an insurance man brought his sister a hundred thousand dollars in cash. You will not be surprised to learn that his wife and three men who claim to be his cousins all confirm his story."

"You believe him?"

"I think they're all lying through their teeth, but I don't think Jochim Torres is a killer. He might cheat his brother-in-law out of his last dime, but I don't think he would kill him."

"Paloma believes Gilda killed Ramón."

"She may be right."

"Any leads on where Gilda may have gone?"

He shook his head. "She's evaporated."

I looked at the kitten and felt a little tug of disappointment. If Paloma wasn't leaving town, she might want the kitten back. Well, so what? I didn't plan to keep her.

"Will you take the money away from Paloma now?"

"The money will stay where it is until we know who killed Ramón Gutierrez, and so will Paloma and Jochim. If Jochim is innocent, the money belongs to Paloma."

Ella settled on my bare feet and sent a nice warm wave up my ankles.

I said, "Any idea who the man was who delivered the money?"

He stood up. "Not a clue. Do you?"

"Not unless he's the man I saw at Ramón's funeral. Young, slight build, short dark hair, dark glasses. His suit looked too big for him, like maybe he'd lost weight recently. I almost thought I recognized him, but if I've ever seen him before he must have been heavier."

He looked down at me for a long moment as if he wanted to talk about something else, then changed his mind.

"If you see him again, let me know. In the meantime, we're focusing on finding the nurse. We've had some promising leads, and she can't stay disappeared forever."

Without waiting for my reply, he opened the French doors and left me with nothing but the sound of his snappy Italian loafers thudding down my steps.

At three-thirty, I got dressed and took Ella down to pee again on the beach. Before I left for my afternoon rounds, I got a disposable cardboard litter box from the stack I keep in the Bronco and shook a quarter-inch layer of clay into it. I put it in my bathroom and made sure Ella knew where it was. My head was pain-free, but I didn't want to add more stress by taking her to a shelter just then.

It was also too soon for a run with Billy Elliot, so I sailed on by the Sea Breeze. I sailed by Ken Kurtz's driveway too, with a mere neck swivel to look toward his house.

The marchers weren't there. Either Guidry had told them to leave Kurtz alone or they'd all rushed off to pray in front of a screen door with a hole shaped like the outline of the Virgin Mary.

With most of the house hidden behind the row of areca palms, all I could see in my quick glance was the row of garage doors. In my imagination, I recalled the first time I'd gone up the walk beside the first garage and saw that huge fireplace through the clear glass. It had been a long walk. Seen from the outside, the long wall along the first garage seemed to be part of the west wing of the house, and I doubted that anybody else had noticed that it seemed too long.

An awareness suddenly plunked itself into my head, neat as a pin turning in a lock, and my skin prickled in astonishment that I hadn't known it before. That *nobody* had known it, when it was right there staring us in the face.

Ethan had said the builders had been obliged to retain 30 percent of the original structure in order to avoid public scrutiny of the house plans. Suddenly I knew where that original structure was and why the four garages were so deep. The reason was that they weren't. More than likely, all the garages were standard size, but there was about fifteen feet of space between their back walls and the back wall of the southern corridor where the wine room was, and I knew why.

Even moving slowly, I was finished with the afternoon pet visits in plenty of time to get ready for the evening with Ethan. I decided it would be better to put off taking Ella to a shelter until the next day. No sense in rushing it. I looked toward the Kurtz house again as I drove home, but there was nothing to see except a thin column of smoke rising from his chimney. I wondered how many times Jessica had driven past and looked toward the hedge. If what she'd said was true, her time was running out before she had to make a decision between the man she loved and the law she'd sworn to uphold.

My own time had run out too. I had to go to Ethan's. I was a mature woman and it was time to act like one.

When I got home, I took one of the packets of emergency kitten food that I keep in the Bronco upstairs for Ella. She was waiting at the door for me, as if she'd known all along that I was coming home exactly at that time. She really was an exceptionally smart kitten.

I left her eating in the kitchen and took a quick shower to get rid of all the clinging pet hairs. I had left the bathroom door open, and Ella came in and watched me blow my hair.

I said, "I guess I'll just let my hair hang straight. What do you think?"

She blinked at me in what seemed a female-to-female sign of approval.

I sprayed perfume on the backs of my knees and on my navel. I said, "Don't get any ideas about that. It doesn't mean anything. This is just a date. You remember I told you what a date is."

Her ears twitched. She knew what the perfume meant. It was embarrassing to be so transparent.

She followed me into the office-closet, where I put on a black lace bra and bikini. I figured she knew what that meant too, but I was a grown woman and she was just a kitten, so who cared what she thought?

I put on a short black skirt with a white cotton turtleneck. I took off the white turtleneck and put on a black turtleneck. I took off the skirt and the turtleneck and got myself into an old dress that zipped up the back. I nearly broke my arm zipping it up, and when I stood in front of the mirror I remembered wearing it with Todd, and nearly broke my arm unzipping it. I stuffed my feet into high-heeled sandals for inspiration and stood in my underwear surveying my pathetic wardrobe. I hated everything I owned, and what I didn't hate was either out of style or worn bald.

I said, "Everything I have is shit."

Ella turned and gnawed on her back ankle, a sure sign that she thought humans were incredibly stupid.

My lower lip was beginning to push out in a little-girl sulk at the whole business of gift-wrapping myself to go eat dinner with a man. The kitten was right, it was too dumb to credit, especially when I wasn't sure I even wanted the dinner or the man. I kicked off the sandals and pulled on a pair of clean jeans and the black turtleneck, then climbed back onto the heels because it was a date after all. Now that I felt more normal, I slicked my lips with pink gloss and grabbed my purse. I would eat Ethan's food, but I would not go gooey just because he was gorgeous and I hadn't had sex in four years.

I picked Ella up and pressed my nose to her nose. I said, "Don't pee on anything. I don't know when I'll be home."

On the way to Ethan's place, I passed the Kurtz house again. The marchers hadn't returned, and smoke was still curling from the chimney. Maybe Ken Kurtz was in his living room sitting in front of a roaring fire. Maybe Jessica was with him. Maybe they were discussing how they could escape both the FBI and BiZogen and ZIGI and run off to Argentina and take tango lessons and live happily ever after. Or maybe Gilda had come back and was administering the antidote to whatever Kurtz had, and maybe the two of *them* were planning to run away together.

Personally, I wasn't going to run away with anybody to anywhere. I was simply going to have a quiet dinner with a man and come home. Maybe I would make out a little bit. Kiss some, touch some, but that was it. I ignored the proven fact that I had never wanted to stop if the kissing and touching were good. I was older, now, and wiser. At least older.

Ethan's house turned out to be an ultra-modern cypress hidden behind a thick tangle of oaks and sea grape and palms on Fiddler's Bayou, where John D. MacDonald used to live. When I eased the Bronco down Ethan's shelled driveway, he was outside with a gray-muzzled bloodhound on a lead. The bloodhound was on the scent of something, with his head so low his eyes were hidden under drooped folds of skin and his ears were sweeping the ground. Ethan waved at me and then was jerked forward by the bloodhound.

I slid out of the Bronco and yelled, "What's he trailing?"

Ethan grinned. "Ghosts, I think. I've seen him go hard on a trail that ended up at a rock."

I went over and stood beside Ethan and watched the hound sniff the ground. With his liver-and-tan coat, he cut a fine figure. The hound, not Ethan. Except for my high heels, Ethan was dressed in pretty much the same clothes I wore.

I said, "I didn't know you had a dog."

"Something else I inherited from my grandfather. He always had bloodhounds, wouldn't even think of any other dog. Sam is the last. He actually did a little bit of police tracking when he was young, but he's ten now."

He didn't need to add that a ten-year-old bloodhound won't be around much longer.

I said, "He looks healthy and happy."

"Yeah. I think he misses my granddad, though."

And right then I decided that I might not leave after dinner after all.

We went inside after Sam found his quarry, which was a rotted knot of oak buried in dead leaves. Ethan praised him liberally and gave him plenty of time to climb the curving steps to the front porch, then held the door for Sam and me. We went into a large round room with a dark wood floor and mostly glass walls. With the exception of a couple of curved walls that I assumed hid bathroom and closets, the entire house was one big room. With soft uplights illuminating the green foliage against the glass, it was like being in a snug tree house.

I said, "Wow. This is fantastic."

"Thanks. My brother built it. He's a genius."

The kitchen was marked by curved cabinets and black polished countertops, and a bed with tall pilasters draped with sheer white linen announced the bedroom. A grouping of white linen chairs and sofas sat around a white shaggy rug. A glass-topped dining table flanked by Japanese benches sat on another white shaggy rug. A clear glass vase of paperwhite narcissus was in the middle of the table—not a poinsettia plant like ordinary people all over the country had, but paperwhite narcissus. I mean, how cool is that?

Leaving a discreet trail of drool on the dark floor, Sam drooped over to an elevated dog bed and crawled into it with a contented sigh.

Ethan tossed a paper towel on the floor and skated it along Sam's drool trail.

"Want some wine?"

Of course I wanted wine. I wanted to sit on the white linen sofa and drink wine in that enchanted room for the rest of my life. Ethan flipped on soft music and poured two glasses of red wine without even asking if I'd rather have white, which was somehow very satisfying. We sat on the white linen furniture and talked about bloodhounds and cypress houses and genius brothers, and I forgot that I was on a date.

After a while, Ethan went in the kitchen and clattered around for a while, and I carried my empty wineglass to the curved counter and watched him dish out steaming lasagna onto plates. A salad bowl of oil-coated greens sat on the counter next to salad plates, so I showed my domesticity by putting salad on the plates and carrying them to the table.

When we sat down, I said, "You cooked this?"

"Are you kidding? I bought it at Morton's and heated it."

"Oh, good. I was afraid you'd cooked it. I mean, not that I was afraid it wouldn't be good if you cooked it, it's just that everything else is so perfect I couldn't stand it if you were a good cook too."

I didn't even care that he laughed. Dating was fun. I loved dating.

The lasagna was delicious, the salad was sublime, and dessert was chocolate-tipped strawberries, of which, so far as I'm concerned, there is no whicher.

I helped him clear the table and put away leftovers, and then he poured us teeny cups of very strong coffee to take with us to the white linen furniture grouping. The coffee was flavored with cinnamon and it was delicious too, but it wasn't exactly romantic. It was more like something to give wine-drinking guests before they drive home. The music wasn't romantic either. It was the kind of music you listen to when you're working, the kind to keep you alert. Like a not-so-subtle announcement that romance wasn't on Ethan's mind.

I sneaked a quick look at my watch, which said it was close to midnight. I stood up and carried my cup to the kitchen counter.

I said, "I have to get up at four, so I'd better say good night."

He said, "I'll walk you to your car."

Sam raised his head and thumped his tail goodbye as we went out the door, and for a moment I felt like falling on the floor and having a fine leg-banging tantrum. Here I'd worried all week about how I would handle the sex thing, and there wasn't any sex thing. I'd been invited to dinner and that's all I'd got. I hadn't even been offered a choice, just like I hadn't been offered white wine.

At the Bronco, I turned to Ethan and said, "It was a lovely evening. Thank you."

He didn't answer. Just put his hands on my arms and leaned down and kissed me, long and hard.

"Good night, Dixie. Drive safely."

I poured myself into the driver's seat and started the Bronco and backed out while Ethan stood in the headlights and watched me. I didn't begin to breathe until I was on the street.

I was surprised my breath didn't come out flaming.

# 26

The world seemed to have taken on a new clarity as I drove home, as if the evening with Ethan had sharpened my senses. The streets were bright with both moonlight and man-made light, with deep pools of shadow under oaks and clumps of palms, many of their trunks outlined by teensy Italian Christmas lights and weighed with plate-sized bursts of night-blooming cereus. I put the Bronco's windows down and inhaled the salty night air drifting from the sea. I felt oddly deflated and exhilarated at the same time, as if I'd failed to get something I greatly wanted and was wildly grateful for failing.

I thought about the kitten waiting for me at home, and it felt good. I wasn't planning on keeping her, but a kitten waiting for you to come home is a spot of love in your life, and that's nice. It's actually very nice.

Approaching the Kurtz house, I automatically swiveled my head to look down the moonlit driveway. As I did, another part of the puzzle fell into place. I not only knew there was another room between the garage and the wine room, I knew what kind of room it was and how it was being used. I also knew without a shadow of doubt why somebody had tried to steal Ziggy, and what Ken Kurtz was up to in that house. The realization caused my hands to shake on the steering wheel.

Another thing about being a little bit off-center is that it robs you of your ability to justify things that are just flat wrong. Normal people come up with all kinds of political explanations and religious rationalizations and rose-colored social delusions when they're confronted with things that shouldn't be. Slightly loopy people can't do that anymore. Like the kid compelled to blurt out that the emperor was naked as a jaybird, we can only see things as they are and tell things as they are.

The way I saw it, I had no choice but to go inside that house and find what I knew was there. I didn't think past that, I just knew I had to do it.

Every sensible bone in my body told me to call Guidry and tell him what I'd figured out. Every experienced bone in my body said no judge would give him a search warrant to look for something that nobody knew existed except me, especially since I had nothing to go on except intuition and a knowledge of iguanas.

In the not-so-distant past, I would have gone home first and got a weapon, but I couldn't do that now. Not just because Guidry hadn't returned my .38, but because I knew I couldn't live with myself if I killed anybody else.

I eased the Bronco around the curve in the driveway and parked in front of the garages. I was careful not to let the door make a loud click when I closed it and then covered the pavement as fast as I could to get between the long garage wall and the privacy hedge in front of the house. I wished I had spare Keds in the car. To keep my high heels from clacking, I had to walk almost on tiptoe.

When I reached the glass wall of the living room, I kept my pace steady, as if I had legitimate business there. Through the glass, the living room was in darkness but I could see a subdued glow in the great fireplace, as if Kurtz had left a fire burning and gone to bed. Okay, so far so good. I tippy-toed back down the walk and turned the corner to skitter past the row of closed garage doors. In the bright moonlight, I felt like the sky was shining a spotlight on me. If anybody was watching the house, they could surely see me.

Ducking into the narrow alcove to the side door, I fitted one of Kurtz's keys into the lock and eased the door open. Once inside, I left the door slightly ajar in case I needed to make a hasty exit. I was banking on the second key being to the wine room. I looked down the southern corridor toward Kurtz's bedroom, where everything was dark and silent. Creeping down the southern corridor past the wine room, I stuck my head around the corner and looked into the living room to verify that it was empty.

The room was quiet, the only sound the sighing and subtle crackling of white-hot logs in the fireplace. My guess was that a big fire had roared there about an hour ago, and without care it had dwindled to a hot memory of itself. I stopped for a minute and considered my options. The most sensible one was to retrace my steps, get in my Bronco, and drive home. But no matter how much my head told me to do that, my feet turned toward the wine room.

Holding my breath, I slipped the second key into the lock and turned the doorknob. Closing the door behind me, I flipped the light switch to fill the room with a ghostly red glow, and almost tripped over Ziggy. He was stretched on the floor just inside the door, and when he felt me he raised his tail and whipped it back and forth. I leaped out of the way, and he lowered his tail. Not because he couldn't reach me, but because he was too weak to lash at me. In the chill of the wine room, Ziggy was closing down. His normal bright green had darkened to ripe avocado, which meant he hadn't been in the room very long. My guess was that Kurtz had moved him to the wine room at about the same time he'd left the fire to burn itself down.

I whispered, "I'll get you out of here later, Ziggy, but right now I have to find a secret door."

I moved to the back of the room and began looking for a hidden control that would open a passage to the room that I knew lay between the wine room and the garage. I felt along the underside of every wine shelf and on each side of every supporting column, but I didn't find anything. I was making my second sweep down the back wall of wine bottles when I tried pulling on the columns. One of the columns moved, and an entire section swung outward on invisible hinges.

With my breath trembling, I faced the dark recesses of the room I'd known I would find. A peculiar iodine odor permeated the room, the same smell I'd noticed on Gilda. I stepped inside and fumbled for a light switch.

Before I found it, I was caught in the beam of a blinding light. I gave a shocked yelp and covered my eyes. Of all the dumb ideas I'd ever had, this one was turning out to be a blue-ribbon prizewinner.

I put my hand up to shield my eyes. "Mr. Kurtz?"

No answer, just the ferocious light.

I decided the lack of shouting and yelling might be a good omen. Maybe Kurtz was so lonely there in the house by himself that he would overlook the fact that I'd broken in.

"Could you move the light? We could sit and talk awhile."

The light held steady for a moment, then swung away to travel crazily over stark white walls and steel tables holding the kinds of things you expect to see in a research lab. Overhead fluorescents fluttered on to reveal a slight young man pointing a .44 Magnum at me. With a resigned sense of inevitability, I recognized him as the same man I'd seen watching Jessica at Ramón's funeral.

I took a half step backward, watching his hand with the gun and thinking furiously. If I ran, he might shoot me in the back. If I didn't run, he might trap me in the lab and kill me there.

In a soft trembling voice, he said, "You should not have come here. Now you have ruined everything."

A cold serpent slithered up my spine.

She had cut her hair and dyed it dark, but the voice and accent were the same. Gilda had returned.

An insulated cooler like people take on picnics was open on one of the stainless tables, with an array of gauze-wrapped vials lying around it.

While I digested the fact that I had caught her in the midst of stealing vials from Kurtz's lab, I could almost see her brain whirling to find the best way to dispose of me.

I said, "Since you don't have any business here either, I don't think it would be a real good idea for you to do anything that would wake Ken Kurtz."

The only sign that she understood my meaning was a narrowing of her nostrils, as if she'd taken in a rush of unpleasant air.

I said, "Are you really a nurse?"

"I am very good nurse."

I heard a hint of proud defensiveness and took heart. People who leap to defend themselves or their work aren't thinking clearly. People who aren't thinking clearly can sometimes be influenced. On the other hand, people who aren't thinking clearly can also panic and blow a hole in your head.

I said, "Then you can clear up a mystery for me. Why does Kurtz have a PICC line in his arm?"

"Is for chelation, to take out metals that cause argyria."

From the way she tossed out the medical word, she had to be a real nurse, maybe even a good one.

Seeing that I didn't understand, she said, "Means blue skin."

"I guess the chelation didn't work, since he's still blue."

Her eyes flashed with a gleam of venom. "I tell him is chelation, is really silver nitrate. He is monster, he should have mark of monster."

I felt a small twinge of sympathy for Kurtz, who hadn't understood why his condition had worsened in the past few months. But things were looking up. Gilda obviously hated Kurtz, and if I could keep her hatred directed toward him, I might be able to convince her I was an ally.

I said, "I've been told that you hired somebody to kill Ken Kurtz. No woman would do that unless she was forced by extreme circumstances."

"It was only way. If the man had done it—"

I pointed to the vials on the table. "But the vials you took from the refrigerator were fakes. If Kurtz had been killed as you planned, that's all you would have had."

She looked chagrined. "Is true. They were there as test. I do not know why he did not trust me."

"Yeah, that's a mystery."

We were silent for a moment while Gilda puzzled why a man she'd been poisoning hadn't trusted her, and I tried to figure out how to get that big gun away from her.

I said, "Why did you take the money to Ramón's widow?"

Her grim expression softened. "There was big mistake and wrong man was killed. I did not want Ramón's family to suffer."

"That was big of you."

I was surprised acid didn't drip from my lips onto my high heels, but her head bobbed so vigorously that I knew she thought I'd given her a compliment.

"Since you're a nurse and you were treating a very sick man, it would have been easy for you to kill Kurtz with an overdose of something. Why hire somebody?"

Her eyes widened. "I am not killer."

"Uh-hunh. Good thing you're rich enough to pay a hundred thousand dollars to hire one."

She laughed shortly. "It was not my money."

I heard a scuffling sound and whirled to look into the wine room's dark red shadows. Ken Kurtz stood inside the blood-hued darkness, and I could see the glint of his teeth bared in a mean grin. He was definitely pissed, ticked off, disgruntled.

I wasn't feeling so gruntled myself.

# 27

Kurtz wasn't wearing his tatty old plaid robe. Instead, he was dressed like a man ready for traveling, in dark trousers and a blue-and-white striped shirt, with tasseled loafers on his bare feet. The blue in his shirt was eerily similar to the blue of his skin. Both blue hands bore angry red welts across their backs.

Ignoring Gilda's gun, he walked to the stainless table holding the pile of vials. He picked up a vial and waved it at her.

"Stupid cow! Did you think I would let you take the work I've sacrificed my life for?"

Gilda's face twisted, and she mimed spitting on the floor. "Pah! No sacrifice! Is all for money!"

"Speaking of money, which pharmaceutical firm is financing you?"

Again, Gilda made a spitting motion. "I work for my people, for the men and women and children on my island."

Holding the vial out on his open palm, Kurtz stepped closer to her. "Then you're even stupider than I thought. What did you plan to do, take these vials home and pass them out on the street?"

She looked from his face to the vial.

I was hoping she would spit again, this time for real, but instead she looked distracted. She actually gestured with her gun as she talked, like a teacher holding a pointer.

"I take them to health department. My government will take them to laboratory . . . they will know what to do with them."

Showing a lot more energy and strength than I'd seen before, Ken Kurtz moved another step closer to her, and I knew that in the next moment he planned to take her gun. I wasn't so sure I liked what I thought he might do once he had it. Gilda might be a thief and she might have tried to hire a hit man to kill Kurtz, but I sort of liked her team better than his.

I said, "I hate to burst all your bubbles, but an FBI team has this house under surveillance and you'll both be arrested."

Ken Kurtz settled the vial in the cooler and looked up at me with a smug smile. "That's like telling Jonas Salk that his parking meter has expired so his polio vaccine is lost to the world. You have no idea how important my work is."

"Sure I do. You've developed a vaccine for bird flu."

Both their jaws dropped in such identical gapes of shock that it was almost funny.

I pointed at a whirling centrifuge. "I'm not a scientist, so I don't know how you make a vaccine, but I know virus-extracting machines can separate a virus from blood and concentrate it."

His eyes narrowed in paranoid suspicion. "Only another scientist would guess at a vaccine for avian flu."

"Oh, please! You don't have to be a scientist to know that iguanas and chickens have identical respiratory and digestive systems. When an iguana is sick, you give it bird tonic. If you transferred a bird virus to an iguana, the virus would weaken because the iguana is a cold-blooded animal, but the iguana would essentially become a vaccine-producer."

Kurtz stared at me with a look of surprised respect, sort of like a dog looks at a human after the human makes barking sounds.

I spread my hands, palms up. "Once you know how, I imagine it's rather easy. You've infected Ziggy with avian flu, he has produced antibodies, and now you're drawing blood from him to spin them out in your vaccine-making machines."

Sounding like somebody who had always wanted to talk about his work to an equal, Kurtz said, "In the beginning, I tried to use silver ni-trate to attenuate the virus. It went much faster when I conceived of us-ing iguana blood instead."

I looked at the welts on Kurtz's hands and knew he had planned to draw blood from Ziggy that night. That had been the purpose of put-ting him in the wine room, to shut him down so he could draw blood without being whipped or scratched. I also knew that when Ken Kurtz was between bouts of debilitation, he was a lot stronger than anybody had imagined possible—strong enough to pick Ziggy up and carry him to the wine room, strong enough to walk out to the guardhouse and shoot Ramón in the head while he slept.

I said, "I don't understand why you killed Ramón."

A flicker of surprise moved across his cheeks. "How did you know?"

"Until this minute, I didn't. But it's the only thing that makes any sense. What I don't understand is why you did it."

"He saw the lab. He would have talked."

Gilda said, "*You* killed Ramón?"

"It was your fault. You opened the door from the wine room to the lab while he was still in the wine room. He saw through the door."

"Bastard!"

I didn't know which one disgusted me more, Kurtz for always blam-ing somebody else for what he did or Gilda for trying to rise to his level of sliminess. From the fury and pain in Gilda's eyes, I had a feeling that Paloma's suspicions about her husband and Gilda might be true.

She backed up a step from Kurtz, got a firmer grip on her gun, and glared at me as if I had been a partner in the crime.

I said, "Some people are damn disappointing."

She waved the gun side to side. "Now you will both go into living room. I will walk behind. If you run away, I will kill you."

She might not have been capable of murder before, but I believed her. Gilda had crossed over her own drawn line, and now she wasn't simply furious and determined, she was full of fine reckless vengeance.

Stepping smartly in my high heels, I clacked through the wine room. Drawn to the living room's warmth and light, Ziggy had moved closer to the door that Kurtz had left open. Careful to stay far enough away to avoid his tail or his claws, I circled around him and stepped through the doorway. Kurtz and Gilda must have followed my lead, because they both got past him without being lashed or clawed.

When I reached the fireplace, Gilda called out, "Stop."

Beside me, Kurtz bent to the basket of wood on the hearth. At first I thought he hoped to fling a log at Gilda and knock the gun from her hand, but instead he carefully arranged kindling and fresh logs on the smoldering fragments to reignite them.

Scientific minds have screwy priorities.

Gilda had a wild-eyed grip on her gun, but I could tell from the way she held it that any shots she got off would be poorly aimed—not that a random bullet isn't as destructive as an aimed one, especially if it hits you. It seemed to me that the situation required somebody with a cool head. Unfortunately, the best we had was me.

I said, "Gilda, the police are looking for you because they think you may have killed Ramón. Once they know you didn't, they'll have no interest in you. But you're in Florida where the death penalty is alive and well, so if you kill either Ken Kurtz or me, you're a dead woman."

I didn't think it necessary to point out that Guidry might arrest her for conspiring to kill Kurtz.

Still looking unfazed by her big gun, Kurtz said, "Gilda, do you really believe you can simply pack up the vaccine and walk away from here? Dixie's telling the truth about the FBI. The minute you go out the door with the vaccine, they'll take it."

He sounded so certain that for a moment I believed him. Maybe the FBI really was out there somewhere in the darkness watching us, maybe they were picking up our conversation on remote speakers. If they were, Ken Kurtz would surely be arrested for industrial espionage and for murder.

If Gilda believed him, it only fueled her anger. "Yes, they will take vaccine and let you go free! They will say I killed Ramón, that I am evil one. They will kill me and make you a hero."

Something uncoiled in my chest, and as I looked at that raving woman with the oversized gun and the outrageous imagination, I knew she might speak the truth. I also knew that I was the expendable one, the fly in the ointment that nobody would miss. It wouldn't be hard to frame Gilda as Ramón's killer. And if they killed me, they could easily say Kurtz had shot me after I'd broken into his house.

The galling thing was that a lot of people, including Guidry, wouldn't have trouble believing I had broken into Kurtz's house. The fact that I actually *had* broken in didn't make it any easier to like the idea of people thinking I had.

# 28

Kurtz and Gilda stood facing me with the wine room behind them. While my brain spun out the possible scenario that Gilda had just described, I became aware of a green movement behind them. Through the wine room's open door, Ziggy had got enough warm air to get his brain spinning too. He was on the move with his tongue flicking forward to smell the air, running silently on the pads of his feet toward the leaping flames Kurtz had restarted in the fireplace. I braced myself. If Ziggy did what I thought he would do, he might be my salvation.

When he was within a foot or two of Gilda and Kurtz, Ziggy's tongue smelled the fire.

His reptilian brain hollered, *Heat is to the right!*

He made a quick turn toward the fire, sensed danger to his side, and whipped his tail sharply around Gilda's legs.

Gilda screamed and threw up her gun hand. In a flash, I leaped to grab it. She struggled, but Gilda wasn't exactly an Amazon and surprise had caused her to lose balance. With her gun in one hand, I only had to shove her hard with the other to cause her to fall backward. She fell like a tree, stiff-legged and stiff-armed, arching her back over Ziggy, whose tail was still wildly lashing. She landed in the perfect location for his whipping tail to slash whatever part of her body was closest to him.

Since she lost her head and scrambled around on all fours, that meant pretty much all of her.

Fighting back the nauseating dizziness of knowing I might kill somebody again, I spread my legs in my damned high heels and stiffened my arms, holding the gun pointed at her with both hands. She was too busy trying to get away from Ziggy to notice.

With his dewlap billowed to its fullest extent and his forelegs stiffened to raise his chest, Ziggy stretched himself in front of the warm fire and bobbed his head. His color was still dull, but he looked quite pleased with himself.

A figure moved across the glass so rapidly I wasn't sure I had seen it, but it set off a contest in my head between euphoric hope—that I'd accidentally been telling the truth and FBI agents were ready to come in and arrest Kurtz—and paranoid fear—that they'd arrest Gilda, kill me, and let Kurtz go free.

The paranoia was too awful, so I went with hope.

To distract Kurtz, I said, "I should have known you weren't that sick. A man that bad off couldn't drink wine."

Scientist to the end, he said, "Not so. Red wine has antiviral properties."

Behind him, the front door eased open half an inch.

I looked around at Gilda to see if she had noticed, but she was examining the ugly slash marks on her arms and hands. The ones under her pants legs weren't visible, but I knew from experience that an iguana's whip burns on your legs hurt like nobody's business.

The door opened wider, and a tall man slipped silently into the room. He wore black jeans and a black long-sleeved T-shirt, so it took me a moment to recognize the fanatic who'd called me a harlot. He was carrying a Colt .357 Magnum, a gun even larger than Gilda's. In his large hand it didn't look out of place.

He winked at me and I almost sagged with relief. I had been right about him; he was FBI.

He said, "I'll take over now."

Shocked, Kurtz spun around to look at him.

I lowered Gilda's gun and handed it the man.

Feeling proud but trying for humble self-effacement, I said, "I took this from Gilda."

Then, to show I was too smart to be taken in by a burlap robe and a fake fanatic act, I said, "That was a great disguise you used. But I knew you were an agent."

I felt like a kid with a gold star. I couldn't wait to tell Guidry how I'd known all along who the good guys were. Me, Dixie Hemingway, was in cahoots with an FBI agent who was there to arrest Ken Kurtz for corporate espionage.

Kurtz said, "Hello, Walt."

I heard a tiny buzz in the back of my skull, as if a gnat had slipped through my bones and got trapped in there.

The monk-turned-agent tipped his chin toward Ziggy.

"You know, Ken, we could have shared him. But no, you had to hog all the credit like some publicity-hungry diva."

The buzzing in my skull grew louder. I looked at the FBI agent's hands and saw crusted claw marks and welts.

Kurtz said, "I'm sorry I didn't kill you last night."

I said, "You're the one who tried to steal Ziggy."

The man gave me a blank look, and Kurtz laughed. For a man with a gun pointed at his head, he was remarkably cheerful.

"She calls the iguana Ziggy," he said. "Sort of an inside joke."

To me, he said, "Dixie, meet Walter Cahill, chief zoobiologist for the Clarex Foundation. I imagine he's the one who knocked you out."

The phony monk had the gall to grin at me. "Sorry, nothing personal."

As if she'd just noticed that our number had grown, Gilda stood up and waved her arms like a traffic cop.

"Monsters! You are monsters, both of you!"

They turned toward her with the lazy insolence of men who can't be bothered by criticism. Cahill held a gun in each hand the way movie cowboys do, his .357 pointed toward Kurtz, and Gilda's .44 Magnum carelessly at his side.

Behind them, Jessica Ballantyne slipped through the open door.

If it hadn't been for the Glock .45 in her hands, she could have been the latest arrival at a happening midnight party. Once again, I vacillated between relief and caution. She was genuine FBI, but she was also in love with the man she had been sent to arrest.

Gilda shouted, "You say you make world better, but is not true!"

Absorbed in her fury, Gilda didn't notice Jessica. Absorbed in themselves, the men were smirking while they watched Gilda's performance.

Jessica had adopted the gun stance that every trained law-enforcement officer uses. Feet spread, knees slightly bent, shoulders back, chin parallel to the floor, both arms extended, the gun in both hands, left thumb over right thumb, trigger finger stretched toward the barrel. She might be a lovesick mess, but the woman knew how to handle a gun.

In a low menacing voice, she said, "Drop the weapons, Walt."

Both men froze, and for an instant a play of emotions rippled across their faces.

Low as an exhaled breath, Kurtz said, "Jessie."

The word held so much love and longing that I forgot about the guns and looked at him. He wore the smile of a happy man, and his eyes burned with new excitement.

Cahill let the guns fall to the floor.

Kurtz said, "God, Jessie, I've dreamed for two years that you came back to me. I thought it was an impossible fantasy. When Dixie told me you were alive, I was afraid to believe it, afraid it would turn out to be a hoax."

Jessica's face remained still, but her eyes showed the turmoil she felt.

Gilda had been ignored as long as she could stand. Still bleeding from Ziggy's claws, her arms windmilled as she bounced in place.

"He killed Ramón!"

The woman's one-track focus was beginning to get on my nerves, but at least she was telling the truth.

I said, "She's right, Jessica. Ken Kurtz killed the guard."

With her eyes still locked on Kurtz's, Jessica said, "Is that true, Ken?"

Kurtz flapped his hand. "Don't get distracted by extraneous details,

Jessica. The important thing is that we're together again. You're a scientist, a brilliant scientist. Together we can do everything we always dreamed of doing."

Jessica said, "I was sent here to arrest you."

"They'll drop it, Jessie. I can name a long list of judges and congressmen and FDA people who've been bought by BiZogen or ZIGI. There'll be some media flap for a while, and then it'll die down. Don't worry about it."

Her voice went even huskier than usual. "I understood how you felt about our colleagues being killed, but I'll never understand how you could deliberately murder a man."

He went very still, as if her words held coded meaning that only an old lover with intimate knowledge of another's pitch and turn of phrase could translate. Then he raised a hand to his face, where spasms moved like small jerking animals under his blue skin. In that moment, he was such a pitiable figure that every eye in the room fixed on his quivering visage. Nobody noticed his other hand plunge into his pocket until he pulled out a small gun. It appeared to be a Smith & Wesson .38 Special, a revolver with a two-inch barrel. Since revolvers don't leave casings, I supposed it was the gun he'd used to kill Ramón, the same gun he'd worn under his robe when I first met him. Now I knew why he'd fussed with the logs in the basket. That's where he'd hidden the gun.

From the corridor, somebody yelled, "Freeze!"

In the next instant, what looked like half the Sarasota County Sheriff's Department exploded into the room from all directions, all with their weapons trained on Ken Kurtz.

Like a highway accident in which a second of chaos seems to stretch into sequential minutes, time slowed to a crawl.

Kurtz pivoted toward the southern corridor with his gun raised and pointed directly at deputies there. At that same moment, Ziggy panicked from all the new smells and sounds and streaked across the room, running straight toward the deputies in the southern corridor. Seeing a small dragon coming at him, the nearest one jerked his weapon toward him.

I yelled, "Don't hurt the iguana!"

With his body still turning toward the southern corridor and his gun still raised, Kurtz became aware of Ziggy's blind run and of the deputy's startled reaction. Instinctively, he leaped toward Ziggy, for an exquisite moment spread-eagled above him. At that precise instant, Jessica put a bullet through his neck.

Kurtz fell on top of Ziggy and rolled to his side facing Jessica. His gun fell from his hand, and in the moment before death claimed him, it looked as if his eyes were focused on her with calm acceptance.

Ziggy scrambled free and scuttled away, his tail dragging through Kurtz's blood to form a red connection between blue man and green beast.

The room went eerily quiet.

With his own gun drawn, Guidry came around the corner from the north corridor.

He said, "Jessica Ballantyne?"

With tears streaming down her face, she handed him her gun. "I'm an agent with the Federal Bureau of Investigation, Lieutenant."

Guidry's gray eyes were watching her intently. "I think you'd better sit down."

"I'm quite all right, Lieutenant."

With his phone to his ear, Guidry came to stand in front of me. Behind him, an officer was arresting Gilda, and another officer was cuffing Cahill and advising him of his rights.

Guidry clicked his phone closed. "Thanks for leaving the back door open for us."

"How did you know I was here?"

"An officer tailed Gilda here, then watched you come in. While he waited for backups, the other two dropped in. You must have sent out invitations."

"Kurtz killed Ramón, not Gilda. The man's name is Cahill. He's a rival scientist. He's the one who hit me, and he tried to steal Ziggy." In sudden alarm, I said, "Don't let anything happen to Ziggy! He's producing bird flu vaccine."

"Don't worry, we'll protect him."

Guidry's level voice was reassuring. Something bad had happened, it was being handled. Other bad things would undoubtedly happen in the future, and they would be handled too. The world keeps spinning, the sun rises and sets, the tides come in and go out, people cope with life.

One of Guidry's men took Jessica's arm and steered her out the front door. As she passed me, our eyes met and we sent each other a silent message that only two women could exchange.

Jessica asked my understanding for sparing the man she loved public humiliation and personal suffering.

I assured her that I would pretend she had killed Kurtz to keep him from taking out a law-enforcement officer.

Then I went to pick Ziggy up and move him to a safe place, because that's what I do.

# 29

I made a frantic predawn call to the head of the University of Florida's College of Veterinary Medicine in Gainesville. When I told him everything I knew about Ziggy, he acted as if he heard bizarre stories like that every day. Four hours later, he arrived with four pre-med students who tenderly carried Ziggy to their van. Before the day was over, he called to tell me he had removed Ziggy's catheter and that Ziggy was fine. He also said he and his wife and kids wanted to make Ziggy a part of their family. Since there was nobody to say he couldn't, I gave my own grateful permission. We didn't discuss Ziggy's vaccine-producing capabilities. That was something for the vet to discuss with research biologists, but I knew he would make sure Ziggy was protected.

On Christmas Eve, I left Ella snoozing in her new kitty bed while I went to Midnight Spanish Mass at St. Martha's. I'm not Catholic and I don't speak Spanish, so it was especially comforting to be with strangers united by a story the credulous take literally and the literate take metaphorically—either way, it transcends dogma or fact. I sat at the back and let the words and music and ritual create a space for my mind to take in the idea of omnipresent love present in every newborn, in every parent, in every man and woman with the courage to trust the wisdom in their hearts. When the service ended, I had moved a little closer to remembering what life and love is all about.

Guidry was at the door waiting for me.

I didn't know what that meant.

Maybe it didn't mean anything.

He looped an arm around my shoulders and we stepped into the dark night together.